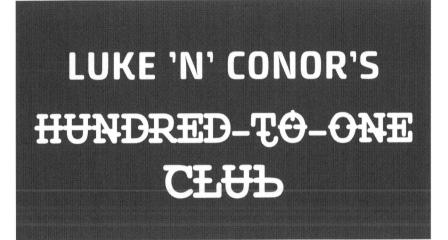

LUKE 'N' CONOR'S HUNDRED-TO-ONE CLUB

J C Williams

ISBN: 9781076693204

First printing June 2019

Cover artwork by Paul Nugent

Proofreading, editing, and interior formatting & design provided by Dave Scott and Cupboardy Wordsmithing

Contents

LEVEL ONE
CAUSTIC KEEP

The scope of a legendary sniper rifle moved cautiously over the rugged terrain, giving a brief glimpse of Caustic Keep. A crisp burst of gunfire startled Luke, causing the usually steady hand to falter. He released the pressure on the trigger for a moment and let his view zoom out, permitting an expansive outlook over the battlefield in front. He shifted his attention away from the game for a moment, reaching forward to take a sip from the strawberry Ribena that'd been sat on his desk for he-didn't-know-how-long. The brief recess gave him a moment to adjust his headset, a headset that had now created a perfect indent into his mop of blond hair — already in disarray from being slept on, and overdue a trim by at least a week.

Back in the game, he cautiously poked his head out from behind the rusting remains of a car before returning to a position of cover, his weapon drawn, and applying enough pressure on the controller's shoulder button to bring into view his rifle's sight.

Luke maintained one eye on the scope and the other on his in-game character's status display — showing he'd been holding steady in 11th position for what seemed like almost an eternity. But a maelstrom was approaching, Luke reckoned, as he knew they appeared at regular intervals and one was about due. He also knew he'd have to make a strategic advance soon, because getting caught in the maelstrom would drain his character's energy to the point of death. It was an ingenious way the game designers had used to ensure all players kept moving along and advancing forth.

Another player, Darius6786, had just made the ultimate sacrifice — being taken out by a shotgun kill, by all accounts, judging by the message at the bottom of the screen announcing his premature demise to the world — and whereby Luke was suddenly promoted into tenth position.

Luke was no stranger to the top ten, but he knew those remaining, in the 1-thru-9 slots above him, would likely be seasoned campaigners. Despite the many hours he'd spent honing his skills, Luke was acutely aware that he was still a novice, a fact highlighted by his "Victory Supreme" tally — finishing the game ranked in first place — which stood at a big fat nil. He was what was referred to in gaming parlance as a "camper." That is, while some players go hell-for-leather running through the various environments, Luke was content to take a position of cover in or behind, whatever was available — a bush, a discarded vehicle, a looted supermarket — with the occasional sortie to pick off an unsuspecting victim like a lion in the jungle.

But there was no way of hiding from the approaching storm. Luke knew his weapons were fully loaded, but that didn't stop him checking for the fourth time.

"Come *on*. Can't hang about," he said to himself, gripping the controller as he pressed on. There was no choice in the matter. With the maelstrom approaching, the area of play on the display map was effectively shrinking, and the world they were in was decreasing in size. This forced all players out of their hidey holes, to fight each other, and it also brought a measure of certainty as to how long a game might last, for otherwise the game could conceivably go on forever.

"No!" Luke yelled reflexively as a figure appeared from nowhere a short distance off in front of him, wielding a shotgun and releasing two blasts from it in quick succession. Quickly realising he hadn't been hit, Luke then toggled his weapons, bringing up his own shotgun and returning fire. But with his opponent taking him off-guard, his accuracy was mediocre at best. Luke's defensive building skills — the in-game ability to construct structures in which to seek refuge — were limited, and so he carried out a series of frantic jumps, leaping about in an effort to shake off his aggressor, and firing blindly in the process as this deteriorated his ability to properly aim even further.

With a quick assessment of the advanced type of 'skin' the character still chasing him was utilising — the kind that could only be earned — Luke knew, despite the missed shot, that he was dealing with a Hundred-to-One veteran. Luke's composure, relatively intact until this point, escaped him quicker than the figure disappearing up the fortress constructed right close by.

His pursuer had played it safe, perhaps not knowing the measure of Luke's possible capabilities. But he was unlikely to be just hiding away. In fact, he was much more likely to be lining up a shot right now under safe cover.

Luke was in a somewhat weakened state, his opponent having managed to connect with a shot before disappearing up the structure he'd just made, but Luke was still standing. He took a deep breath and built furiously himself. However, while his opponent had constructed, in seconds, a tower that could probably withstand a tornado, Luke's paltry efforts in response would do well to bear the weight of a butterfly landing on it.

But at least he was still in the battle. He could see from the in-game display that only six hardy souls remained at this point, including himself, out of the match's original one hundred. Of course this only served to increase his anxiety levels even further. He wanted victory! He was now amongst the final small handful of players remaining in the game, and could *taste* victory — almost *smell* it!

Unfortunately, the defensive position he'd just crafted was obliterated in short order by several pinpoint rounds of ammunition. It was a sad state of affairs that fortresses in the game were never designed to be absolutely impregnable. And a poorly constructed building such as Luke's, especially, could be brought down by nothing more than a few well-placed shots, forcing the inhabitant to scurry away like a rat escaping a sinking ship.

"No, no, no!" Luke shouted at the screen in vain, desperately trying, with his structure now in ruins and useless, to reach cover behind a tree on the nearby hillside.

Several additional shots whistled past his new position. He wasn't sure if another aggressor was now also involved in the incursion, or if it was the same shooter again. Either way, he felt like he was involved in a battle with a jar of black treacle, trying to get its lid off that'd been fixed on there like glue from the sticky syrup — that is, struggling to merely catch his breath, let alone make any sort of progress of any significance. He wouldn't have long to remain in cover as the storm that had been approaching was now upon him, quickly sapping what was remaining of his depleted energy. He had to make a move.

With the others likely occupied in escaping from the maelstrom as well — since even the protection afforded by an expertly-constructed fortress would be rendered useless as the storm descended — Luke seized the opportunity, sprinting into the open, and with one eye on his dwindling energy as the storm took its inevitable toll. He managed to break free from the storm's grip, thank goodness, but knew any additional hits taken from opponents would mean the end of him.

With only four opponents remaining, as one by one they were each being eliminated by the opposition, Luke was unsure whether to go on the offensive now or to hope those more experienced would do him the courtesy of taking each other out of the equation, doing the hard work for him. With so few players left, he could conceivably come out on top. It was possible! As long as he didn't take any more hits... and he *could* end up finding some medpaks, after all... could this be his moment?

If it indeed was, then bragging rights would be his in school — where he could finally declare himself as having bagged a Victory Supreme win. All that stood between him and his destiny was...

A sniper's bullet. That knocked him right off his feet.

And with that, his campaign was over, and his victory would need to wait for another day. Destiny, it would seem, had other plans for him.

"No!" he screamed, throwing his controller up onto his desk — where his TV-as-game-monitor sat — in a fit of rage. He wanted desperately to vent his frustration even more. A few choice swear words were on the tip of his tongue, in fact. But he was on the final warning from his mum in that regard, and so he stopped himself... though with great difficulty.

Ordinarily, he'd watch the conclusion of the battle in observation mode even after being taken out. But the pain of defeat, after having come so close to victory this time — the closest he'd ever gotten — was all too raw for him. He slumped back in his chair, removed his headset, and then, with headset now off, became immediately aware of a quick succession of thunderous footsteps hurtling up the stairs.

"Luke Jacobs!" shouted his mum. He could tell instantly from the heightened pitch of her voice that she wasn't coming in to wish him a good morning. "I've been shouting up to you for the last five minutes!" she said.

"Sorry, Mum, I was just—"

"I know what you were just doing! You were glued to your game console, as usual! It's first thing in the morning!" she said, throwing open his curtains. "And you're sat in here in your underpants playing that bloody thing yet again!" she continued, pointing at the console. "I'll bet you've not even brushed your teeth, have you?" she said, but she didn't wait for a response, likely as she already suspected the answer. "Jump in the shower now, right now! We need to be out the door in precisely thirty minutes, young man! *Remember?*"

"Of course I do!" he offered. "I never forget important things! Especially very important things like this! But, could you maybe... *erm*... refresh my memory? Where exactly are we going again...?"

Luke's mum went ahead and grabbed several articles of discarded clothing up off the bedroom floor, while she was in there, as mums tend to do. "I knew you weren't listening to me, you little monkey!" she said, tucking the clothes under her arm and laughing. "You promised me you'd help me with the bake sale at the church community centre on Saturday morning," she told him, playfully ruffling his hair with her free hand. "And it's Saturday morning."

"It's Saturday morning!" Luke agreed.

"Do you remember now? The fundraiser towards the new roof?"

"How could I not remember!" Luke answered, raising his finger up like a scientist who'd just had a *eureka!* moment. Though the truth of it was, he had no idea what she was talking about. He did, vaguely, remember some sort of conversation or other taking place. But the precise details of it were lost somewhere during the course of the week — where, exactly, he couldn't be sure. To be fair, though, anything that wasn't specifically game-related tended to filter straight on through his brain like a sieve.

Luke's mum, Sally, pressed her glasses up her nose, looking down at his console. A whiteboard with the words *VICTORY SUPREME WINS,* written on it with felt marker, was propped up behind it. These words were accompanied by a zero, scrawled underneath.

"You've not managed it yet, then?" Sally asked, with no real understanding of what *it* actually was. But being Mum, it was her job to be interested, even when she wasn't, particularly. "If you need me to show you how it's done, Luke, you only need to ask, okay? I'm quite the expert on Hundreds-of-Fun, you know. Just ask your dad!"

"It's *Hundred-to-One,* Mum," Luke said with an exasperated sigh. After all, how could she not know the name of the most important game in the very history of history?? Still, he appreciated what she was trying to do. "But you might have more success than I'm having, actually," he went on. "Even Conor has managed a Victory Supreme win by now, and I've been playing longer than he has."

"Alexa! Alarm off!" Sally suddenly shouted, separating Luke's underpants from his chair as his bum abruptly rose up off of it.

"Mum! You scared me!" Luke protested.

"That's the last batch of cakes I need to take out of the oven," she explained. "So, *you...*" she said, pointing straight at him... "Get your skinny carcass into the shower before I *throw* you in there bodily."

"You wouldn't," Luke answered.

"Oh, indeed I would," she said with a wink. It was the sort of wink that implied she meant business.

Sally left Luke to his own devices, but paused at the foot of the stairs. *"Hundreds-of-Fun,"* she repeated, laughing to herself. That was a much more sensible name for the game anyway, she thought, much more jolly-sounding. Then she stood there, listening for any movement from upstairs. She knew her son well, and, unsurprisingly, there was no motion or action of any kind to be heard. "Shower!" she shouted up the stairs, which produced the desired effect, prompting an immediate padding of rapid footsteps as evidenced by the creaky floorboards.

A few moments later, on to the next task at hand, Sally reached for the oven door, taking a moment to appreciate the aroma emanating forth as she opened it. "Don't forget we'll be leaving the house soon, Tom!" she called out to her husband as she placed the cakes on cooling racks she'd set out on the kitchen counter.

Tom appeared in the kitchen doorway, drawn as much by the sweet scent of the cakes as by his wife's reminder. He scratched the stubble on his chin. "Of course," he announced unconvincingly. "Well of course I remember. How could I forget?" he added, surreptitiously tapping the buttons on his phone. And, then, "Ah. Yes. The bake sale," he said.

Sally cocked her head and cast him a look. The confused, *I-don't-know-what-you're-talking-about* gene must have ran through the male side of the family, she surmised, her son obviously inheriting it from his father. "You've just looked at your calendar on your phone, haven't you, Tom?" asked Sally rhetorically. "Yes, the *bake* sale, Tom. Honestly, you and your son are exactly alike. Do *either* of you *ever* listen to a word I say?" she said, shaking her head and laughing.

"Yes, I'd love one," replied Tom. "They smell really good."

"See? That's just what I'm talking about!" Sally scolded him, playfully throwing a tea towel at him for good measure.

The tea towel struck Tom in the chest, snapping him back to the present, and he managed to scoop the towel up — though only just — before it reached the floor. To be fair, when there was food about, Tom could think of little else. Everything else fell to the wayside. This was completely natural, he felt, and quite obviously couldn't be helped. He kept this notion to himself, though, feeling it the wisest course of action.

"People don't listen to each other anymore," Sally was saying. "In fact, the quickest way to arrange a family meeting in this house is when the internet goes off! You can be guaranteed everyone will be in the front room in less time than it takes to toast a slice of bread, checking the router!"

"Toast?" said Tom, his interest suddenly keenly piqued.

"Our son is never off that game console of his," Sally continued. "And I suppose... I suppose we're just as bad, glued to our computers or our phones, looking at pictures of *other* families enjoying themselves, for instance, when we should be out there *ourselves* enjoying life."

"You're right," replied Tom, discreetly putting his phone back in his pocket. "You're right, of course." He felt this was the best response to give whenever his wife was speaking. "To be fair to Luke, though, most of the time he's playing is spent chatting to his friends over his headset rather than actually playing the game. Or in equal measure, leastways. Either way, I'd rather he was doing that from the safety of his room than standing out all night down by the shops, actually, like some of the kids do. But I take your point. We spend far too much time scrolling through nonsense on social media, and the like. I'll make a concerted effort to keep my phone in my pocket a greater percent of the time, I think... if you'll do the same?"

"Agreed," said Sally. "Now go and get dressed into your clown costume. The fundraiser is starting soon, and you need to be ready," she said with a perfectly straight face.

Tom scanned Sally's face for the glimmer of a smile, hoping against hope that she was joking. This clown costume... was this something else he'd agreed to at some point, while pretending to be listening when he actually wasn't...?

Fortunately for Tom — and perhaps the children in attendance at the bake sale as well — Sally's eventual grin revealed that his juggling and balloon animal-making skills would not be called upon and put to the test. At least not this particular day.

Luke hadn't even removed his coat before he was set upon. "Morning, Mr and Mrs Jacobs," offered Conor hurriedly, before virtually dragging Luke towards the notice board. "Have you seen it?" he asked Luke, taking a bite of cake to settle his nerves. "Everybody's talking about it," he prattled on, barely able to catch his breath. "Look," he continued, turning to point, but before he could, both he and Luke felt a firm hand on either of their shoulders.

"Good to see you here helping!" boomed a voice looming over them.

"Hello, Reverend Scott," replied Luke, recognising the voice, and adopting his most polite tone in response. The Reverend was old, possibly the oldest human ever, it seemed to Luke, but always wore a cheery smile.

Reverend Scott peered down, squinting through his thin-framed glasses, adjusting them on his nose as he struggled to focus. "You're Conor, and you're Luke," he said to them, but it could easily have been a question as much as a statement. In fact, he'd misidentified the both of them, calling them each other's name. They weren't terribly offended. After all, they looked somewhat similar — both ten years old, with blond hair and blue eyes — and the Reverend was ancient and with dodgy eyesight. And so neither boy saw fit to correct him.

"Ah," continued the Reverend, turning his gaze toward the notice board. "I see something has drawn your attention? Would that be the poster for the Christmas Carol service I put up this morning?" he asked thoughtfully.

But neither Luke nor Conor had allowed their eyes to venture far enough down the notice board to see the poster the Reverend has so lovingly and carefully designed.

"*Ehm*, yes," replied Conor, shifting from one foot to the other uneasily. "We were just talking about how much we're looking forward to it. Weren't we, Luke?"

"Yes!" replied Luke enthusiastically, and maybe a little too quickly. "I was just going to tell my mum about it, too!" he added, bracing himself and looking skyward, worried he'd get struck by a bolt of lightning from the heavens for lying to a priest — and a kindly one at that.

Reverend Scott clapped his hands together like thunder, resulting in a gentle wobble of his ruddy cheeks — weathered by exposure to many years buffeted by the Isle of Man's salty sea breeze. "Wonderful!" he replied. "Oh, and I trust, gentlemen, that you're going to sell some cakes today and not just eat them all?" he asked, with a friendly, benevolent smile. "Remember, every cake sold is a step closer to getting the roof fixed!" he explained, before moving on to greet the next of his volunteers.

Luke and Conor waited for a moment, until they were certain they could speak freely. "Did you *see* it?" asked Conor.

"Yes!" Luke answered, arching his neck, unsure why an advert directed at kids their age would be pinned so high up the board.

"Here," said Reverend Scott, doubling back, and returning to unpin the poster the pair were *actually* looking at.

"He knew the whole time?" Conor whispered, leaning over to his friend, while the Reverend retrieved the poster.

"He knew the whole time," Luke whispered back, confirming his mate's suspicions, in awe of the good Reverend's powers of observation.

"I still expect to see you at the Christmas Carol service," said Reverend Scott. "Agreed?" he asked, though it wasn't so much a question as it was a decree.

"Agreed!" the pair replied to the now-retreating figure, the Reverend having gone off once again to attend to the other members of his parish.

Luke ran his eyes over the poster now in hand, glanced up at Conor, then returned to read it once more. "No way!" he exclaimed, eyes wide. "A Hundred-to-One tournament! First prize, one thousand pounds!" he shouted, attracting the attention of those in the queue for the ginger cake, nearby. "One thousand pounds," repeated Luke, with a little more composure this time, clutching the poster to his chest.

"Yes way. I know," replied Conor. "That's why I've been waiting for you to get here. So I can show you. And did you read the bottom part?"

Luke returned his attention to the poster, moving his lips along silently as he read along further, until he got to the part Conor was on about. "The winning team will also win an entry into a national tournament!" Luke shouted in an excited whisper. But this was of course knowledge that Conor was already well aware of.

"National tournament," repeated Conor, tapping the side of his head and giving Luke a knowing look. "We could be famous, mate. And rich."

"And rich," Luke reiterated, agreeing. But then Luke's initial enthusiasm dampened for a moment. "Conor, I don't mean to take the wind from your sails... but I'm guessing that this poster has been placed all around the Island. So it's not just us that are aware of this."

"Correct," replied Conor. "And my mum said she heard it on the radio this morning as well. Apparently, some company or other is sponsoring a load of regional heats where the winners win a place in the grand final."

Judging by Conor's gleeful expression, they'd already won the thousand pounds and were on their way to the grand final in his mind. It looked as if he was picturing the attention from the media they'd receive, and imagining walking up the red carpet, beset by the adoring press — who simply could not get enough of them, being the gaming legends that they were.

"There's only one problem," offered Luke, disturbing his friend's daydream.

"What's that?" asked Conor.

Luke put his hands on Conor's shoulders, in dramatic fashion. "I hate to tell you this, Conor..." Luke said, trailing off, but looking into his friend's eyes knowingly.

"Hate to tell me what?" Conor enquired. "Spit it out, man," he said, shrugging Luke's hands away.

"The thing is... we're not awfully good at Hundred-to-One, are we? I mean, we're in the last year at junior school, but—"

"But what?" Conor asked, unsure where this was going.

"We're in the last year at junior school. So we've been around a good long while, obviously," Luke told him.

"Obviously," Conor agreed.

"But there are guys in year five..." Luke went on... "Who could kick our butt."

"Oh," replied Conor, beginning to see Luke's point.

"In fact there's that one kid in year four that—"

"Okay, I get it!"

"No, listen," Luke pressed on. "There's that one kid in year four that destroyed me, right? And hasn't let me forget about it, either."

"Ah," said Conor. "Is that the kid with the limp and the watery eye? I always wondered why he went around calling you a loser to everyone."

"What do you mean, *to everyone?*" asked Luke. "I hope you corrected him??"

"I'm not going to shout at a little kid with a gammy leg, Luke. Dude, how would that look? Besides, he *did* kick your butt. You just said."

Luke shrugged his shoulders. "Yeah, I guess. Whatever. But, anyway, that's the point. We're not very good, is what I'm saying, if even this Tiny Tim kid with one watery eye—"

"Is that why he used the eye patch?" Conor interrupted.

"What?"

"The kid in year four. With the watery eye. Is that why he wore an eye patch before?"

"Before what?" asked Luke, confused.

"Just before!" said Conor.

"I guess so?" answered Luke.

Conor pondered this for a moment. "I thought it was just his thing, like maybe he had a thing for Jack Sparrow or something. I didn't know it was a medical thing."

"What?" Luke began. "Jack Sparrow never wore a—"

Conor clenched his fist and tapped Luke's arm with his knuckles. "Okay, enough about Blackbeard or whatever. Look, we can win this thing with you on deck, Luke," he assured Luke. "You're our secret weapon!"

"I am?" asked Luke, somewhat flattered, yet totally confused. "How do you figure that, exactly?"

"Well," replied Conor, with an *isn't-it-obvious?* sort of expression. "You've got twenty-three Victory Supreme wins, dude!" he exclaimed, bursting with pride over his best friend's truly magnificent record. *"That's* why you're our secret weapon. Duh. With you on board, we can beat *anyone*. You could give the rest of our squad *lessons*, practically."

Luke glanced over at the stained-glass windows of the church, of which Reverend Scott stood directly underneath. Luke felt his cheeks flush, and he bowed his head. He could feel the good Lord's judgement burning into his very soul.

"See, now here's the thing about that," Luke confessed to his friend. "I, *em*... well, I may have been a bit generous in my description of how many wins I've actually achieved, and, *erm*... exaggerated just slightly."

"What?" replied Conor, shaking his head from side to side in both disappointment and dismay. "So what are you saying, then? How many have you actually got?"

Luke held his hand out in front of him, extending each finger in turn as if counting, bobbing his head along in time as he did so. "Well... if I factor in what I did last week..." he said, the forefinger of one hand laying over the extended pinkie finger of the other, where he'd apparently left off counting.

"Yes?"

"... And then the ones I got this morning..." Luke went on, looking up and to the left, as people do when they're deep in thought.

"Yes??"

"Precisely none," said Luke, looking back down, his eyes returning to focus.

"None?? As in *none*? Like, *none*, none? As in, *totally none??"* asked Conor in disbelief.

Luke touched each of his fingers again, as if the act of counting again might somehow produce a different result. But of course the answer was the same, and he turned both hands over, palms-up, in defeat. "A big fat zero," Luke admitted, with a deep exhale. "I've been *trying*, though, Conor. Honestly I have. And I managed a top-four finish just this morning, right before we came!"

But Conor was less than impressed by Luke's professed top-four finish. "I should have known," said Conor, now circling Luke to emphasise the shame he should be feeling. "I should have guessed. Every time we play, you're always camping, always hiding behind something, always hoping to get a shot off," he said. "Aww, crap," he added, sighing a heavy sigh, realisation setting in. "I thought we were really going to win that thousand pounds."

Luke raised himself to his full height of four-foot-four. "We can practice, Conor!" he insisted. "We can get better! And, besides, you've got a Victory Supreme win, right? So we can't be that bad, right? I mean, not *completely*. Right...?"

"Right, so that's one Victory Supreme win between us. That's brilliant. Only..." Conor began.

But Conor didn't finish his sentence. And now he, too, was bowing his head in a penitent manner.

"Hang on, you haven't got a win either, have you?" asked Luke, to which Conor scrunched his mouth to the side of his face.

"I can't believe you lied to me!" Luke exclaimed.

"*Me*? What about *you*??" Conor returned.

"That's different!" Luke replied.

"How is it different?"

"It just is!"

"That doesn't even make any—"

Luke raised his hand to the air, signalling he'd had enough. "We both lied, I guess. I thought it was girlfriends we were supposed to lie about having, not wins on Hundred-to-One? Anyway," he said, his confidence returning. "We've got, what, six weeks? We can practice, Conor! Come on, we can do this, yeah?"

"We can..." replied Conor, drifting back to his daydream, in which he was lifting the cheque up for all to see, and smiling to the TV cameras. "Right, then. Okay, so for a squad we need four people," he added, returning to practical matters at hand. "Right. So who else should we get? What about the kid in year four who kicked your butt? The one with the gammy leg and the watery—?"

"No chance!" snapped Luke, but then reconsidered. "Well, having said that," he went on, more reasonable now. "*Hmm*, I suppose if we want to win, we ought to consider it. Wait, hang on, how about this? How about we hold an audition? You know, like a pop group looking for a new drummer? We could set up our very own Hundred-to-One club. We could—" Luke began, but stopped short. "Oi. Where do you keep pulling these cupcakes from?" asked Luke, in reference to Conor being midway through demolishing yet another one — and it looked good, too, the cupcake.

Conor wiped away a rogue crumb from his chin, but continued to hold the pose, the back of his hand pressed against his lips, deep in thought. "I like it," he considered. "Yeah, we can definitely do that audition thing. But..."

"But what?"

"Well, the only problem I see with that is that the people auditioning might be loads better than us?"

"Why would that be a problem?" Luke asked, confused.

"It's just they might not want to join our team if they know we're rubbish, see?" Conor explained.

Luke nodded his head, understanding now. "Well, that wouldn't be hard. Them being better than us, I mean," he said. Then he cast a glance over to Reverend Scott. The

Reverend was on the other side of the room. Even so, Luke was worried he'd know — somehow, he always *knew* — the words about to come out of Luke's mouth. "We'll just keep that fact to ourselves, right?" he said, turning back to Conor. "No one needs to know we're rubbish at the game, yeah?"

"Agreed," replied Conor, offering a hand to seal the deal. "And I can see it now, Conor and Luke, in charge of the... the..." he said, searching for inspiration.

"The Momentous Melee Hundred-to-One Club!" Luke came in, raising his finger in triumph.

"Ohh, I like it," replied Conor agreeably. "It's got a certain ring to it, for sure," he said, but was now distracted by the appearance of another cupcake now somehow, like magic, in his possession. "Conor O'Reilly. President of The Momentous Melee Hundred-to-One Club," he considered aloud, enjoying the sound of the words, and licking his lips in appreciation of both the cupcake and his new self-appointed title.

Luke eyed him suspiciously. "I think you meant to say *co-*president?"

"Sure, whatever," replied Conor. "Co-president is fine. It's just that *president* rolls off the tongue better, you know? But, actually, I don't even know what a president does, to be honest. Anyway, I hope you've not upset that kid in year four as we may need his services if we're going to win this thing. Ah, I can just see it now, Luke... stood on a stage... me holding a cheque for one thousand pounds..."

"*Us* holding a cheque for one thousand pounds," Luke corrected him.

"Yes, yes, of course," Conor assured him. "You needn't get too bogged down in the details. This cheque might not be very large. It could be rather small in size. So it might be better if *one* of us was to hold it. That's all I'm saying."

"Fair enough," Luke answered his friend, chuckling. "As long as we both get to spend it. And right now the only thing stopping us is the fact that neither of us are particularly good at the game."

"Minor details, Luke. Minor details," Conor told him. "First, we set sail," he said. "And, then..." he went on, in search of a proper analogy. "And then we..."

"And then we win!" said Luke.

"And then we win!" Conor agreed, laughing.

LEVEL TWO
FOREST FURY

The teaching staff of Braddan primary school was well versed in dealing with the unexpected. They were seasoned professionals, able to handle any situation thrown before them. And yet the vision of Conor O'Reilly and Luke Jacobs sat on the playground wall, swinging their legs, *half an hour before school started*... Well, it was nothing short of baffling, and they found themselves at a bit of a loss. One of the teachers even questioned as to whether the boys had actually gone home from the day previous. How else to explain this anomaly?

How else indeed?

"Ah," offered Mr Benson, the boys' teacher for the year, taking a sip from his coffee as he joined the rest of the faculty peering through the cold glass panes of the windows overlooking the playground. "Masters O'Reilly and Jacobs asked me if they could use the ICT room for an audition they were looking to host. They appeared enthusiastic enough, but I'll be honest, I didn't think they'd see it through. I was happily proven wrong, however. They even had flyers printed for the occasion! But I must mark them down on their English, as it would seem they've used the word *addition* rather than *audition*. Still. I've actually allowed them to use part of the first lesson period to encourage their initiative."

It was a particularly chilly 1st December morning, with the feeling of an imminent snowfall in the air. Mr Benson left the cosy confines of the staff room to address his two students. "Come on, you two!" he shouted across the playground. "I can't have you sat out here freezing yourselves to death! The parents of the last students to do so were particularly unimpressed the previous time that happened!" But his attempt at humour, such as it was, went straight over the heads of his enthusiastic students. "Are you all set up?" he asked them, once they'd made their way inside.

Conor nodded, smartly revealing a notepad to show his teacher. "I've brought this to take notes," said Conor. "We'll be interviewing a fair few candidates, I expect, so I wanted to keep track of who was who."

"Impressive," replied Mr Benson. "So are you lads going to show me what this audition is all about?" he asked, a boyish grin across his face.

"Sure," replied Luke, removing a baseball cap from his backpack. "This might help," he suggested, handing it over.

Mr Benson looked the hat over, examining the custom stitching.

"My mum made them," said Luke by way of explanation. "I forgot to tell her that I needed them this morning, so I think she was up most of the night. She wasn't happy, but she likes to sew."

Luke paused in his explanation, his mouth held open, his eyebrows raised. This meant an awful pun was likely about to follow. Sure enough...

"... Sew no problem," Luke continued, laughing merrily at his own, fabric-based, joke. He looked to Mr Benson for his reaction, and then over to Conor. "See? I *told* you it was funny, Conor," he said, in reference to the obviously rehearsed line, and to Mr Benson's pained, obligatory chuckle.

Mr Benson found himself the proud custodian of a beige baseball cap, festooned with the words *The Momentous Melee Hundred-to-One Club* embroidered across the front.

"We're thinking of selling them, actually," said Luke. "I've not mentioned it to my mum yet. But I'm sure she'll be keen enough on the idea."

"I get to keep this? I'm honoured," replied Mr Benson. "And particularly impressed with the initiative shown, I must say."

Conor set up a number of seats outside the classroom door, in the hallway, for the comfort of those who'd soon be waiting for their big opportunity to impress. He hoped it would be enough to accommodate the teeming throng certain to appear.

"It's all about the experience," explained Luke, meanwhile. "If you'd sit there, Mr Benson?" he offered, directing him like a cinema attendant to the designated gaming chair he'd arranged.

The overhead lights were turned off, and Mr Benson stared at the dark screen at the front of the room until the Hundred-to-One game suddenly burst into view.

"Now, you lads do realise you're only allowed access to the game for the purposes of your audition, don't you? I just want to make that clear."

"Yes, yes," Conor assured him, back in the room.

"Of course," Luke chimed in.

Conor placed a controller in the teacher's empty hands. Mr Benson stared at the device as if it were an artefact from another world. Which, to him, in essence, it probably was. "So, now... what is it that I do here...?" Mr Benson asked.

Conor realised that it'd likely take his teacher an age to access the game, unfamiliar as he apparently was with gaming. "Should I do it for you?" Conor asked, removing the controller from his teacher's hands for a moment before Mr Benson could respond. "Here, I'll get you in the game," he told him. "To save time." As he was doing just that, he explained further...

"Okay, so the audition is simply down to who impresses us, right? *Us,* being the judges. As for you, you'll be playing a solo game here — that means by yourself, no teammates — where there'll be one hundred real people online. Your mission is to shoot as many of them as you can. Extra points will be awarded for building skills and for kills achieved."

"I'm sorry?" Mr Benson came back, clearly puzzled. "Wait, hang on," he said, a thought occurring to him. "It's eight-twenty in the morning. There's no way you'll have one hundred people online at this time of day playing the game, surely?"

Conor and Luke looked at each other, and then laughed out loud at their teacher's naïveté. Not in an unkind way or anything. They just knew he wasn't clever enough to be making a joke like that, and that he really meant it, so they felt kind of sorry for him, actually. But he'd soon see.

"Anyway, Mr Benson," Conor told him, placing the game controller back in his hands. "This is the Hundred-to-One Hotel you're in now, the starting area, in the hotel foyer, where all the players assemble before the game starts, okay? Don't worry, though, it won't take too long."

"He means it won't take long for enough people to get to the foyer, and for the match to get going," Luke added helpfully. "Although the match itself, at least for you, likely won't take long to complete because..."

"Here! This fellow just struck me with an axe!" Mr Benson protested. Their teacher stared blankly at the screen in disbelief as one of the first arrivals began to attack him for no sensible, justifiable reason that he could fathom. "Here, is he meant to do that? That's quite poor sportsmanship! Very bad form!"

Luke and Conor couldn't help laughing again. Poor Mr Benson. He honestly didn't have a clue. He'd been staying cloistered away in school so long he had no idea how things worked out in the world.

"That's the point of the game," Conor told him.

"That's the whole point of it," Luke confirmed, agreeing. "Besides. You're still in the hotel foyer. So you can't take any damage just yet. It's just this player messing about, so it's not anything to be concerned with."

"So it's just hitting, this game?" Mr Benson asked, trying his best to get a sense of the whole thing. "People hitting each other...?"

"What else would it—?" Luke began.

"It's quite good fun to dance," suggested Conor helpfully, not wishing to hurt his teacher's feelings. After all, it wasn't his fault he didn't know much. To be fair, most adults didn't.

"In fact, we're giving bonus points for the best dance," Conor went on, proud of this new idea he just came up with on the spot. "Five bonus points."

"Nice," said Luke, nodding appreciatively.

"Dancing, is it?" Mr Benson asked, uncertain as to how dancing might possibly enter into the affair, but game nonetheless at this unexpected development. "Well," he replied, lowering his controller. "It's been a while, but I think I can give it a go," he said, his left shoulder beginning to move in time with the game's background music. A moment later his right shoulder joined the party, followed shortly thereafter by his head, which bobbed to the beat of the automated soundtrack. "Not too bad for a stuffy old teacher, eh, wot?" he asked. "I've still got the moves, I should think," he added with a grin, rather pleased with himself.

"Mr Benson..." said Luke, mortified.

Conor, though, didn't blink. "You dance in *there*, Mr Benson," he said, as politely as he could, pointing at the AV screen. "In the *game*. Not out here."

"What? Why would I...?" Mr Benson began. But before he had time to consider how he might reproduce his dance moves in the game, and for what purpose, he was suddenly being jostled about as the other players in the foyer began heading for the hotel lifts. "What's happening?" he asked. "Why is everybody leaving? Is the game over already?"

"No, it's only just starting now," said Luke. "Are you joking or are you...? Oh. Oh, you're serious. Okay. Okay, so right now everybody's heading to the lifts," Luke went on. "See all the lift doors with the area names on them? You pick which area you want to go to, and then go get in that lift to get there." Luke felt this should all be obvious, but he explained it as politely as he could.

"Ah," replied Mr Benson, eager to redeem himself. "Jolly good. Splendid," he said. "So, *ehm*... which door shall I pass through, then? That is, which corresponding area should I be travelling to...?"

"Whichever one you want to go to," suggested Conor, seeing the perplexed look on Luke's face, and stepping in.

"Ah, well, yes. Yes, that's precisely what I'm asking, I'm afraid. Which area *is* it that I should want to go to?" asked a thoroughly befuddled Mr Benson.

"Whichever area you *want* to go to," Conor answered him, confused as to why his teacher was confused.

"It doesn't matter which," said Luke, finding his voice once again. "You can pick any door. It doesn't matter."

"Splendid!" replied Mr Benson. "Well, then. *Forest Fury* certainly does sound enticing, doesn't it? What fabulous wonders might it hold? What adventures lie there in wait? What possible surprises could it—?"

"Forest Fury is fine!" Conor and Luke both said at once.

"Right. So when the lift door opens, you'll want to check your parachute, and—" Luke started to say, resuming his previous instruction.

"Hang on, how's that? Parachute? I don't understand," interrupted Mr Benson.

"To get down to the area," Conor offered. "To get down to Forest Fury."

"But I'm taking a lift," said the teacher. "The lift doesn't take me straight there? Why would I need a parachute? It's just that I'm in a lift, not an aeroplane, so where does this parachute enter into things?"

Luke and Conor both laughed. Mr Benson was being silly. But he didn't mean to be.

"The lift doors will open," Luke carried on. "The lift doors will open, and you'll find yourself high up above your target destination. And then you'll need to jump out and parachute down."

"*Hrm*. How very peculiar. How very peculiar indeed. I should think it would make far more sense to simply arrive at my destination directly," Mr Benson considered aloud.

"It's just the way these things are done," said an increasingly exasperated Luke. "It's just the way games are played."

"And it's more fun, besides," Conor added. "Mr Benson, I'm guessing you've not played this before?" Conor gently suggested.

Conor looked at Luke, and Luke looked at Conor, both unsure if maybe they were on a reality TV show. It was the only logical explanation for this kind of behaviour they were witness to.

"You assume correctly, young Master O'Reilly," came the eventual reply.

Luke wasn't sure how much more of this he could take. He moved closer, pointing to the controller. "Right. So the lift doors have just opened. Now, if you press the button marked 'A' you'll jump out," he offered.

"Oh. Oh, dear. It's quite a long ways down, isn't it?" the teacher said, peering over the edge. "It isn't dangerous at all, is it?"

"Yes," Luke answered him, but then quickly continued, "Well, no. Later, yes. But, here, no. Not this jumping part. Because you'll have a parachute."

Having been assured he wasn't to be falling to his death, Mr Benson did as he'd been instructed, and he pressed the button he was directed to press. He was soon dispatched from the lift, gliding gracefully via parachute towards the forested area far below, guided along, as it happened, with the assistance of a giant — though very helpful and friendly — wild wallaby.

"It's quite a nice view from up here!" Mr Benson remarked. "And at least there's no more hitting at present," he added, enjoying his descent. "This reminds me of my grandfather on my mother's side. Lovely chap. And the stories he used to tell! He was a paratrooper in the war, don't you know..."

Conor and Luke listened politely as their teacher yattered on about the war exploits of his grandfather on his mother's side as a paratrooper. Neither of them knew which war was being referred to as that was ancient history. They could have asked, but it didn't really matter. They knew, of course, that service to one's country was something to be proud of. Only they just couldn't really understand why people ever fought in real life when you could do it in a video game instead with nobody ever actually getting hurt. Maybe they didn't have video games back then?

"... Although I'm quite certain my grandfather didn't have a giant wallaby to accompany him," Mr Benson was now concluding. "What's the purpose of this furry fellow again?"

"You can customise the game with certain add-ons," Luke told him. "And Conor—"

"I like wallabies," explained Conor.

"Ah. Jolly good," replied the teacher, just as his in-game character was touching down. "You know, I rather liked that part, I have to say. That last bit, especially, I almost felt like Mary Poppins."

This received no reply.

"Mary Poppins?" their teacher said again. "Wafting down gently with her umbrella, yes...?"

"Okay. Right," replied Luke. He didn't know what else to say. Luke glanced at Conor. Conor wasn't blinking again.

With Mr Benson's character safely on the ground, his wallaby companion hopped away and disappeared, its duty fulfilled. Their teacher took a breath, working out, at least, how to move the joystick around in order to survey his surroundings, and taking a few leisurely moments to do just that.

"You're near Forest Fury," advised Luke helpfully. "You may want to move, as it's a busy area and you might get shot at very quickly."

But Mr Benson didn't move. Beyond being able to simply look around, it was obvious he was at something of a loss as to how to proceed.

"Should I show you how?" asked Luke. And in a case of role reversal, Luke spent several minutes instructing his teacher on the finer workings of the game. He patiently explained what each button did — how to aim and shoot, for instance, how you broke into a sprint, and how he would eventually go about building. *If you ever make it that far*, Luke thought to himself. But Luke was proud of his ability to outline the game to a novice, at least. "So, Mr Benson. You have a go, and see how you get on," he said, after concluding his tutorial.

Precisely six seconds later, the screen went black. "Oh, dear!" Mr Benson exclaimed. "Have I been done in already?"

Conor chewed his lip. "*Ehm*, no, Mr Benson. It looks like you've mashed the controller and somehow managed to turn the console off in the process. I didn't even know that was possible, so... cheers for that?"

"Ah. So I'm guessing that I'm not going to be shortlisted for the final squad?" their teacher proposed.

"Sadly not," replied Luke. "I'll give you a couple of points for the dance at the beginning, though."

"Five points for that," Conor added.

"And you do get to keep the hat," Luke reminded him.

"Well, then. If I've not got a future playing Hundred-to-One, I suppose I'll need to resume my teaching duties," said the teacher, handing back the game controller. "Good luck, gentlemen," he told them, and then tapped at his watch. "Don't forget you've only got the room for one hour," he reminded them.

Conor and Luke spent the next twenty-five minutes conducting further extensive field research — which loosely meant they played Hundred-to-One. The audition was due to begin five minutes after the first bell, but to raise the tension Luke suggested they extend this to seven minutes after.

With a glance at the clock, and the appointed time near, Conor took his chair and faced it towards the classroom door... but then flipped it around backwards, sitting down again the wrong way, with his chest pressed against the back of the chair and his arms hanging over.

"Why are you sat like that?" asked Luke, making his way to the classroom door.

Conor shifted his bum in the seat. "I'm sure I've seen important people on Netflix sitting like this, and, as I'm a president, I thought it was a good idea."

"Co-president," corrected Luke. He stuck his head through the opened door, peering outside to the temporary waiting area they'd designated.

"How many waiting?" Conor called over, now struggling with the chair digging into his armpits.

Luke pulled his head back in and closed the door. "Well..." he replied. "In total?"

"As opposed to what? Yes of course, *in total*, what else?" replied Conor.

"Alright, in total, then... Nobody," Luke came back.

"What? *Nobody?* This is the hottest ticket ever! How can there be nobody? Did you forget to put the posters up or something?"

"Of course not. You were there with me putting them up!" Luke answered him. "Give it a couple more minutes. I'm sure everyone's on the way. And put your hat on, too. My mum spent ages making them, and plus we need to make things look official, and... Hang on, what's wrong with your hands? They look really weird. Like, all pale and everything," said Luke.

Conor flapped his hands, like he was shaking water from his fingertips. "I think the flow of blood got cut off. I, *ehm...* I think I'm going to sit normally," he said.

"I think that would be a good idea," Luke cautioned him. "The school nurse might not be in yet, and we don't want any complications here."

"No we don't," Conor agreed, regaining feeling to his extremities once again. "Hey, wait. I think I just heard a noise at the door. Do you want to check again?"

"Sure," Luke answered, and he made his way over and tentatively eased the door back open, hoping for the best. And to his immense pleasure, he caught sight of two pairs of feet before him. "Come on in," he announced cheerily, until looking up and realising the feet belonged to a girl from reception class — one of the little'uns — and the other pair to a woman, likely her mother.

The woman held up a piece of paper. "I'm here to see the headmaster," she announced.

Luke's shoulders dropped. "So you're not here for the...? Nevermind. Headmaster's office is around the corner. I can show you if you'd like?"

With the school visitor safely directed to the correct office, Luke trudged back on his way to their rather disappointing auditions — disappointing in the sense that there was a distinct lack of any. Salvation, possibly, however, was skulking around the corridor in the form of Jimmy Redmond. He was a familiar face, a good friend to Conor and Luke. And, whilst not the most proficient at Hundred-to-One, he'd certainly make a worthy substitute player for the squad, to step in at a moment's notice should the need arise.

"Oi. Jimmy," said Luke. But there was no response. Jimmy was engrossed at the task at hand, whatever that task may have been. "Jimmy," he repeated, through gritted teeth. "Are you lost?" Luke asked.

"Lost?" said Jimmy. "No. No, not at all," he said, appearing quite aware of where he wanted to be.

Luke pointed up the corridor, to his destination. "Jimmy, the auditions are in the ICT room. Back that way," Luke made clear. "Conor's in there. We can count on you, right, mate?"

Jimmy laughed, shaking his head with a quick side-to-side motion. "Sorry, Luke. But Harry Newbold had the same idea as you and Conor. So, no. See, he's also had an audition. Not really as official as yours or anything. He set up in the sports equipment room. But he was paying ten pounds to anyone who made it into his squad. Everyone was there trying out, even that limping kid from year four. You know the one I'm talking about? He's—"

"Yes, yes. I know who he is," Luke replied, in no need of an explanation. "I can't believe you've dropped us for Harry Newbold, though. That's pretty cold, Jimmy."

"Well he *is* kind of good at Hundred-to-One, mate. He's got nearly as many Victory Supreme wins as you, remember. And then of course there's the matter of the ten quid."

Luke took the half-compliment, thinking it best, without correction or complaint. "So, you've joined his squad, then? And pocketed ten pounds in the process?" he asked.

"Sadly, no," Jimmy said, pulling his front pockets inside-out to show they were unhappily empty. "I didn't stand a chance. I only lasted about five minutes, to tell you the honest truth. Some of the people he's got there are bloody brilliant."

"Ah. So, you'll be coming along to our audition?" Luke proposed, hope rising again within him.

"No," replied Jimmy.

"No? But why not?"

"See, here's the thing, Luke," Jimmy explained. "Harry Newbold is paying me five pounds to take all of your posters down, right? So I'll need to finish that first, so I can get my money. It's five pounds," said Jimmy again, as if that should clear up any confusion. "Maybe I'll come along after I'm done, though," he offered. "Have you had many people turn up so far?"

"No, not many, Jimmy," Luke replied. "But that's hardly a surprise, now is it? I think I may need to evaluate my circle of friends, Jimmy," Luke told him, narrowing his eyes for effect.

"It's five pounds," Jimmy repeated cheerily, smiling, and by all appearances happy with his efforts for the day. "Do you want them back?" he asked, holding out a wad of papers rolled together. "Only I have to turn them in, still. Otherwise I don't get paid. Plus I've still got some left to collect," he said, eyeing a certain spot on the hallway wall again.

"No, you're alright Jimmy," Luke assured him, motioning for Jimmy to hold onto the posters he'd already gotten. "It's a bit late now. The damage is already done," he said. "Thanks for your support, though," he added sarcastically. "You're a real pal. I'll be sure to ask Conor to thank you when he next bumps into you."

"It's five pounds!" Jimmy replied, more to himself now than Luke. And he started singing a little song to himself as he set about pulling the nearby poster down. It was a happy little tune, the lyrics consisting of *It's five pounds*, repeated over and over again melodically.

Luke returned to the ITC room, grumbling under his breath the entire way, and kicking imaginary obstacles out of his way as he went. Once he arrived there, he saw their makeshift waiting room — or waiting hall, as it were — was still distinctly lacking in occupants. He opened the classroom door, half wondering if there'd been a last-minute influx of eager candidates. But the vision of Conor performing a handstand against the wall (rather well, it must be said — the boy was skilled) confirmed their audition had been an abject failure.

"We've got competition," announced Luke as he entered, chucking the rolled-up poster he'd just pulled down from the door into the bin.

"Yeah, I know," replied Conor from his upside-down vantage point, his head turning the colour of a beetroot. "There'll be loads of competition. But we'll beat them, and claim that cheque. Or at least that's the plan."

Luke twisted his neck and his body around like a contortionist, so that he was looking at Conor's face the right way despite its wrong-way-round position. "You really should stop doing that, Conor. Your eyes are actually bulging," he said, straightening up again. "And I think I just hurt myself," he added. "Anyway. What I meant was, we've got competition closer to home. Harry Newbold has set up his own audition, and is conducting it presently. And it looks like he's already managed to pick up the best gamers in the school."

"Well that hardly seems fair," Conor answered, pushing his feet off the wall, one at a time, and collecting himself into a standing position again, like a toy Slinky. He wobbled for a moment as he gathered himself together and the surplus blood exited his face. "I thought we'd have at least a couple people turn up, though. We did place those posters all over the school, after all."

Luke considered revealing his conversation of a moment ago, but was worried that, if he did, Jimmy might end up nursing a fat lip if Conor heard what he'd done, and Jimmy remained a friend, despite everything. "There's been some complications," was all Luke finally said.

Conor shook his head, which made him wobble a little more, his circulation still sorting itself out as it was. "My sister said she'd be on board," he offered. "If that helps?"

"She's what, six?" asked Luke, collapsing into a chair. "We'll need to go a bit further afield than the school, I think," he mused. "There are a few guys from the other schools that go to the community centre at the church. Maybe we could get them on our team?"

"They'll probably be in squads in their own school?"

"Probably," sighed Luke. "We may just need to settle for the ones Harry Newbold didn't select? His cast-offs?"

"Okay, gentlemen!" barked Mr Benson, making his reappearance. "That's time up, and ready to get back to classes!" He took a quick scan. "Are all your candidates away already?" he asked, in reference to the empty room, but before waiting for a response, he moved closer to Conor. "Are you all right, Conor?" he asked, his concern evident. "Only your face looks awfully peculiar. Do you need to see the nurse?"

Conor felt his face, pressing his fingers into his cheeks. "What's wrong with it?" he asked, certain the blood flow would be back to normal by now.

"That's the way it always looks," Luke suggested.

Mr Benson stared a moment longer, until Conor just shrugged. "That's the way it always looks, I think," he agreed, shrugging his shoulders a second time.

"Did you get anybody signed up, then?" Mr Benson asked, moving on.

Conor held his fingers up in a 'V' shape — the nice version, not the other one. "Two," he announced, glumly.

Mr Benson smiled. "Ah. But that's good, isn't it? You've now got the four you need, isn't that right?"

"No," replied Conor. "I meant the two people already here. Me and Luke."

"And maybe Conor's little sister," Luke added, with no enthusiasm at all.

"Nobody turned up," Conor explained.

Mr Benson could easily have just ushered the boys on their way, but he could see the dejection written all over their faces. "Look, boys," he said. "I know you're a little disappointed at the moment," he went on, thoughtfully. "But you've impressed me with the professionalism you've demonstrated. You've shown some real business acumen that I'm sure we'll see more of. You've got another few weeks, so I'm sure you'll get the other two people you need. Failing that, I'm sure I could offer my services?"

Conor grinned like he'd got wind. "Eh, thank you, Mr Benson, but we'll have to, perhaps, you know—"

"There's an upper age limit, sir," Luke cut across. "Sadly, that would rule you out," he explained, sparing his teacher's feelings — and Conor's squirming — in the process.

With that, the two would-be entrepreneurs plodded unhappily back to their regular class. But they knew Mr Benson was correct in one respect — they still had some time yet in order to collect the additional teammates they needed. So all was not lost. Their faltering egos couldn't have picked a worse time to walk past Harry Newbold's class, though. And they stopped dead in their tracks as they witnessed the spectacle of Harry and several other students tearing a collection of Luke and Conor's posters to bits, laughing merrily as they did so.

Conor once again held up his fingers in a 'V' shape, but this time it wasn't the nice version he used. It was the rather more rude version.

Luke grabbed Conor's arm before anyone saw, and he pulled his friend to the side, out of view. "Look, we need to forget about them, and focus on making sure we're the best we can be," he began, in a sort of motivational masterclass. "Sure, Harry and his squad are probably the best in school. But we're not exactly useless at the game, are we? And think about this— If we've been lying about how good we are, then chances are they have too, right? Right. So we need to set to work, practising all the time, and watching what other people who really know what they're doing play the game."

"Twitch," said Conor, simply.

"What?"

"Twitch," Conor said again.

Luke didn't understand the *why* of it, but did as he was instructed, blinking several times in quick succession, followed by an impressive flurry of nostril flaring.

Conor took a step back, away from the crazy person before him. "Okay, I... I'm not even going to ask what that was."

"You told me to—"

"You need to watch Twitch, is what I'm saying," Conor said. "All the top gamers go on there and livestream their games. There's some who aren't really all that good, of course, and so nothing special. But then there's others who are absolutely unbelievable."

"That's it, old chum," said Luke, punching his own fist like Batman. "We just need to spend every waking minute practising Hundred-to-One or watching other people playing Hundred-to-One. There's nothing that'll get in our way. Not even that idiot Harry Newbold."

Conor raised his hand, even though he clearly didn't need permission to speak. They were in school, so it was likely force of habit. "When you say there's nothing that'll get in our way..."

"Yes?"

"I think you're being a little... what's the word? ... optimistic. Yeah. Optimistic," Conor told him.

"How do you mean?" asked Luke.

"Optimistic," Conor began. "It means—"

"No, I know what it means. I mean, why do you say that, is what I'm asking."

"I'm pretty sure that my mum and your mum are not really going to buy into the extent of our research strategy."

"How do you—?"

"I mean I'm not sure how keen they'll be on us spending every waking hour online," explained Conor.

"Oh. You could be right there," groaned Luke. "In fact my mum was just going on about reducing time on electronics the other day. So, yeah. You could be right." Luke thought for a moment, considering options. "There's only one thing for it, Conor," he said eventually. "We'll have to run away from home."

"Yeah?" replied Conor, weighing this up.

"Oh, and tell your sister that she's on the reserves bench," Luke added. "At least for now."

"Yeah."

LEVEL THREE
BADMINTON TOURNEY

uke's mum had taken to giving him five minutes' notice before anything was required of him, be that teatime, shower time, or we're-going-out-for-family-time. The process worked sufficiently well, for the most part, and gave Luke time to wrap up whatever he was doing. Now, as to what he'd be doing, you'd be forgiven for imagining that Luke spent every conceivable minute on his game console playing Hundred-to-One. It might very well have been a reasonable enough assumption until only recently. But ever since Conor had introduced him to the world of Twitch, Luke also spent every conceivable minute watching *other* people playing Hundred-to-One on *their* consoles as well.

Rather than Twitch encouraging Luke, however, it ended up having quite the opposite effect on his confidence. From Luke's perspective, it sort of reminded him of the time earlier in the year when his dad caught his mum watching the bloke next door chopping a tree down, the bloke's sweat-embossed muscles glistening in the sun with every swing of the axe. That's the way his mum described it, anyway — much to Luke's horror. Anyway, Luke's dad felt somewhat inadequate by comparison, and even ended up going to the gym for the next few weeks thereafter. Well, Luke laughed at the time, of course. But now it was his turn to feel inferior by comparison. Luke was marvelling at people playing Hundred-to-One at a level he could only dream about. These guys could one-shot a rival at three hundred yards — whilst hopping one-legged on a roller-skate if they wanted to. They were on an entirely different level altogether, and Luke was feeling even more dejected knowing he was a million miles away from where he needed to be.

"Five minutes until badminton!" shouted Mum.

Ordinarily there would be a succession of several more reminders forthcoming, but on this Tuesday night Luke switched off his electronics without any further prompts.

It'd been weeks since he'd last played badminton with his dad, and Luke had to wipe a layer of what looked very much like dust from the cover of his racquet, but he was ready in short order.

Tom did a double-take as he found Luke present and correct at the front door, eager to go. "I'm looking forward to this, Luke," he told his son. "It's been too long since you ran your dear old dad ragged around the badminton court."

His father was being kind, and Luke knew this. In point of fact, his dad was one of the finest players on the Island. So getting beaten by his dad was to be expected. But Luke did enjoy the games played with his dad. He maybe didn't so much enjoy getting beaten on a regular basis, mind, but his performance improved each time they played, at least. And teaming up with such a skilled player did have its distinct advantages, as he and his dad having won the annual tournament the year before could attest.

For his part, Tom was eager to retain the parent/child tournament's annual trophy once again. But he didn't want to appear as one of those 'pushy' parents, forcing their kids into something they didn't want. So to see Luke ready and willing — and actually champing at the bit, no less — meant a great deal to him.

The badminton league was held at the National Sports Centre, a short drive from their house, and Luke spotted several of the usual badminton faces walking in from the car park upon their arrival.

"Does the competition start tonight, Dad?"

Tom took a sheet of paper from the car's glovebox. He flicked on the overhead light, and then ran his finger over the text. "The Christmas knock-out tournament starts next week, apparently. It's the singles league next week, and doubles the following week, which includes the parent-child competition. So it looks like we've got a couple more weeks to hone our skills, Luke. So, we'll just play for a bit of fun tonight, all right?"

Luke smiled, but he knew full well his dad was even more competitive than he was, and that deep down his dad would happily walk over hot coals or more to retain the trophy.

"Evening, guys!" shouted Roberta, longstanding stalwart of the Isle of Man Badminton world, as the pair entered the building. Roberta was a treasure, running the badminton clubs for little or no reward other than the pleasure and satisfaction she took from doing so.

"Tom, if I can ask you and Luke to partner up on the court at the far side of the hall? That would be lovely. We've got a new couple tonight, so it might be quite nice if I put them with you, as long as you don't mind?"

"No problem, Roberta," replied Tom, walking towards their appointed court, intermittently performing several deep lunges along the way to stretch his legs — and looking like a routine from The Ministry of Silly Walks in the process. Tom made his way to the net, extending a warm handshake through the tall gap under the netting once there. "I'm Tom, and this is my son, Luke," he announced with friendly enthusiasm to the fellow on the other side. The greeting was sincere, but Tom would have taken the opportunity to size up the opposition.

"Hey, great to meet you both," said the man. "I'm Stuart Robinson. My son Eric should be with us in a few moments. We can start without him, if you'd like?"

Tom knocked a gentle one across to get them warmed up, and within a few hits, Luke could see it was clear his dad had the edge over this new chap, Stuart. It was only a friendly game, but Luke figured it was likely they'd meet in the main competition, so there was certainly no harm in giving them a good thrashing at this point early on in their relationship.

As for Luke, he was at the top of his game. He'd been playing a computer game for months that drew out your ability to be calm under pressure, and giving you the reactions of a cat, so this actually helped a great deal. He knew those long hours in front of the TV were the ultimate preparation, so when Stuart knocked the shuttlecock over to his side of the court, Luke bent his knees and leapt up like a salmon swimming upstream against a raging current, swinging his racquet gloriously, with a force that produced an audible *swoosh* through the catgut latticework. Luke was setting his stall early, and as the strings made contact with...

... fresh air. The strings made contact only with fresh air, actually, with Luke missing his target completely. And to add insult to injury, the shuttlecock slapped into his forehead, just before the momentum of his efforts sent him tumbling unceremoniously to the floor.

"Nevermind," said Tom, with an enthusiastic slap on the back once he was up on his feet. "And no problem. You just need to get your brain working as quick as your hand."

To compound his embarrassment, though, Luke caught sight of a boy walking over to their court — a boy who'd undoubtedly witnessed his arm flailing like a windmill a few seconds earlier.

"Ah, here's Eric," announced Stuart. "My son."

Eric approached the court slowly, and Luke wondered if this might be a deliberate tactic to draw out the suspense. Only when Eric came closer into view did Luke realise the pace of his arrival was dictated by the fact he had a dodgy leg, suggested by a slight, yet noticeable, limp.

It was the kid from year four.

"Nice shot," remarked Eric sarcastically, announcing his eventual arrival.

Despite his embarrassment over his fumbled shot, Luke struggled to contain his excitement. This was the perfect opportunity presenting itself, to avenge his defeat against this little kid — two years his junior — who'd destroyed him online, but now in a real-life game. The top of Eric's head came up only to Luke's shoulders, plus he had a physical impediment. Whilst Luke would never admit it openly — especially the physical impediment part — these two points, he felt supremely assured, were the perfect combination of disadvantages for badminton, ensuring his own dominance over the boy.

"Here you go," offered Luke with renewed confidence, starting the match. Luke knocked it over the net, offering his dad a smug yet discreet rolling of his eyes in the process, confident as he was as to the outcome.

Eric hardly reacted, easily flicking out at the shuttlecock like he was swatting a fly. In a tight, controlled manner, he produced a brilliant, deft drop shop — a shot hit softly and with finesse to fall rapidly and close to the net in the opponent's court — that cleared the top of the net by mere millimetres, leaving Luke scrambling in futility. Even if

Luke'd had a skateboard and a jetpack, there was not a hope in heaven he'd ever have reached it.

For an ostensibly friendly game, Luke was soon dripping in sweat. His legs turned to a mixture of lead, then jelly, and then back to lead again. He was breathing with the ragged difficulty of a four-pack-a-day smoker with only one lung left to his name. Everything he returned over the net came back to him twice as quickly, and with expert precision. The surface of the court appeared to have doubled in size, and he was struggling to adequately cope, since at this rate a normal-sized court would have been enough of a struggle by itself.

Everything he stretched for was out of reach. It was as if not only had the court expanded to outsized proportions, but his racquet had shrunk down to the size of a soup spoon as well.

"Time out!" suggested Tom after a bit, taking out a couple of water bottles from his kit bag, and handing one over to his son. "Don't worry, Luke," he said encouragingly. "You've not played for a while. You've just lost a bit of match fitness, is all. Keep your chin up!" Tom knew exactly why Luke had lost his match fitness — too much time spent with a game controller in his hands and not enough time spent with a racquet in them — but that wasn't his observation to make.

Luke drained the water bottle's contents in seconds, after which he replied, "Dad, I'm ten years old! How can I have lost my fitness? I mean, I should be at my physical peak!" he said. "And, anyhow, what's *with* that kid?" he whispered, making sure his volume was low enough that the others couldn't hear him.

"How do you mean?" asked Tom, smartly performing a couple of star jumps to keep the legs ticking over.

Luke motioned his father over so he could continue to speak in confidence. "He goes to my school," Luke began, once his father had re-joined him. "And everything he touches, he's *good* at," he explained, looking over his shoulder to make sure he wasn't overheard. "He's got something wrong with his leg. Did you see? Did you see the way he walked in? It almost seemed like he was struggling to even walk as far as our court. And then, two seconds later, there he is sprinting around the court like an Olympic athlete! Honestly, Dad, I'm starting to think this kid is related to Yoda or something. I can't understand it!"

"Well... And don't take this the wrong way, Luke... But maybe he doesn't spend every waking moment sat in front of a TV, glued to his game controller? It's possible he spends his time on other pursuits. Like practising badminton, for instance."

Luke knew his dad was talking sense, but that didn't help matters any. If Luke didn't up his badminton game, and quick, it looked like Eric was going to have bragging rights over Luke the next day in school. Again.

Back in the game, once he'd worked off some of the cobwebs, Luke was exceptionally grateful to see some of the old magic return. The partnership of Luke and his dad was eventually bearing fruit once more, and the most *competitive* 'friendly' match they'd ever found themselves playing in resulted, eventually, in a very hard-fought victory for Team Jacobs.

"I can hear my heart beating in my ears," said Luke to himself, crouched over with his hands on his thighs.

With the match over, the two dads engaged in cheery small talk, centred on how Stuart and his family had only moved to the Island eighteen months prior. Eric, for his part, unlike Luke, hadn't broken a sweat and looked like he was ready to play another five games.

Luke extended a friendly hand. "Good game, Eric," he said, once he'd gotten his breath back.

"Thank you," said Eric, taking the hand offered. "I've only been playing for five months. So I might give you a better game next time," he promised.

Luke turned up his nose. "I'll look forward to it," he said, before walking away to wipe the gushing sweat from his head. "One thing," he added, turning back to face Eric. "You know how we played Hundred-to-One? And you...?" he began, not sure how to say it, exactly. And so he just said it. "Well, you kicked my butt is what you did."

"Did I?" replied Eric, cocking his head quizzically. "*Hmm.* I do that a lot. So often, actually, that I couldn't remember if you were one of the ones I beat."

Luke narrowed his eyes, unsure if Eric was mocking him. "Well, you did. And thanks for telling the whole school about it, by the way. Anyway, Eric..." Luke said, moving back in, closer... "I wanted to ask you. Did you know about my auditions for the Momentous Melee tournament?"

Eric looked at him blankly. "No," he said, simply.

"Ah. That'll be thanks to Jimmy taking our posters down, I expect," Luke replied.

Eric didn't say anything, so Luke carried on. "Okay, so me and Conor, my friend Conor O'Reilly, are setting up an elite Momentous Melee Hundred-to-One squad to enter the regional tournaments. I heard through the grapevine that you'd auditioned for Harry Newbold's squad already. But what I was wondering... Well, what I wondered was if maybe you'd like to join our team instead?"

"How are you elite?" enquired Eric.

"What?"

"You said you were elite," Eric explained. "But, if I'm only in year four, and you're year six, and I still managed to kick your butt so easily, I'm not sure that would qualify you in any way as elite...?"

Luke scratched his chin. "Alright, I take your point," he said. "How about we remove the 'elite' part and just call it our squad, then? Either way, there's a thousand pounds up for grabs. So what do you say? Would you consider ditching Harry's squad and joining ours instead?"

"Harry's an idiot. I don't like him," explained Eric. "There's no chance I'd ever join his squad."

"But I thought you went to his auditions?" asked Luke, confused.

"I did. Yeah," Eric told him. "But only because they were giving away free cake."

Luke made a mental note to give away cake at his next audition.

"So, Eric..." Luke said, adopting the friendliest tone he knew how. "Can we count you in for our squad?"

"No," Eric said once again, without elaboration.

"I'll buy you cake, Eric. Lots of cake?" offered Luke, with a hint of desperation now in his voice.

The offer of more cake appeared to bring Eric pause, and he pondered the notion for a tick, before ultimately giving the same answer. "No. I haven't got the time. Sorry," he said, turning his back and heading for the exit.

On the journey home, Luke's father could see that Luke wasn't his usual self. "Everything okay?" he asked. "You've not said much of anything, and usually I cannot shut you up. Did you enjoy badminton?"

"I guess," replied Luke morosely. "I think I need to get in some more practice, though," he said after a long pause.

Tom laughed, but not in an unkind way. "That kid was pretty special, Luke. You shouldn't let it bother you that he was so good. I've been beaten plenty of times by people younger than me. In fact, I suspect you'll be beating your old dad soon enough."

"We *did* beat them, Dad."

"I know, Luke. You *are* good. You just need to remember that. Your main problem is when you lose a couple of points, you get frustrated with yourself and sulk. But when you learn how to harness those feelings, it'll make you a better player, right? Just stay focused and calm. Remember, if you lose control of your emotions, your thought process will become erratic and you'll throw away more points, then become more annoyed, and so it continues. Understand? Also, a little bit more fitness wouldn't hurt. But you'll get that back in no time."

Luke nodded in agreement. He knew his dad was correct, but he'd always been a little hot-headed. He needed to work on that. Plus being slumped in his gaming chair for hours on end was certainly not helping his athletic prowess, that was true.

"There's a badminton club in school on Fridays, I think I'll sign up for it, Dad," Luke decided, announcing it to himself as much as to his father. "I'll get a bit of practice in that way, and it'll also give me a chance to try and find out where I left my other lung."

The badminton match, and subsequent discussion with his father, wasn't lost on Luke. He reflected on the points his dad had made, and could relate it to a significant portion of his life, actually, and not just badminton specifically. Every time something went against him, for instance, Luke had the habit of letting his frustration get the better of him. He did it in school if he got a question wrong, he did it in sport when he missed a point, and he especially did it when playing Hundred-to-One.

The inward reflection would prove valuable. Luke made a conscious effort from then on to use his energy for positive purposes, and so he did. It was difficult at first, but by golly soon enough Luke was beginning to reap the rewards. Where previously he'd get frustrated and want to kick furniture or any other inanimate object, now he was focused, quickly analysing the error of his ways, and taking corrective measures. He was genuinely starting to see the benefits of this new approach, and his confidence was starting to return. Sadly, however — at least in the case of the upcoming tournament with his dad — it was Hundred-to-One Luke had mostly adopted this approach to, as opposed to honing his skills on the badminton court.

"Hey! You lot! Have you recruited the rest of your squad?" shouted Harry Newbold derisively, across the length of the playground. Luke pretended he couldn't hear him, but Conor's hearing, it would appear, was more finely tuned.

"We could beat you without even any batteries in our controllers, Newbold!" Conor shouted back.

"Game controllers don't *use* batteries in them, you nitwit!" Harry corrected him.

"With the charge run down to nothing, then!" Conor sputtered. "You know what I meant!"

"He doesn't know what he's talking about," Luke assured Conor, once Harry had sauntered off. "*Our* controllers *do* have batteries in them. He must be playing on a different console or something."

"So I'm not crazy?" asked Conor.

"Well let's not get carried away, mate," Luke answered him with a chuckle.

Harry could be a pain at the best of times, but with his crack elite squad formed and in training he'd now become intolerable. In fact, Harry and his friends were one of the reasons Luke was eager to move up to high school so they wouldn't have to see them as often. Harry himself, oddly, was one of those people whose head appeared too big for their body. It may have just been his scruffy hair that needed a trim. Or perhaps he just really did have an unusually large head. Either way, it did seem rather appropriate somehow, Luke thought, as Harry was so annoyingly big-headed.

Luke clenched his fist. "Seriously, though. I'd love to beat that idiot in the tournament. I'd also love to take my badminton racquet and beat him directly over the head with it," he added.

"Are you sure?" said Conor. "That might not be such a good idea."

"Why not?" asked Luke.

"Well, with that fat head of his, you're sure to ruin your racquet. It's your racquet I'm worried about, is all."

"True, true," Luke laughed, but then, "Oh, no!" he said suddenly, slapping his forehead in dramatic fashion. "Speaking of my badminton racquet, I just remembered I've got badminton club after school today but I've forgotten my stuff!"

Conor wagged his finger, gently admonishing his friend. "Now, now. You hardly need to be busying yourself with badminton anyway, young man. Not when we're going to be world champions."

Luke sighed, reflecting on that point for a moment. "I know, but, Conor, I've got this thing coming up with my dad, and I said I'd get some practice in. I might see if Miss Hemsley has got a spare racquet I can borrow. Yeah. I think I will. I'll catch up with you later, mate."

Luke muttered in frustration while jogging towards the school building. He wasn't just doing this for his dad. He actually enjoyed playing badminton. And so the fact he'd forgotten his stuff was even more infuriating.

The corridor was empty but for the sound of Luke's footsteps, mirrored by another set of slightly-slower and somewhat-shuffling footsteps, which echoed on the polished floor tiles. Luke caught a glimpse of Eric, and he briefly considered asking if he might possibly have a spare racquet. But then another sound manifested itself suddenly — another, much less welcome, sound.

"Look who we've got here!" boomed a familiar voice. The corridor was, unfortunately in this case, perfect to enhance a booming voice.

Luke dropped back, staying out of sight, as Harry Newbold, and now the rest of his squad, took up position in front of Eric. It was Eric they'd spotted and not him, thank goodness.

Luke knew eavesdropping wasn't polite, but he assumed they were all going to talk shop, so to speak. And the prospect of overhearing the group's Momentous Melee tactics was too good to pass up. Also, now discovering who was on Harry's squad would give him, in effect, a list of names of those he could possibly poach for his own team.

It quickly became evident, however, that the conversation was not to be a friendly one. Nor would it be about discussing gaming tactics.

Luke watched on as Harry circled his prey, sneering, eventually coming to a stop behind Eric's backpack. "What's this, Eric? A squash racquet?" he said, in reference to Eric's badminton racquet poking out the top.

Before Eric could stop him, Harry had pulled his pack off him, unzipped it, and pulled out Eric's racquet.

Eric, unmoved by this display of aggressive posturing, and unwilling to give Harry the satisfaction of a reaction, simply rolled his eyes in response, stating flatly, "It's a badminton racquet. Obviously."

"What do you need a badminton racquet for, Eric?" Harry taunted him. "Do you use it as a walking stick or something? What with you having one leg shorter than the other, that is? Oh, and what's this?" he asked, rummaging around in

Eric's pack and pulling out an eye patch. "Oh, I know," continued Harry, looking over to his friends, who, to their credit, did not appear to be exactly revelling in Harry's antics. But this didn't seem to deter Harry, serving only to redouble his efforts instead.

"Is this your pirate costume?" Harry carried on, the pitch of his voice rising and becoming unnaturally shrill. "*Arrrggh, me hearties!*" he shouted, clearly pleased with his genius insults.

Eric didn't speak at this point, which only riled Harry further. Harry took the racquet and placed the tip of it down to the floor. "I know what this is for, Eric," he announced. "I'll bet you use this as a walking stick due to the limp," he said again, apparently forgetting he'd already made this same comment. "Or maybe, with you being a pirate and everything, you've actually got a wooden leg?"

At this point, Harry began hobbling around, making a great show of using the badminton racquet as a cane, and then, as a crutch, holding it under his armpit, even though it didn't reach the floor this way, interjected periodically with an addition "*Arrrggh!*" here and there for proper effect. When this didn't produce the desired result, however, he took things up a notch by actually using the racquet as a sword, taking a swipe at Eric's gammy leg with it... and missing.

Eric, with perfect timing, had simply taken a step back, out of reach of Harry's swing.

"You think you're too good for our squad, do you, Eric?"

Eric shrugged his shoulders. "Well, yes. I told you that at the time, Harry," he answered. "Do you not remember, or does your limited IQ mean you forget things?" he said. "Maybe you should write it down, Harry," he suggested calmly. "Assuming you know how to write?"

Back up the corridor, Luke took great pleasure in the annoyance he saw on Harry's face — evident even at this distance — but as far as confrontations went, this was an enormous mismatch. Harry was two years older than Eric and about a foot taller.

Luke recalled the athletic agility witnessed on the badminton court, and he waited a moment longer, unsure if he was about to witness something spectacular. Eric was like Yoda with a badminton racquet, he knew. So, perhaps he was some sort of Jedi master versed in the skills of some ancient form of jiu-jitsu or similar, and would dispatch a beating of biblical proportions with a series of spinning kicks?

Luke held his breath in anticipation as Eric, by the looks of things, was gathering himself up, readying his attack.

But Eric only took one step in Harry's direction, before merely crouching down in order to pick his discarded eyepatch up from the floor. At this, Harry swung his foot, knocking the patch in the direction of the nearby radiator. But Eric didn't react.

"Harry, you are such a tremendously unpleasant person!" shouted Luke, who'd seen enough — and his word choice might have been very different were he not in school. He marched with purpose up the corridor. "I mean, seriously," he said, once in front of the group. "You're picking a fight with a kid who's two years younger than you, half your size, with a limp, and with a watery eye besides," he berated him. "Uh, no offence, Eric," he added, turning briefly to Eric.

"None taken," replied Eric. "Facts is fact, after all."

Luke cast his eye over the rest of Harry's gang. "Seriously, you guys? Seriously? You're just standing there watching this plonker picking on a little kid, and doing nothing? Have a word with yourselves, will you? I know that—"

Luke was just gaining momentum, like a steam train getting to speed on the tracks, but his tirade was suddenly cut short by way of a precision punch to his abdomen. He barked in pain as the wind rushed from his lungs, before falling to one knee.

Harry nudged Luke with his foot, pushing him the final distance to the floor, where Luke lay in the foetal position, clutching his stomach.

Harry placed the racquet, still in his possession, over his knee, bending it like a really lousy strongman until the fibreglass snapped in two under the strain. "Here's your racquet back, then," he announced when finished. "Gosh, so sorry, Eric," he said sarcastically. "I've no idea how that happened. Somehow it's gotten a bit *squashed*," he added, emphasising the last word. But as soon as the words came out of his mouth, a look came over his face indicating he realised he'd got the wrong sport again. "I *meant* to say that," he insisted, floundering.

Eric shook his head in disappointment. "You truly are an incredible idiot," he said.

Before either of them could say anything more, a leather football hurtled past Eric's head like a cannonball, coming to an abrupt end once meeting with Harry's face. And for a kid with such a big head, it was remarkable to see how far the impact bent his neck back.

"Sorry, Harry!" shouted Conor from the other end of the hall, a short distance away. "I always forget I'm supposed to tell you catch! You'd really think I'd learn!"

Dazed and somewhat confused, it wasn't clear Harry even knew what had actually hit him, such was the velocity the projectile struck.

"Oh. And if you touch either of these two again..." Conor went on... "It won't be my football bouncing off your chin! You understand my meaning??"

Harry, at this point, apparently deciding discretion was the better part of valour, took his leave. That is to say, he ran away.

Conor walked up to Luke, extending his hand. "Come on, mate. Up you get."

"One second," groaned Luke from the floor. He stretched his hand out and grabbed the eyepatch now sat behind the radiator. "Here you go, Eric," said Luke, returning to his feet. "Here's your patch," he offered, holding it out to him.

Eric was strangely indifferent to the assistance provided. He collected his eyepatch, straightened out his racquet, closed up his bag, and casually wandered off — presumably to badminton practice, despite his ruined racquet.

Luke glanced at Conor, then back to the now-departing Eric. "Ahem, Eric..." he called after him, gently jogging to catch up to him.

Eric turned around.

"Eric, just a quick one," Luke offered. "I was just thinking..." Luke began, trying to work out how to say what he wanted to say.

"Yes?"

"Well, it's just... now we're all friends and everything... and you've seen what an idiot Harry really is... I mean, what better way to dish out revenge, right? than by kicking his butt and joining our squad for the tournament...?"

Eric pursed his lips, scrunched up his left eye, and tilted his head to one side. "You're right," he replied, after several seconds of careful deliberation.

Luke smiled over at Conor, and then looked back to Eric. "I am?" he asked, hopefully.

"Sure. Harry really *is* an idiot," Eric agreed. "I mean, a squash racquet looks nothing like a badminton racquet."

"Right. So... about the tournament?" Luke said, pressing gingerly for an answer.

"No. Again, no. But thanks," Eric replied. And then, without saying another word, he pivoted around, continuing on his journey, and leaving a bewildered Luke in his wake.

"Maybe we should forget the whole idea," suggested Conor, once Luke had joined him again. "I mean, all of our other friends are absolutely useless at Hundred-to-One, right?" he elaborated. "And I think I need to take a break from practising anyway. It's actually starting to cause hallucinations! It's weird. I've got too much Hundred-to-One in my brain, I think. Like, every time a door opens — in real life, I'm talking about — I'm expecting someone to throw a grenade at me! Or build a wooden fort! And I even found myself doing one of those silly dances from the game in the lunch queue yesterday! I didn't even realise I was doing it. It was only when the dinner lady asked me if I wanted beans that I snapped out of it and stopped."

Luke slapped his friend on the back. "Still. All that practice has improved your aim spectacularly."

"It has?"

"Sure. That's the best kick of a football I think I've ever seen!"

Conor smiled, bursting with pride. "Thanks, mate. As soon as it left my foot, I knew it was going to be something special."

LEVEL FOUR
THE HUNDRED-TO-ONE-SHOTS

hristmas cheer rang out from the car radios of those sat in traffic in the morning rush hour. One cheery soul had entered the season of goodwill, properly getting into the spirit of things, by offering a lovely hand gesture to another motorist who wasn't progressing with his journey quickly enough. However, beyond the occasional grumpy motorist, Luke and Conor's school was a different matter, though, and a place where expressions of holiday cheer could be found to be more genuine...

Conor sprinted across the playground, causing the bobble on his Santa hat to erratically chase after him. "Where've you *been*, Luke?" he shouted. "I've been messaging you for the last hour!"

Luke pulled down the scarf that covered his face once Conor had made his way over to him. "Nice hat, Conor," he remarked.

"Thanks! 'Tis the season to be jolly, after all!" Conor replied.

"Anyway, how've you been messaging me?" Luke asked him.

"On your phone," Conor told him, making the universally-accepted *phone* sign, thumb and little pinkie extended to ear and mouth, even though people didn't talk like that on the phone anymore, not since the olden days before mobile phones. "I've been texting you."

"I haven't got a useable phone at the moment, Conor," Luke informed him. "It's on the blink ever since I dropped it down into the toilet bowl. That'll be why I didn't message you back."

"How did you—?" Conor began, but then corrected himself. "You know what, nevermind, I don't need to know." Conor took out his own phone, prodding the screen. "Look. I've got you listed as *Luke New Number* on my phone."

Luke came over, standing shoulder-to-shoulder, and peered down at the phone's display. He read the number out loud, which resulted in a flicker of recognition. "Ah. That would be my dad's number. Remember we had to call him to pick us up after computer club last week? That's probably how it's gotten there on your phone."

"Your dad's number?" The blood drained from Conor's face. Panicked, he scrolled through his 'Sent' folder, re-reading the outgoing texts. He quickly put his hand to his head, causing his bobble to wobble. "Luke, I'm pretty sure I won't be invited for Christmas dinner when your dad picks up his phone," he said. "He's got a good sense of humour, I hope...?"

"Well?" asked Luke, clapping his hands together and rubbing his palms against each other for warmth.

"Well, *what*?" Conor asked. "The messages?" he said, looking worried.

"Yes, the messages. You've been trying to get hold of me, remember?"

"Oh, those," Conor replied, appearing relieved he didn't have to get into the contents of the *other* messages at the moment.

"Yeah. So what was so important you had to tell me that you kept messaging me?"

"Here, let me show you, seeing as how you're standing right in front of me now," Conor said, pulling out a scrunched-up piece of paper from his bag, and handing it over for inspection.

Conor allowed Luke to read through the notice for a few moments before continuing. "To enter the tournament," he went on, summarising the contents, "You have to register with the company that's organising it. Oh, and that reminds me, we need to come up with a proper team name, as well..." he added, trailing off, before another thought came suddenly to mind. "Did you see the bit...?" he asked. "Just there," he said, pointing to the relevant passage. "The bit that says you're supposed to be at least twelve to play Hundred-to-One?" he asked, incredulous. "I never...? I mean, what in the...?"

Luke screwed up his face. "Well there's no chance of that, surely? I mean, that makes no sense. Everyone we *know* plays it, and they're not twelve."

"I know, right?"

"So is that going to throw a spanner in the works?" Luke asked.

"It's not the end of the world. Not completely," Conor explained. "It's only our team captain that has to register, and they need to be at least twelve. Oh, and the maximum age for our category is fourteen, by the way."

"But neither of us are twelve yet. So that's a problem. Maybe... I suppose we could tell a tiny little fib?" suggested Luke.

"Yeah, I was going to," Conor told him. "But the captain of the winning team will need to show their proof of age, otherwise they'll be disqualified. And as I'm pretty certain — in fact, *totally* certain — that we're going to win the thing..." said Conor, employing the principle of positive thinking... "We'll need to play by the rules on this occasion, I think."

Luke threw his hands in the air. "Marvellous," he said, not sharing his friend's optimistic outlook. "We can't get anyone to join as it *is*. So what hope have we got of finding a twelve- to fourteen-year-old Hundred-to-One legend, and more specifically, one who wants to spend their time with a pair of bloody losers who haven't got even one Victory Supreme win between them?"

"Yes, but—" Conor began.

"Hang on. What you just said before... I thought we'd agreed on the team name?" Luke interrupted him, before Conor could finish.

"We did?"

"Yes," Luke told him. "The one my mum came up with, and was particularly proud of? The Pied Snipers?"

"I don't get it," Conor said, not getting it.

"You know. Pied *Piper*... Pied *Sniper*?"

"Ah. I get it now. Okay. We'll go with that, then, I guess, unless something else comes along," Conor agreed. But then, not even a moment later, he added, "No, wait! I've got it! How about, *The Hundred-to-One-Shots!*"

"The Hundred-to-One-Shots? *Ehm*, have you thought that through, mate...?" asked Luke.

"How do you mean?" replied Conor, confused.

"How do I mean?" answered Luke, confused as to why Conor was confused.

"Yes, because it's brilliant, don't you see?" Conor told him, his enthusiasm unwavering. "The game is called Hundred-to-One, right? And it's all about shooting, see? And so that's where the 'Shots' part enters in. So you see? Brilliant!"

Luke sighed. He didn't have the heart to tell his friend that 'hundred-to-one-shot' meant they didn't have a prayer of winning. He sighed again, deciding it wasn't worth all the trouble of trying to explain, and simply said, "You know what? The Hundred-to-One-Shots it is, then. That's fine."

"Anyway, that wasn't everything I was going to tell you. I wasn't finished with the telling," Conor said, waving his hands around like a really cheap magician.

"There's more?" Luke asked. "Wait, so just how many text messages is my dad going to end up finding?"

"Quite a few, to be honest," Conor answered him. "Maybe... okay, a lot, actually. When you see him, just remind him that it was me who lent him the bicycle pump when he had a flatty, yeah? It may get me in his good books. Anyway, listen..."

"I'm listening."

"... The person we were watching on Twitch last night? The one from the Isle of Man? You know the one I mean?"

"*Yeeeesss...?*" replied Luke, drawing the word out to invite further explanation.

Conor duly obliged. "You know how they were like the best player we've seen on Hundred-to-One? Well, certainly in the Isle of Man, at least?"

"*Yeeeesss...?*" replied Luke again, and then yawned on purpose. "We break up for Christmas in a week, Conor," he reminded his friend, implying that... "You should probably get to the point?"

Conor accepted the challenge, raising his forefinger. "What was their username?" he asked pointedly, introducing, as it were, his point.

Luke twisted up his face like someone had farted and he was trying to work out who it was that had done it. "I can't remember," he said eventually. "Aquadude? Aquablade? Something like that? But I know where you're going with this, Conor, and there's not a chance we can sign someone like that up. They're good enough to win it on their *own*. They certainly don't need *us*."

Conor leaned in, moving his head closer to Luke's, as if he were either conspiring something nefarious in purpose or sharing a great secret. He took that same forefinger he'd employed only a moment ago, this time matching it up with Luke's line of sight, and then using it to scan slowly and purposefully across the playground, like a cursor, until finally it settled on a small figure currently by the school's main doors. "Eric," announced Conor, with a virtual double-click.

Luke pulled that funny face again, as if he'd accused the wrong person previously and had reopened his bottom-burp investigation. "Yes? I can see that's Eric. And...?"

Conor nodded with significance. "The username you were trying to think of just now is... Aquaeyepatch."

This time it was Luke's turn to not get it. "What?" he said, not getting it. "I don't get it."

Conor paced now like a TV detective. "Aquaeyepatch," he repeated as he padded back and forth. "Aquaeyepatch, my good fellow," he said, puffing on an imaginary pipe.

"I heard you, Conor. Yes, Aquaeyepatch," said Luke, but the name meant nothing to him.

Conor ceased pacing, stopping in his tracks dramatically, and pointing the tip of his imaginary pipe in Luke's direction. "Think, man," he said. "Use your noggin," he instructed, using the pipe now to tap at his own cranium, before placing the phantom implement back into his mouth and taking a long, simulated draw on it.

"Conor, have you been drinking your dad's whisky?" Luke enquired.

"Correct!" Conor replied, completely ignoring the wrong answer that Luke had just given. "Good show, old bean! Why, it's none other than our very own Eric!" he exclaimed. "It has to be!"

Luke appeared unconvinced.

"Who else do you know with a watery eye that wears a patch?" Conor, asked, now himself again, as opposed to the pipe-smoking detective. "And aqua," he said. "As in water. Or in Eric's case, watery."

Conor folded his arms over, waiting for the cogs of recognition to catch up in Luke's brain — which, eventually, they did.

"No way!" replied Luke.

"Yes way," replied Conor, grinning.

"We've got a Hundred-to-One Twitch legend in our very own school!" Luke exclaimed, clutching Conor's arm, before the realisation of the situation hit him, dampening his brief enthusiasm. "But, Conor, I'm not sure how that's going to help us, exactly," he said. "We're looking for a twelve-year-old, remember? And, besides, Eric has rejected us, what, three times now? So the situation there is starting to feel like the time you tried to ask Hannah to the school dance."

"You didn't need to bring that up again, Luke. That's still raw," Conor admonished him unhappily.

"It was a year ago!" Luke told him.

"Right. Still raw. Like I said," Conor replied.

"It's even more annoying how good this kid is," Luke said, back on point. "But I don't think there's anything more we can do. We can carry on watching him on Twitch, at least. You know. Learn from the best, and all that. But, other than that, I'm not sure what else—"

"We could blackmail him?" suggested Conor, with very little consideration for the words coming from his mouth.

The blank expression on Luke's face and lack of response was taken by Conor as an invitation to continue outlining his master plan.

"We could tell Eric that we'll unveil his true identity," Conor went on. "That is, unless he joins our Hundred-to-One squad," he suggested in a moment of evil genius.

"But how does being revealed as a gaming legend work in our favour? What's the downside to that?" replied Luke. He began walking towards the school hall. He'd heard enough. Conor trailed behind.

"The slightly embarrassing name...?" was all Conor could offer, calling after his friend.

"Conor, he chose that name for himself. And besides, it's not as if we're dealing with Clark Kent, or secret identities, here," Luke told him, once Conor was alongside him again. "And we can't exactly go blackmailing an eight-year-old anyway. Think what you're saying. There must be another way. What do we know about Eric? There must be a way we can convince him other than blackmail."

Conor closed one eye. He did that, amongst other things, when he was thinking. Or, it could've just been the cold air was bothering him. "I think he's got a sister in year five and moved to the Island recently," he announced proudly, after a moment of careful consideration.

"That's not exactly high-level intelligence, Conor," Luke told him. "We were told that when they were introduced on their first day. And so he's got a sister. How does that even help us, anyway?" he said. "Look, we said it the other day, we need to forget about Eric and come up with another plan. And the priority at present, as it stands now, would appear to be a team captain who's at least twelve years old. That's what we need to focus on."

"That'll do, boys and girls!" shouted the headmaster from the front of the sports hall. "Quiet, if you please!" he added, bringing the youthful exuberance to a controlled hush. He pursed his lips, strolling the length of the raised stage giving him a vantage point over his seated audience.

"Good morning, children," he began. "I need to start off this morning's assembly on a negative point, I'm afraid."

With that, a quiet murmur arose throughout the audience.

"Most unpleasant," the headmaster went on. "It seems we've had an incident targeting a year six pupil, one which we're fully investigating. It would appear that someone — another student, presumably, with considerably ill intent — had seen fit to wire a car battery to the individual's bicycle, which resulted in a rather nasty electric shock. Fortunately, there will be no long-term damage to either the individual or the bicycle, though both will require a bit of aftercare to get them sorted out."

What reaction the headmaster might have been expecting was unknown. Rather than concern or dismay from the students, however, as one might imagine he'd have hoped for, their headmaster's revelation resulted in a general round of laughter from those assembled.

"Apparently the kid's got no eyebrows left," muttered one child to his friend. "The shock blew the kid out of his shoes," muttered another, followed by, "Smoke coming out of his ears," by still another.

Conor turned to Luke. "Why are we only hearing about this now?" he asked. "We're the cut and thrust of this school, after all, so we should have known about this. Even the little'uns from reception class look like they were aware of this... so why weren't we?"

Luke shrugged his shoulders, but it was clear he was equally as concerned at their lack of insight. "Who was it?" asked Luke, turning to those sat around him. "Anybody know?"

An ordinarily timid girl the size of a field mouse piped up first. "It was the boy in year six with a head like a watermelon," she announced to those around her, proud to have overcome her fears and looking very pleased with herself.

Conor and Luke were beside themselves with shock that this wee one in front of them had her finger so firmly on the pulse of the school, whereas they did not.

"Harry Newbold?" asked Conor, with a glimmer of hope in his eyes. "Wait," he said. "Was he the perpetrator or the victim?"

The little girl nodded at the word *victim*, and then fanned out her fingers, mimicking an imaginary explosion, and offering an audible "*Boooom*" for good measure.

Instinctively, Luke peered toward Eric, on the opposite side of the hall, who appeared rather blasé about the whole affair, Luke couldn't help but notice. A careful observer might have gone even as far as to suggest he looked perhaps somewhat smug, what with there being the faintest hint of a grin emerging on his face and all.

"Have a little look over at our friend Mr Aquaeyepatch," Luke whispered to Conor. "He doesn't appear too surprised to hear about Harry's misfortune."

"You're right. He doesn't," agreed Conor. "Although I have to say I find the whole sordid affair rather... shocking, to say the least."

"That's not bad, Conor, I'll give you that one," Luke replied. Puns were good. It was never not a good time for a pun.

Later that morning, year six were called upon to aid the teaching assistants in putting up the Christmas decorations around the school, as well as decorating the impressive tree that dominated the area just inside the main entrance. It was one of the highlights of the school year, and a visual indication, once having been completed, that the Christmas holidays would soon be upon them.

Conor and Luke, specifically, were tasked with hanging tinsel around the picture frames hung near the staff room.

"What do you think they do in there?" Conor wondered aloud, attempting to sneak a glimpse inside.

"Drink coffee, mostly. Lots of coffee, I expect. Judging by some of their breath, that is," replied Luke. "Anyway, here's some of this for over there," he said, throwing a shimmering section of tinsel Conor's way.

Conor snatched up the tinsel Luke had offered, though he didn't break his careful surveillance. And then another thought came to him, as thoughts sometimes did...

"When they're alone in there... the teachers, I mean... when they're alone in there, by themselves, the teachers, when no one else can hear... Do you think they call each other by their first names? Or is it still *Mister* this or *Missus* that, like normal?"

"I can't say I've really given that much thought, one way or the other," Luke told him. "I'd guess they probably call each other by their first names, now I think on it. It *is* pretty weird when you hear your teacher being called by their first name, though, and that's for certain."

"Yeah," Conor agreed, with the tinsel secured temporarily in his mouth, while he stretched over so that he could place it in the desired position. "Hey, get this. I saw Mr Benson at the supermarket once," he said to Luke by way of interest. "And he was wearing jeans!"

"That's just unnatural," Luke remarked in reply. "There ought to be regulations saying they can't do that, I should think. I mean, they shouldn't be allowed to go around dressing like regular people. It's... its..." he said, searching for the right word.

"Misleading," Conor offered, to which Luke shook his head in agreement. "Yeah, it was definitely the strangest thing ever," Conor added. "Hold on," he said. "Guess who I've just spotted?"

Conor turned — now sporting, adhered all around his mouth, a thin layer of glittery residue from the tinsel — to address Luke directly. "Over there," said Conor, picking up a Star of Bethlehem, and using it to point the way. "It's Harry, sat in the Nativity scene, next to the horse," he told Luke, not waiting for Luke to figure it out himself.

"No. That's a donkey," Luke corrected him.

"Here, that's a bit harsh on Harry, don't you think? Don't forget, he's had a bad day," said Conor, thinking fast.

"You're on a roll today, Conor," Luke offered. "Hey, does Harry look a little subdued to you?" he asked. "I'm sure I saw him twitching just now. Which made me think of something," Luke went on. "I watched this documentary before, where they used to electrocute people to make them better if they had problems in the head. Like Harry does. So maybe that small electric shock has stopped Harry being a complete idiot? What do you reckon, Conor?"

"If that was the case, Luke, he'd need much more of a shock to set him right. More like a lightning strike, probably," said Conor, a fair point to which Luke had to concede.

"Right," said Conor. "Throw me some of the red tinsel, will you? Let's mix it up a bit."

"Gotcha," came Luke's answer.

After more work, and with an appetite built up and the picture frames near the staffroom looking more festive than they'd ever looked — such was the attention they received whilst Conor was covertly spying — lunch was a welcome distraction.

"Over here," suggested Conor, pointing to one table in particular.

It wasn't their usual seats they were taking, but Luke could understand straight away why they were being a little adventurous, seat-wise. Eric cut a solitary figure, sat quietly, looking through the window out onto the playground.

"Hey, Eric," said Conor, announcing their arrival. "Mind if we join you?" he asked, even though they were already seating themselves.

"What do you want?" asked Eric suspiciously.

Conor looked offended for a moment. "We just wanted to see how you were doing. Did you see the Christmas tree we— Right. So did you do it?" he asked, changing tack abruptly, trying to catch Eric off-guard.

"Do *what*, exactly?" Eric asked disinterestedly, turning his attention to his cottage pie.

Conor looked at Luke, then back to Eric. "You know what I'm talking about," he replied with a grin. "Come on, now. You can tell us," he said, like the 'good' cop in a good cop/ bad cop scenario. "Can't he, Luke?"

"You better tell him what he wants to know, there, fella," Luke told Eric, not sure he was playing the 'bad' cop correctly but giving it a go.

"Ignore my partner," Conor went on amiably. "We're all friends here," he said, smiling. "Go on, then. You can tell us."

Eric held his fork midway to his mouth, pausing there to stare out the window again. "Of course it was me," he said after a moment, not looking at them. "It required precision engineering, and a steady hand. The rest of the school are hardly capable of that kind of craftsmanship, and lack the proper intellectual acumen," he went on distantly, as if he were talking more to himself than to them.

Eric did not speak like your typical year four student.

"They couldn't change a light bulb, let alone construct what I did," added Eric. "And so of course it was me." And, at that, he turned his head back around, satisfied, and allowed his fork to resume action, taking, in the process, a mouthful of cottage pie and chewing.

"Wow. Well with that friendly attitude, I'm surprised you dine alone," Conor put forward. "Anyway, we just wanted to drop by and congratulate you on a job well done."

Eric looked at them now, blinking. It could've been that his gammy eye was irritated. Or he could've been collecting his thoughts. Either way, he softened his next response...

"I'm sorry for being rude. Not everyone here is an idiot. You're not idiots. I didn't mean to imply that. And I actually like being in this school. I'm not particularly good at mixing, as might be obvious. But, even so, a lot of people have been good to me, and you two included. So thanks for that."

Luke patted Eric on the shoulder, happy to abandon the 'bad cop' persona. "Don't worry about it," he said. "And we're not going to say anything about you being the culprit, so don't worry about that either. To be honest, they should be painting a portrait of you, hailing you as a hero."

"We could put tinsel around it," offered Conor.

Eric looked over each shoulder, then leaned in closer to Luke and Conor. "Harry knows it's me," he told them. "Well, he saw me a few moments before he jumped on his bike and lit himself up, and then he put two and two together. Even a cretin like him can do basic arithmetic, it would seem."

"He told the teachers?" asked Luke.

"No. But he said he will, unless..."

"Unless what?" pressed Luke.

"He said if I joined his rubbish Hundred-to-One squad, then he'd forget about the whole thing — he wouldn't tell the teachers and we could happily go about our separate ways afterwards, with no hard feelings."

"Blackmail?" Conor interjected. "What kind of lowlife would resort to blackmail? Oh, bad form!"

Luke rattled his fingers on the table, casting Conor a look. "As much as we don't want you to join his team..." he said, turning to Eric again after a moment of consideration... "It's a bit of a no-brainer, I have to say. Join his team and then all this goes away. Our friend Sparky McSparks doesn't tell the teachers, and you don't get expelled. Simple?"

Eric was holding his knife this time, and he stopped mid-motion again. "No, not simple, I'm afraid."

"How so?" Conor enquired.

"The thing is..." Eric began, looking a little embarrassed for a change. "Look, the thing of it is, I may have told a few people I'd kicked their butt on Hundred-to-One. Maybe more than a few, actually."

"Sure. Bragging rights," Conor told him.

"No, but, well, it wasn't actually true, exactly," Eric replied, waving his knife to make his point.

"But it was," Luke reminded him. "I was one of them, remember. And plus we've seen you on Twitch and you're bloody spectacular," he said. "Oh, and I love the name Aquaeyepatch, by the way. It's very clever," he added.

"You're mistaken," explained Eric. "Well, partly mistaken. Aquaeyepatch *is* me. Or, at least, it *was* me."

Eric's explanation only served to confuse Luke and Conor, generating two blank stares in response.

"Okay, it's like this," Eric explained further. "My brother plays Hundred-to-One, see? So I thought I'd have a go at it. He set me up an account, and trust me, that username wasn't my choice. Anyway, I played a couple of times, yeah, but it ended up just not being my thing. I prefer more practical, hands-on hobbies."

"Like electrocuting fellow pupils?" suggested Conor.

"Exactly. And so the truth of it is, I'm absolutely useless at Hundred-to-One. And this would become immediately apparent should I join Harry's team. And the end result of which would be him telling the teachers it was me that electrocuted him, and I'll be expelled."

Conor and Luke shared an expression indicating they were not entirely clear on this whole thing.

"I'm not sure I understand," ventured Luke after a long pause. "So if you're Aquaeyepatch, but you don't actually play Hundred-to-One..."

"Then who does?" Conor entered in, finishing Luke's thought for him.

"Your brother?" Luke asked.

Eric shook his head. "No. My brother's got his own set-up. Aquaeyepatch, the person who kicked your butt, Luke, and the one playing that you see on Twitch..."

"*Yes...?*" said Luke, the suspense doing his head in.

"... Is actually my sister Daisy," Eric told him.

Luke didn't register what he was being told at first. But then the harsh reality of it set in. "Hang on," he said. "I thought I'd had my butt handed to me by an eight-year-old boy. Which was bad enough as it was. And now, in actual fact, it was an eight-year-old *girl*??"

Conor, being a supportive friend, was now laughing to an extent that snot bubbles were forming about his nostrils.

Eric grinned. "No, Luke, you've got it wrong. We're not twins. She's nine, not eight. So it was a *nine*-year-old girl that handed your butt to you. If that makes you feel any better at all...?"

Luke placed his head on the dinner table in despair, and defeat. "I'm never going to live this down. Not ever," he moaned. "I think I'm going to confess to Mr Benson," he said. "I'll tell him it was *me* who wired up the bike, and I'll get myself expelled. It would save me the shame of having to face any of the other students should they find out. Because it couldn't possibly get any worse than this. It really couldn't."

LEVEL FIVE
SUDDENLY SUSAN

A six-foot-tall plastic tube made up to look like a thermometer stood in the church entrance hall. It'd been festooned in twinkling fairy lights and served as a warm welcome, in addition to the neighbouring Christmas tree and the generous application of decorations peppered around the walls, to those entering. On the front of the tube were drawn lines in black marker at regular intervals, with "0" written at the bottom and "70" at the top, and finer lines in between them, and with the upper main mark having an image of a roof next to it. However, unlike mercury used in traditional thermometers, the contents were sand, and with each of the primary lines the sand would reach representing a thousand pounds raised towards the church roof fund.

"Good evening, Reverend Scott," said Luke, being careful not to startle him, for the Reverend was perched halfway up a ladder with a beaker of sand in hand.

Conor moved his nose closer, captivated by the sand trickling into the tube. "How much are you on now, Reverend Scott?" he asked.

"*We*, young Conor. How much are *we* on. This is a community church for the benefit of us all," said Reverend Scott, but not in an unkind way. He raised his finger for

Conor to hold that thought, while he emptied the remaining sand like a gardener watering their flowers. "There. Done. That's the total up to date for now, so you tell me," he invited, climbing back down the ladder to admire his handiwork.

Conor counted up, aided by the fact that every tenth line was marked out with a rounded numerical figure. "Ten, twenty, thirty, forty, fifty, one-two-three-four," he said, catching his breath at the end. "You're... *we're*, I mean... on fifty-four pounds?"

Reverend Scott laughed a belly laugh. "Each one of those bold lines represents one thousand!" he explained. "Even so, we've a long way to go, as you can see. And we may need to make the number at the top even larger, as it turns out, since the builders are now saying it's a bigger job than they'd originally thought."

"What?" interjected Luke. "Fifty-four thousand pounds? What's the roof made from, gold bars??"

"Fixing a roof of this size and complexity is an enormous task, and one that comes very dear, I'm afraid," came the reply.

The boys left Reverend Scott to his own devices, milling about for a bit. The Reverend, it must be said — accompanied by a small team of helpers — did a wonderful job of converting the church into a youth club on Friday nights. Church pews were pushed to one side, replaced by table football games, ping pong tables, and even a snooker table. A further draw for those present was the tuck shop — where the items were discounted, for the younger age group in attendance, by God himself.

Luke and Conor settled themselves in the darkest corner of the room, elbows on the table, sat next to each other and staring intently at the front door. Conor, in particular, was doing his best to appear pensive, moody, and interesting —

like a teenager — to those who looked over, wondering why they were sat doing not very much. Occasionally, Conor would bang down on the table for no reason, shaking his head as he did so, and then raise his hands to the heavens.

"What on earth are you doing?" asked Luke, edging in his seat slowly away.

"Some bloke in a suit kept doing that this one time we were in a coffee shop," replied Conor. "He was on his phone making a load of noise, and my dad said he was a prat who thought he was overly important or something. We need to appear important. So I guess that's what you do...?"

"Please don't," suggested Luke. "You just look mad as a box of frogs. And we don't want to be asked to leave, okay?" he cautioned his friend. "Oh, hi. Sorry, Susan," said Luke, pointing to the two empty chairs on the opposite side of the table from them. "You can't sit there, I'm afraid. We've got a business meeting and we need the seats, okay? Cheers."

But Susan — from year five — had bright red cheeks and no intention, it would appear, of listening to instruction. "I need to sit down," she said, flaking out into the chair. "I've been skipping for twenty minutes. Nonstop." She examined her hands, before holding them out to Luke and Conor. "Look. I've got blisters on my fingers. That's how hard I've been skipping rope."

"That's a lot of skipping," Luke had to admit.

"Only we've got an important meeting, and this is our office," explained Conor, pointing to the piece of lined paper, at the ready, that he'd set down on the table. "I've even brought a pen along. It's a fountain pen," he said, holding it up for examination. "That's just how important this meeting is."

Susan dabbed at her forehead theatrically with her shirtsleeve, even though there wasn't actually any sweat there, as she was quite proficient in the art of skipping rope.

"Well I need a seat, and I've chosen this one," she said, with little sympathy. "Of course, if I had a drink of something to cool me down, I could be on my way even quicker," she proposed, thinking fast. She was, after all, quick on her feet. "For two important businessmen, such as yourselves, that shouldn't be a problem?"

"Go and get her some water, mate?" Conor instructed Luke, using his pen to point the way to the kitchen. "If you don't mind, that is."

Susan took hold of one of her blonde pigtails, pointing it, as Conor had done with the pen, and then shaking it in a disapproving fashion. "I don't think water is going to do the trick," she told him. "I *have* been skipping for a dreadfully long time, after all," she admonished him. "A fizzy drink would be more thirst-quenching, I should think. Something fruity," she said. "Oh, and some Jaffa Cakes as well," she added. "You know. Just to replenish the energy levels."

Conor shook his head in mock dismay, disgusted at the way two hard-working professionals were being exploited in such a manner by the masses. "You should be ashamed of yourself, Susan," he told her, before dutifully turning to Luke. "Luke, go and fetch her a fizzy drink. Something fruity. And some Jaffa Cakes," he said to Luke, instructing his partner again. But this time there was no *if-you-could-see-your-way-clear* or similar.

"What? Hang on, why me?" Luke protested, now there was money involved in this equation. "Why's it *me* who's paying for it??"

"With power comes difficult decisions, Luke. I stepped up and made the hard choice. It's called taking initiative. You can thank me later," came Conor's reply.

Muttering to himself, Luke was dispatched to the tuck shop and Conor tasked with minding the remaining seats.

With goods in hand a short time later, Luke knew he shouldn't do it, but he couldn't help himself. He took the fizzy drink and shook the can so much his neck hurt. His evil smile evaporated, however, when he turned back to the table where Conor was minding the seats. Susan was now joined on the seat next to her by her friend Helen. On the seat that Luke had just vacated was another of the girls' friends, Libby.

Luke didn't dislike girls, as such. They were a peculiar breed, but they had their uses, he supposed. But the timing of this gathering was not the best, usurping as they were Conor and Luke's workspace.

Luke placed the Jaffa Cakes in front of Susan once back at the table, then turned to his friend. "I thought you were supposed to be keeping the seats, Conor?" he asked. "It's just I can't help but notice we now have fewer seats than before I left. And with my own seat taken, as well, on top of it," he observed.

"Oh, that. Well I was showing the girls my fountain pen," offered Conor sunnily, by way of explanation.

Susan reached out, extending her arm in Luke's direction. "Is that my fizzy drink, then?" she asked. "Give it here."

Luke started to hand the fizzy drink over to her before changing his mind, pulling it back and giving it instead to Conor. "Sorry, Susan, this one's for Conor," he said.

Conor's eyes lit up at this surprise turn of events. "Cheers, mate. Business partners should look out for each other, after all," he said, as Luke moved backwards a pace. "Although, for future reference, I do prefer a Fanta," Conor advised.

Shortly thereafter...

... It appeared the quickest way to shift three girls from your office was to have a fizzy-based atomic explosion. Luke handed Conor a napkin to wipe the liquid from his face, arms, hair, clothes... pretty much everywhere. "I'm terribly sorry about that, Conor," offered Luke, perhaps not entirely convincingly, pointing back over his shoulder to the tuck shop. "They must have been shaking it before I bought it. Very cheeky, if you ask me."

Just as Conor was finishing sorting himself out, a familiar creaking noise was heard as the ornate wooden entrance door — with a rounded top in the shape of an arch — opened, and a figure entered. "Ah. Here he is," said Luke, waving Eric over to their temporary office. They were joined a few moments later by Harry Newbold as well.

"Thank you both for coming," said Conor, in his most professional-sounding voice. The two guests filled the vacant seats, with Harry offering a cautionary glance at Eric.

Conor was still dabbing at himself, with a fresh napkin now.

"Why are you all... sticky?" enquired Eric.

"Ah. There was... a bit of an accident," said Conor, a little flustered. This was not how he wanted to present himself at such an important meeting.

"Speaking of which," said Harry, still eyeing Eric. "Accidents, that is. Thanks to you sabotaging my bike, I've still got a ringing in my ears. And my left foot keeps kicking out, for no reason at all, whenever it feels like it."

Rather than an apology, Eric grinned, and, to be fair, so did Luke and Conor. "You're lucky I stopped at a 12-volt battery, Harry," was all Eric had to say for himself. "Or it could have been much worse."

Luke raised his hands, bringing the meeting to order. "Okay, gentlemen. We know why we're here," he said. "So we'll keep this brief."

"Good. I've got things to do," Harry said brusquely, attempting to regain control of his dignity by employing a bad attitude.

"Harry," Luke went on. "You've agreed to forget about the entire incident involving your bike. In addition, you'll tell the headmaster that it was all a big mix-up, and that your injuries were actually, in fact, accidentally self-inflicted. When you've done this — and one of us has to actually hear you telling him — then Eric will agree to join your Hundred-to-One squad for the purposes of the upcoming tournament."

Conor leaned forward, elbows on the table. It was his turn now. He held his fountain pen aloft with one hand, twirling it around with notable dexterity. That is, until he dropped it and it clattered unceremoniously onto the table. Conor pretended this didn't happen, or that he'd done it on purpose, and placed his hand over the pen, covering it up. The lined paper he'd brought along had been ruined anyway, with the fizzy drink, so it's not like he could've done any writing anyhow even if he wanted to. This was serious business, so he carried on, undaunted.

"Also," Conor began, resuming his role as co-business-mediator. "Regardless of how good or bad any of you perform in the tournament, the entire bike incident is forgotten. Forever. Agreed? And if you try and muck us around, Newbold, I might need to remind people of the unfortunate bed-wetting incident when you stayed over at Liam's house."

"Bloody *Liam*! Bloody big mouth!" Harry said through gritted teeth, cursing out his friend. "And that was when I was four years old, besides," Harry protested to those in front of him.

Conor took up his pen once again, tapping it purposefully on the tabletop. Thank goodness he was getting some good use out of it after all. "I might very well forget to tell people how old you were, Harry," Conor warned him. "Or I might accidentally say you were in year four, as opposed to four years old. And you know what school is like. That won't take long to get around."

Harry nodded his assent to the deal. He wasn't happy about it. But he nodded. "Agreed," he told them. "Just one thing," he said.

"And what's that?" Luke entered in.

"How am I meant to tell the headmaster that it was self-inflicted? The electrocution, I mean."

It was Eric's turn to chime in. "You could tell him that you'd read a picture book about an electric-powered bike. You could then tell him that you thought that by wiring your bike up to a car battery that this would make your bike electric," he said.

Harry scoffed. "There's no way the headmaster is going to believe I'm that stupid."

"Umm," said Eric. "I think you'll find he probably could. And would. Quite easily, too."

"Ay! There it goes again!" gasped Harry, as his left foot kicked out involuntarily, like a doctor had just applied one of those weird-looking little hammers to his knee to test his reflexes.

"Could be Tourette's," Eric offered flatly.

"Okay so I'll speak to the headmaster on Monday," Harry continued. "You can stand near me when I tell him," he said to Luke and Conor, before his attention turned back to Eric. "You promise you won't back out of the tournament?"

"Oh, no, Harry," Eric assured him. "Wild horses couldn't drag me away. And I promise you I'll give this tournament every ounce of my Hundred-to-One expertise. You can be certain of that. Every single ounce, not one held back."

Harry gave Eric a hard stare of impressive intensity, which he held for what seemed like an age, though which probably lasted for only a few seconds. It seemed much longer, though, such was the quality of it. He got up to leave, and, halfway to the door, gave an additional suitably cold glance over his shoulder. It was a wonderfully moody exit that impressed both Conor and Luke — and Conor, especially, was taking a mental note so he could add it to his repertoire should he have need of employing it in future.

Alas, Harry's dramatic exit was made considerably less so when his leg kicked out again unexpectedly, resulting in him nearly falling over.

"Alright, I should go as well, actually," said Eric, once he'd stopped laughing. "Remember, you two need to be at my house tomorrow at two p.m. as it's the only time I could get my sister and brother available at the same time. They seem fairly up for the tournament, but they want to meet you and make sure you're not a couple of muppets." With that statement, Luke gave Conor a cautionary glance that said, *don't muck that meeting up.*

"You should stay," suggested Conor. "You said it yourself, Eric, you're a bit of a loner — some may say *weirdo* — so you should stay and make some new friends. They're not a bad bunch here. And Luke will even go and get you a fizzy drink. Just tell him what kind you want, is all. He got me something else, for instance, when I really prefer Fanta. Although I didn't end up drinking the fizzy drink he gave me anyway..." he said, trailing off, not wishing to relive that memory.

Eric wasn't one for socialising, as he freely admitted, and the current environment had caused his head to shrink into his neck like a tortoise. His eyes shifted furtively around the room, while his hands tapped on the table out of impatience or perhaps nervous energy. He soon relaxed, though, appearing to make a decision. "Some people think I'm a weirdo?" he finally said.

"Not all," replied Luke. "Only some," he assured him. "And why is it me who's been tasked to go to the tuck shop again?" he protested to Conor, though he had already given in and was standing up to go and do just that anyway.

"I think I will stay for a bit, if that's okay?" announced Eric. "It looks like it could be good fun. Oh, and by the way— Let me know who said I was a weirdo. But keep in mind, it's not just bikes I can wire up to car batteries."

Conor laughed the sort of laugh that indicated he wasn't at all certain if what he'd just heard was a joke or a threat.

"I'll take a Vimto, if they've got it. Thanks," Eric said to Luke.

"I'll take a—" Conor started to say, but Luke was already off.

"Come on. Let's go and play some table football," Conor suggested, turning to Eric. "Just don't electrocute me, okay? Promise?"

"No," replied Eric simply. "That's a promise I could never make."

LEVEL SIX
THE KNIT & NATTER

It's a well-known fact to children of all ages that mums like to chat with other mums. This is usually done amidst activities or endeavours where the child didn't actually want to be involved in the first place and with the act of talking often resulting, from the child's point of view, in dragging out the unfortunate situation even longer. Examples of this include but are not limited to:

☞ Shopping centres, usually when it's cold or particularly busy and when she's given you a heavy bag to carry.

☞ Hairdressers, when you pop in for a quick trim but the ensuing conversation between mums lasts three times longer than the actual haircut.

☞ Petrol stations. But, in this situation, the irate driver waiting impatiently behind may serve to bring this conversation to a premature conclusion with a toot of the horn or angry hand gesture.

☞ The next is the most common and quite possibly the biggest general threat to children's sanity ever: the supermarket. The frustration is amplified as the mums have the ability to see each other on every separate aisle, running into each other again and again. Here, they will remember something else to say that they'd forgotten about in the vegetable section but that's come suddenly back to them in the dairy section. And even if they've got nothing further to discuss, there's always the inevitable, *"Fancy meeting you here"* — which is said because they'd seen each other precisely seventeen seconds ago when their shopping trolleys virtually collided. They'll usually both chuckle at this and likely repeat the same scenario at least three more times on their eventual journey to the frozen foods aisle. Now, you may think you're safe once shopping is done and when the final bag has been hauled from the trolley and into the boot of the car. You're about to step inside the car to escape from the biting cold when the familiar voice of one of your mum's *other* friends comes belting across the car park. The most likely phrase you'll hear is, *"I've not seen you for ages"* — which is a bit of a gentle fib, as likely they'll have seen each other or spoken within the previous several days. And it's truly amazing how much mums will find to talk about after the span of only a few days. At this point, you should probably smile and climb into the car, if this should happen, and enjoy the radio for twenty minutes or so until the mums' conversation has run its course.

And then there were those times set aside *exclusively for chatting*. There could be some activity as an excuse to gather, but the activity was secondary to the main goal of chatting. As such, Saturday mornings was the official get-together for some of the school mums that liked to knit and crochet, in addition to talking — something they were exceptionally good at. Luke, Conor, and some of the other children had been regular attendees at Knit & Natter — the name of this weekly craft club held at the local coffee shop — but eventually both parties, mums and children alike, mutually decided that children were no longer obliged to attend. It meant the mums could chat and knit without interruption, and also that the children didn't, well, have to suffer through listening to their mums chat and watching them knit.

To the casual observer or even the particularly nosey, the group of women in the coffee shop produced an incessant chatter that didn't ever appear to break, not even for breath. When one of the mums stopped to take a sip of coffee or perhaps to activate the crochet hook, another of the mums would jump in to fill the verbal gap. It was an extraordinary display, if a little disorienting.

"Refill, ladies?" asked Fiona, the chirpy café owner armed with a coffee pot ever at the ready. "What are we working on?"

Fiona's question produced a further round of chatter, followed by an intermittent bout of laughter, more sipping of coffee, and more action with the crochet hook.

After a bit, Luke's mum, Sally, switched her attention from the hat she was knitting, and from the gossip at hand, to the poster stuck to one of the shop's front windows. It was facing outwards, but the paper stock was white, and so Sally could make out the bold text on it as the sun shone through. She cocked her head, and with some effort she could manage to read the reversed lettering.

Conor's mum, Lisa, saw Sally's silently moving lips, and followed along her line of sight. "We're not that boring, are we, that you're reading a poster backwards?"

Sally laughed. "Well, sometimes," she joked, before her attention returned to the window. "But, no. I just recognised the logo on that poster. It's that game I can't ever pull my son Luke away from. Hundred-to-One."

Ordinarily, if you mentioned the name of what was, essentially, an online video game meant solely for the younger crowd, to a group of women in their... well, nevermind how old, as it's not polite to ask... you'd have received collective blank expressions in return, with glazed-over eyes. In the case of Hundred-to-One, however, there was a collective murmuring of recognition and agreement that — despite the general Knit & Natter theme — wasn't at all woollen-related, as it should happen.

The general consensus was one of abject frustration.

"It's a nightmare trying to get my son off it," suggested one mum...

"I know, right? It's as if mine goes into a trance or something, and heaven forbid if we try to get him off it during a game!" said another...

"All I hear is shouting from behind his closed bedroom door," said another...

"Mine is up all hours of the night, and then getting him up for school the next morning is like pulling teeth!" said one of the mums.

"My daughter was playing it the other night at the *same time* as watching *other* people playing it on her iPad!" said still another.

It was clear this was a topic of particularly keen interest, as all crafting projects had been lowered and needles stood down — a rare occurrence indeed. What remained uncertain, however, was what the actual solution was for this type of phenomenon. And then there was the question of whether it was really a problem that needed solving in the first place — or, at least, how *much* of a problem it was, precisely. Sally managed to chip in first, in this regard...

"Luke is always playing the game, forever and always, it seems. But I've had this conversation with my husband, and we've agreed Luke is in his room, playing with his friends, in a safe environment. Whereas he could just as easily be out on the street instead, getting into goodness knows what kind of mischief. So it could be worse, right? I mean, so there's that, yes?"

There was some murmuring again, along with some nodding of heads, as the others considered what was being said. Sally continued...

"And we still do other things, mind you. We do. We have movie night, for instance. And we do jigsaws, and we go for walks in the countryside. And he's out every other weekend metal detecting with his dad or playing badminton. So it's not like he's doing nothing else, then. But then so why do I feel like such a negligent parent when he's playing it...?"

Fiona added her two pence, at this point. And, as she had a coffee pot in one hand and a plate of cream scones in the other, she was wisely given priority to speak...

"My son is exactly the same, and I felt the same as you did," Fiona said to Sally, though it was clear, with a wave of the scones plate, that it was addressed to all. "We were always arguing about it. Eventually, we had a family meeting about it. And, there, we came to realise, once we began talking about it, that the only time my son was playing was when everything else he had to do, like homework and such, was done. And this would be while my husband and I were sat downstairs watching the telly, or browsing at nonsense online. The only thing the boy was doing different was that he was sat in his room rather than next to us, on the sofa. Anyway, the point is, as long as all of the other daily things that need doing are done, then I don't see what the problem is."

Now she had her say, Fiona set down the scones, for which the women were blessedly grateful.

Lisa nodded her head, looking around to check the reaction from the other mums. "I think, maybe, the reason we feel bad about it..." she entered in. "Is that we think our children should be doing something creative, like playing the piano, painting a watercolour, or writing a book. The truth is, though, as parents, if we're not doing these things ourselves, then why should we think to penalise our children if *they're* not doing them? Is that fair? As long as nobody's getting hurt in the process, and they're not skulking around shop doorways drinking or smoking, I suppose, then what's the harm?"

More murmuring and nodding of heads.

"Anyway," Lisa went on. "I'm guessing that poster is for this tournament that Conor's been prattling on about for weeks. And I've seen how much work and effort he's put towards it, to be honest. It's been remarkable, and his teacher has even said as much also." She thought for a tick before continuing. "It could be the problem is that we, as parents, just don't get it because we ourselves don't play it," she added, finally.

"Maybe we should," replied Sally, with a confident bob of her head.

"Hang on, what?" returned Lisa. "That's not really what I was—"

"Yes, but maybe we should," Sally said again.

Lisa wasn't sure she was hearing her friend correctly. "You actually think we should give up crochet and take up playing video games instead...?"

"Well, I never said anything about giving up the crochet," Sally answered her.

"Oh, thank goodness. For a moment there, I thought—"

"I meant not entirely give it up. But I do think you're onto something in that we, as parents, don't really understand too much about this Hundred-to-One thing. And that the only way we *will* understand it is to play it for ourselves."

"Yes, but I didn't mean to imply—"

"And according to the poster..." Sally carried on, despite Lisa's protests... "There's a tournament for those less than fourteen years of age, and a tournament for those *over* fourteen. Now, I'm pretty sure we're all over fourteen years of age..."

"Though not *too* far over," one of the ladies suggested.

"Or at least you'd never know it from the way we look," said another.

"Exactly what I meant, yes," agreed the first.

"Anyway, so what I'm actually thinking is..." Sally went on, concluding... "Why don't the Hundred-to-One mums enter a team of our own into the tournament?"

Lisa raised her crochet hook, holding it aloft as if to mark her place as she rolled her friend's idea around in her head. "You know, Sally," she said, after careful deliberation. "That might not be as entirely mad an idea as I first made it out to be. In fact, it might even be some jolly good fun. I say... why not? Yes, I'm in," she declared. "Though with one caveat," she added. "That you meant what you said about not giving up the crocheting entirely...?"

"Of course," Sally assured her. "That *would* be mad. And there'd be little sense to it."

"Right, then," said Lisa. "Agreed." And with that, she held out her crochet hook. Sally, following suit, did the same, crossing Lisa's crochet hook with her own, like the leaders of two great clans touching swords to mark a pact, and with the others quickly joining in as well.

"Agreed," echoed Sally, but added one concern. "The only thing—" she began.

"I know what you're going to say," Lisa cut across. "Who's going to tell the boys? Although... who says we need to tell them at all?"

To which everyone laughed, and, now the matter was settled, set to work crocheting once again lest the afternoon should be wasted.

Daisy Robinson, Eric's sister, was a master. Ordinarily, two businessmen — such as Luke and Conor — would take offence at being kept waiting for such a length of time as they were presently being kept waiting. But not today, as they were content to watch on as Daisy finished up her current Hundred-to-One match. Eric handed his guests a glass of lemonade each, but they didn't avert their eyes, rather taking a step closer, watching the screen for so long without blinking that their eyes dried out.

Daisy, though a year older than her brother, was even smaller than Eric — and Eric was small. Her gaming chair had all but swallowed her, and from Luke and Conor's rear vantage point, all that was visible was a pair of hands mashing buttons on the controller in a blur. She was operating at a level completely alien to Luke and Conor. They weren't observing a timid girl from year five. No, they were in the company of *Aquaeyepatch*. And she did not disappoint.

Luke and Conor were mesmerised. For them, it was the equivalent of watching a moon landing; they were in the presence of greatness, of Great Things. Daisy's character — in the wonderful Berserker Devastation skin she was presently employing — appeared to float gracefully through the game in a controlled, fluid motion that radiated confidence. One aggressor after another who dared to cross her path was each, in turn, dispatched with precision. She was in the top three, currently, with seven kills credited to her so far, and throwing up defensive positions as effortlessly as if she'd had an army of labourers at her command.

And, now, as the boys watched on, she was crouching down, alert to some sort of impending attack, and taking a bolt-action sniper rifle from her inventory. Before Luke and

Conor had even caught sight of the aeroplane — the object that Daisy had somehow detected in advance of them, with seemingly supernatural ability — Aquaeyepatch zoomed in for merely a split second before releasing a single round from two hundred metres, catching the unsuspecting pilot of the aircraft (who had up till just now been very intent on an aerial strike) in the side of the head with a glorious one shot, and taking in the process her tally of kills to eight.

It was unfair to say there was minimal effort, but that's certainly how it appeared. Ordinarily, if Luke were to somehow find himself in this advanced position of the game, he'd be on his feet, hammering the controller with all composure gone completely out the window. Daisy, on the other hand, was cool as a cucumber, and a few minutes later, the words appeared on screen that Luke and Conor could only dream about: #1 *Victory Supreme.* And she'd done it without so much as breaking a sweat.

Daisy removed her headphones, placed the controller on her desk, and then spun round in her chair like a James Bond villain. A small white stick protruded from the side of her mouth, which was, presumably, attached to the head of a lollypop further inside. She twirled a ribbon of ginger hair in her fingers, looking Luke and Conor over like a butcher eyeing up a slab of beef.

She removed the lolly from her mouth, and she pointed it in Conor's general direction. "You're the inept catastrophe from year six whose butt I kicked at Hundred-to-One?"

Conor shook his head in the negative, offering a half-extended thumb to his friend. "That was him," he told her.

"Ah. Well," she said, turning her attention towards Luke. "You'd be the one who plays badminton, then. I hope you're better at that than you are Hundred-to-One?"

Conor chuckling at this point was not helping matters any. Luke cleared his throat. "Daisy, first of all, that was truly inspiring," he began, pointing at the screen, thinking it best to lay down a foundation of flattery. "We're very grateful you agreed to see us," he went on.

"I didn't," she snapped back. "Eric told me about half an hour ago that you were coming, and you'll need to be quick as I've got other things to do."

Conor could see his business partner was on the ropes, so stepped up like a true friend should. "He's not always a... inept catastrophe," suggested Conor, remembering Daisy's exact words, and setting out his stall, with hands held out in an entreating fashion. "Well, he is sometimes, but not—"

"There's nothing says you're not a pathetic loser as well," Daisy interrupted him. "So don't think you get off scot-free here."

Conor ignored the insult, his pride taking second place to the greater goal, at present. He said, "Daisy, we're setting up a team for the Hundred-to-One—"

But Daisy cut him off by throwing her lollypop at him. It was a cracking shot, with the sticky green confectionary end making perfect contact with Conor's forehead — where it held fast. For a brief moment Conor resembled a Dalek, before the grip eased and the lolly fell downwards, succumbing to gravity, and coming to an eventual end on his shoe.

"I know exactly what you pair want," said Daisy, reaching to a jar on her desk for a replacement lolly. "You've entered a team into the competition heat and have realised you're generally pretty useless and need my help. Am I correct?"

Conor went to move but thought better of it as he didn't want to knock the discarded, weaponised lolly onto the carpet. "That about sums it up, Daisy. Yes," he admitted.

"It's a fair cop," Luke agreed. "Still—"

"It's true about the *us-needing-your-help* part," said Conor, not finished yet. "But not so much about us being useless," he clarified, his pride unwilling to shoulder this continued assault. "We're not half bad, actually. And we're getting better all the time," he told her.

"All the time," Luke reiterated.

"So what do you say, Daisy? Are you up for joining us?" enquired Conor. Well, pleaded, actually.

"Your brother Sam has already agreed to join us. We just spoke to him," offered Luke. "Or Conor did, at least. He'll be team captain, as he's over twelve," he added, hoping this might be a selling point.

Daisy narrowed her eyes and drummed the fingers of her right hand on the armrest of her gaming chair, before declaring, simply, "No chance," and then turning the chair back around to indicate the meeting was now over.

Luke and Conor shared a despairing glance. "Come on, Daisy," asked Luke desperately. "There must be something we can do to convince you?"

"*Weeeelll...* now you mention it," Daisy replied, spinning back round slowly. "Eric tells me you and your dad are one of the favourites in the badminton competition?" she asked, with no real intention of waiting for the answer. "You need to lose early on to give my dad and Eric a chance to win."

She said this as if she'd already planned on saying it. Which she had. This was like a game of chess to her, and she was easily several moves ahead of them. "Yes, you do," she added, even though Luke, stood there dumbfounded and gormless, hadn't even had chance to protest yet. "And if you play against them directly, well, you know what you need to do..." she told him.

"He'll do it!" came Conor's immediate response, happy to speak for his friend, and offering Luke a slap on the back by way of confirmation.

"No he *won't* do it!" yelled Luke, regaining his voice. "Not a hope in hell will he do it, actually! And by *he*, I mean *me*, just to be perfectly clear. Come on, Conor, I've had enough."

Conor was in two minds as to whether to peel the lolly off his shoe or simply storm out with it still stuck to the one trainer. They were his good ones, the trainers, and he was worried about the suede leather being stained by continued contact with the sticky greenish-blue partially-rendered sweet. He wasn't for quick decisions, however, and by the time he'd finished deliberating in his own head, Luke was by the door already preparing to leave, and Daisy was in the Hundred-to-One hotel foyer — the place where players congregated until enough gamers were online to constitute a viable match — getting ready for another game.

"Enough!" screamed Eric, and for a young man of very limited stature he certainly carried some volume in those lungs of his. He reached over to Daisy, plucking the earphones off her head with one hand whilst hitting the power button and turning the game console off with the other. But before Eric continued further with Daisy, he briefly turned to Conor. "Just take the bloomin' lollypop off your shoe, will you, Conor?"

Conor did as instructed, but was then faced with the problem of what to do with the thing. He removed a small dusting of fluff from the lolly's surface and then, examining the confection's salvageability, and in the absence of any other apparent, available options, popped the lolly into his mouth.

"Now, *you*," Eric said, pushing his sister's chair so she was facing him. "Daisy, what the heck are you on about the badminton tournament for? What has that got to do with any of *this*?"

Daisy pointed at Eric's leg, her slight frame disappearing into her chair even more than previous. "I was trying to be *nice*, Eric," she told him, somewhat ironically, given the circumstances. "I just wanted you to win at something, is all, because, well, you're not the..." she said, trailing off.

"I'm not *what*?" demanded Eric.

"You're not the most..." she said, searching for just the right words to use. She was very clever. Even more clever than Eric. That wasn't the problem. She just wanted to choose her words wisely, so as to remain as delicate as possible...

"You're a bit odd at times, Eric," she said, finally. "And not very successful. So I thought winning at badminton would perhaps put a smile on your face."

"He doesn't need your help, Daisy," interrupted Luke. "Trust me, even though Eric has a limp, or whatever it is, that kid is a bloody genius on the badminton court. He won't be easy to beat, let me tell you. At *all*."

"Also," said Conor, removing the lolly from his mouth with a pop, in order to add his own observation. "I've never seen anyone so good at absolutely everything they do. Eric is brilliant. Hundred-to-One, it seems, is the only thing he's *not* good at. Also... who else have you met that can turn a bicycle into an electric chair?" Conor took a moment to slow-clap his appreciation for that particular display of ingenuity.

"Ah. I *knew* that was you," said Daisy to Eric. "When I heard somebody had been electrocuted, I knew that was your handiwork. And if you don't get your friends out of here and leave me alone, I'm going to tell Mum and Dad just what sort of mischief you've been up to in school," she advised.

Luke motioned to Conor, offering Eric a raised eyebrow in sympathy and support for what he obviously had to deal with on a regular basis. "Come on, Conor. We'll leave them to it," he said.

"You didn't even ask why I electrocuted him," said Eric softly, to which Daisy shrugged her shoulders.

Luke and Conor paused, deciding, at least for the moment, to stay and hear this out as it was obvious Eric had more to say.

"You said it yourself, Daisy," Eric went on. "I've always been a bit, well, different, I guess you could say — odd, even, if I'm being completely honest — and always been that kid at school nobody particularly wants to do things with. The thing is, the reason I did what I did, Daisy, is because I was being bullied. And it's not the first time, either, and not just with Harry. It's been going on for years. But what I did to Harry Newbold, Daisy, is as a result of being picked on and made to feel stupid for these past several years. A culmination, if you will, and I'd simply had as much as I was going to take."

"Good word," Daisy had to admit, pursing her lips and nodding with approval. "*Culmination*, I mean."

"Thank you," said Eric.

Eric took a breath before continuing, at which point Conor offered him his lolly, which was politely refused.

"Daisy," Eric went on. "This pair, here, are the nicest people I've met at school. They're the only ones who looked past my limp to see me for who I am. And if it wasn't for these two, I'd be expelled by now. It's only thanks to their efforts that I'm not."

Daisy glanced over at Conor and Luke but didn't say anything. Her demeanour may have been softening, or it may not have been. It was difficult to tell.

Eric carried on...

"Did you know, Daisy, I went along to the youth club for the first time the other night? I did at that. And I was ready for leaving after five minutes. But this pair of pudding-heads... *em*, no offence, lads..."

"None taken!" said Luke and Conor cheerfully.

"This pair convinced me to stay. And I actually ended up enjoying myself for a change! And did you know I made more friends that night than I've ever made in my entire life put together? It's true. And I've even signed up to help with the church fundraising for their new roof! And, again, it's all thanks to these two pillocks here," said Eric, motioning towards Conor and Luke, adding, "No offence, guys."

"None taken!" said the pair, again, cheerfully. Because, really, there was no offence to be taken, as insults such as this were simply how boys showed each other affection.

"Daisy, not once have I ever thrown this in your face, and you know I haven't, but remember it's your entire fault that I've got this rubbish limp in the first place," Eric reminded his sister. "But these two muppets..." he said. "No offence, chaps..."

"*Erm...* none taken?" came the slightly less enthusiastic response this time. Throwing insults at each other was all good fun, after all, but this was maybe taking things too far?

"Well, as I said, they looked straight past the limp," Eric continued on. "At the risk of sounding overly dramatic, I have to say that these two are like a lighthouse beacon cutting through the fog. For the first time in years, I've got a purpose, and I've got people I can finally call friends. And so the point of this whole diatribe..."

"*Diatribe*," Daisy repeated, nodding her head in approval again.

"... Is that you're doing this for me, Daisy. Joining the team? You're doing this for *me*," Eric concluded.

Daisy lowered her head, and Luke and Conor gave her room, as they were rather unsure what was coming next. It was an emotionally charged occasion, so there was always the threat of tears. And the two of them were not the best with emotional women, or emotional displays in general for that matter.

"Whatever," said Daisy abruptly, clearly a girl of few words now. She rolled her eyes and placed her headset back on. "I'll join your stupid squad," she said. "Now get lost. I've got things to do."

The three of them retreated before Daisy had chance to reconsider. Once clear of her, and safely out of earshot in Eric's room, Conor offered a raised hand ready for high-fiving. "We've got a team!" he shouted, dancing a jig on the spot.

But Luke was a bit more reserved.

"What is it, Luke? I thought you'd be happier about this?" Conor enquired.

"Firstly, I wish people would stop calling me and Conor losers and such," Luke said, as a general observation.

"*Inept catastrophe*, I think were her exact words," said Conor.

"Losers, in essence. And, to be fair," said Eric to Luke, "Conor *is* eating a second-hand lolly."

Luke nodded in agreement. "You're not wrong there, Eric," he conceded. This, however, only produced a shrug from Conor, as Conor carried right on attacking the lolly with gusto.

"I'm just a bit concerned about how much thought I actually gave to throwing the badminton tournament just to get Daisy to join our Hundred-to-One squad," Luke went on. "Despite what I said, I very nearly gave in to her demands."

"Well you don't need to now," Conor reminded him happily. "And we've got our squad to get us into the finals!" he said, unable to contain his excitement. "I cannot wait to kick Harry Newbold's butt, gentlemen," he said, putting his arms around both Luke and Eric.

There was much nodding of agreement.

"Oh," added Conor, pulling back now. "Just one more thing, Eric. Does your sister have a date for the Christmas dance?"

"Just try it..." growled Eric... "And I won't be the only one around these parts with a limp."

LEVEL SEVEN
FOOLING HARRY

'm leaving in precisely thirty seconds, Luke!" shouted Sally, using her right foot to prop the front door open. With no sound of movement from above, and with heat escaping out the open door, she removed the foot from its position, stamped it down, and marched up the stairs with one eye on her watch. "Luke, this is ridiculous," she called out in advance of her arrival. "I've told you at least six times that we need to go, otherwise we'll miss your dad's singles final! And you're sat up here playing Hundred-to-One again! Or still! Or something! Or..."

She threw Luke's bedroom door open, casting her eyes directly over to his television set, the screen of which was, to her great surprise, in darkness. "Oh, my," she said, placing her hand over her mouth, as she found her son, not playing video games, but sprawled out on the floor instead. It took her a moment to readjust, and to take in what it was that she was seeing.

"Sorry, Mum. Just finishing this up," said Luke.

"Luke," she said, easing down onto one knee to get a good look. "That's absolutely wonderful," she told him. "I think he'll quite like that."

Luke gave her a smile, and then applied the finishing touches. "There," announced Luke. "That's done. What do you think?" he asked, now standing up and holding out his poster like one of the female round announcers at a boxing match. He'd evidently spent a good couple of hours creating the lettering and colouring it in, which read:

GOOD LUCK, DAD!!!

"Do you think he'll like it?" asked Luke. And, then, shortly thereafter, "Hang on, are you crying, Mum?"

Sally dabbed at her cheeks, to clear away the moisture that had somehow indeed collected there. "I think he'll be over the moon with that, Luke," she told him, ruffling his hair. "Now let's get down to the tournament, shall we? Otherwise, it might be over before he has a chance to see that lovely poster of yours..."

Luke sat in the car, nursing his poster like a new-born baby. "Oh. Mum. We need to make one stop along the way, if you don't mind," he informed her.

"Why do we need to stop?" she asked, before her eyes were drawn to an enthusiastic child leaping on the spot in front of the church at the bottom of their road. "Ah, I guess we're picking up Conor, then," she said, answering her own question, and shortly bringing the car to a stop.

"Hiya, Mrs J," offered Conor, jumping into the back of the car.

"Morning, Conor. Nice to have you with us. I didn't think you were one for badminton, though?"

"It's not my thing, to be honest," replied Conor. "But when Luke said his dad made it to the singles final, I wanted to come along and support him."

"You're good lads, you two. Don't ever forget that," she said, and worried her tear ducts might let go another issuance of watery materials.

Conor whipped a notepad out of his backpack. It was covered in what looked like arcane markings — ancient runes, perhaps — scrawled in ink. Of course it was just Conor's enthusiastic, but messy and barely legible, handwriting. "It will also give us a chance to discuss Hundred-to-One tactics, Mrs J."

Sally sucked in through her teeth as she eased the car away from the halt sign and back onto the road. "About this tournament, boys. I need to speak to you about that."

"You're not going to say we can't go in it, Mum?" pleaded Luke. "Please don't say that!"

"What? No. No, of course I'm not," she assured him. "But there's something that I've been meaning to speak to you about, Luke. And now seems like as good a time as any to tell you."

Luke blinked uncertainly. This sounded serious. And parents didn't usually make it a point to inform kids of things, like she was now, unless the situation was somehow dire...

"You may have noticed that I've been popping out of the house most evenings this week?"

"Oh. Have you?" came his reply. Luke's vacant expression indicated he perhaps wasn't the most observant of children. Or it could have simply been the case that he was perpetually lost in his own world, as most boys that age were.

"I have," she continued. "And thanks for noticing. It's good to see I was missed," she chided him gently. "Anyway, I've been sneaking about because I'm doing something that I couldn't talk about," she told him. "Well, it's not that I *couldn't*, exactly. It's more that I wanted to wait until things were more..."

Luke turned down the radio. "If you're going to tell me you're getting a divorce, then this isn't the best time," he said, pointing to his travelling companion in the rear. "I know Dad snores something wicked, but he's not all bad!" he began at pace, his mind racing, and casting out possible imagined motives in quick succession for said upcoming and imminent divorce.

"No, it's—" Sally began.

"Or is it because he's always stinking up the bathroom all the time?" Luke went on, fearing the worst, not giving his mum a chance to respond.

"No, it's not—" Sally attempted.

"Or is it because he has smelly feet? Because if that's the reason, it was only that one time, and it went away after he got that special powder, remember?"

"No, it's not that—" Sally tried.

"Or is it because he produces so many bottom burps?" Luke carried on. "Oh, wait, that's me, actually..."

"No, it's not that at—" Sally tried yet again.

"Or is it because he's always talking to the woman down the shops with the big pair of—?"

"Luke!" yelled Sally. "My goodness, let me speak!"

"Gosh, you don't need to shout," Luke protested. "It's not *my* fault you're getting a—"

But this time, again, it was Luke who was not allowed to finish. "We're not getting a divorce! And what would even make you think such a thing??" asked Sally. "My goodness!" she said again.

"I just said," offered Luke weakly. "All the things I just..."

"Sweetie, we're not getting a divorce," Sally told him gently, not yelling anymore. "So you don't need to worry about that."

"Oh," said Luke. "Oh," he said again, confused. "Then I don't... then what...?"

"Me and a few of the other school mums were talking about Hundred-to-One and the ridiculous amount of time you kids spend playing it."

Luke opened his mouth to say something, but thought better of it, opting instead to let his mum continue.

"We all realised that we don't know the first thing about this game of yours," said Sally. "And that the only way we'd be able to *truly* understand the appeal of it was to..."

"Was to what?" Luke asked, unsure where all of this was headed.

"Was to, well, play it for ourselves," she told him. "Luke, we've formed a team and entered a squad into the Hundred-to-One competition," she concluded.

Luke sat there at something of a loss. He didn't even know how to respond. What she was saying didn't make any sense. Mums didn't play Hundred-to-One. Obviously. That was nonsense. He couldn't wrap his mind around it, and he almost wished his parents *were* having a divorce, because that would've been easier to process. Easier than this.

"Are you not too old?" ventured Conor bravely, puncturing the silence.

Sally curled her fingers into a fist and shook it playfully. "You're lucky I'm driving, Conor!" she told him. "And no, we're *not* too old," she informed him. "And, you should also know that *your* mum is in the squad as well," she added.

Now it was Conor's turn to be silent.

Luke, by this time, had been able to digest this revelation, for the most part, and concluded it wasn't some sort of cruel hoax or joke in very poor taste. "No harm to you, Mum," he offered. "But you've never been the best with technology."

"That's not true at all!" she protested.

"Mum, when we first bought this car, Dad convinced you that you could unlock it with your voice. You spent the first two days talking to the car as Dad, meanwhile, used the remote control to open it, making it look like the car was responding to your commands. The people in Tesco's car park thought you'd lost the plot."

"So you can't unlock it with your voice?" Conor asked, confused, because unlocking the doors with your voice sounded totally plausible to him, actually.

"Okay, I'll give you that," Sally replied, responding to her son's comment. "But it doesn't mean I'm not the best with technology. A little gullible, perhaps. But that's all," she said. "Anyway, you'll be pleased to know that we've been playing Hundred-to-One all week and we're not half bad, actually. In fact I managed to come in fourth position in one match, with four kills."

"Pleased...?" said Luke.

"Hang on!" laughed Conor, almost clambering over the car seat. "Luke," he said, barely able to contain his delight. "Luke, that's the same as you, and you've been playing for months!"

"That's actually pretty good, Mum," Luke had to admit, his eyebrows now rising in appreciation. "But, Conor," he added, arching his neck to get a look at his friend, even though Conor was sat right behind him. "Just remember that I can kick your butt on Hundred-to-One. And with that in mind, that pretty much means that my mum can kick *your* butt also, now doesn't it?"

"Anyway," Sally went on, looking over her shoulder and reversing the car into a narrow parking space, as they'd reached their destination. "We're actually enjoying the game. And as much as I hate to admit it, I'm starting to realise why you want to spend so much time playing it."

"So, I can play it even more...?" asked Luke, in hope rather than expectation, but his mum's expression told him all he needed to know.

"Come on, boys. And, Luke, you should make the most of this badminton match as it's likely the last time your father will be able to play competitive sport due to the problem with his leg."

"What? Dad's injured?"

"Not as yet," replied Sally, climbing out of the car. "After what you told me about the girl down the shops, though, I've got a funny feeling he's going to end up with some broken bones when I get him home, is what I'm saying." She closed the door and turned around to face the car. "Lock doors!" she commanded to her wing mirror. "I'm kidding," she added, taking the keys from her handbag, but Luke remained unconvinced that she was, in fact, kidding.

"At least I now know why your father never complains when I send him down to the shops," said Sally, holding a playful fist up in the air and shaking it about once more.

Luke and Conor, and now Eric, perched themselves on the moveable partition that divided the sports hall in two — which allowed different sports to take place simultaneously — with a direct view over the badminton tournament, and with all six legs between them swinging in unison.

"It's no good," moaned Eric. "I'm going to get expelled from school, and then what am I supposed to do? And look," he said, pointing to his face. "My eye is watering again. It does that when I'm stressed."

"Nice shot, Dad!" Luke said, cheering the match on, and in reference to his dad, who was presently throwing himself around the badminton court after a particularly fine shot. Luke held his poster aloft, giving it a gentle jiggle for good measure. "And you're not going to get expelled, Eric," Luke added, turning to his friend. "Now you need to stop panicking, right? Otherwise, we're going to have to get a mop and bucket for that," he said, nodding in the direction of Eric's eye, as his hands were still occupied holding up the sign he'd made.

But Eric was not for consoling. "Harry Newbold has organised his first squad practice session for later this afternoon," he explained. "As soon as he realises I'm about as useful in the game as a one-legged man in an arse-kicking competition, he's certain to go straight off to the headmaster and tell him I electrocuted him. And I haven't even got an account on Hundred-to-One. So what am I meant to do in the first place??"

Conor rubbed his chin with purpose, until he became aware of Luke and Eric's eyes on him. "Ah," he said. "I've got nothing. I was just rubbing my chin because it was itchy. Sorry if you thought otherwise."

"Marvellous," exclaimed Eric, with hands raised to the heavens.

Luke, waving his poster about after yet another sublime shot by his dad, lowered it back down. "Hang on, what do you mean you haven't got an account?" he asked. "Oh, wait, I remember," he said. "Aquaeyepatch is your sister's account, isn't it? Well, it wasn't originally. But it is now," he added, fitting the pieces together. "Alright, so don't worry. We'll just get you set up on a new account and can tell Harry some nonsense that you've lent the other log-on to your sister for reasons that he'll hopefully be too stupid to ask for. So, no problem," he said, leaning in for a closer look to see if the eye had stopped watering. It hadn't.

Eric gave Luke a perfect *are-you-really-that-stupid?* type of glance. "You may have forgotten," Eric told him. "And apparently you have. But I cannot play the stupid game!"

"Oi!" said Luke.

"Hey, hey!" Conor protested. "There's no need for that, mate!"

"Not for calling the game stupid," Luke clarified, for Eric's benefit, and shaking his head in horror.

"Sorry," replied Eric. "It's just that I'm completely useless, like I said. So he'll be realising in less than seven seconds that I'm utterly hopeless and likely cancelling our deal. And then I'll be out looking for a new school and possibly a new home when I get chucked out."

"Just tell Harry that he has to put things straight with the headmaster by no later than Monday, otherwise the whole deal is off," Luke instructed. "Then you should be safe no matter what."

"I'm fairly certain..." said Eric, glancing at the imposing digital wall clock... "The deal will be off well before then. In about three hours' time, actually."

Luke lowered his sign, focussing his attention squarely on Eric. "Relax, Eric. I've got a plan."

"You have?" asked Eric, a flicker of hope shining in his eyes — and glistening in one of them, it being all watery as it was. "Well why didn't you tell me before?"

"Because I just thought of it," Luke told him.

"Oh," said Eric.

"Right," said Luke.

"Well?" said Eric.

"Well what?" said Luke, blinking.

"The plan!" said Eric.

"Oh. Right. Okay. So you come back to mine, yeah? And we set you up a new account for you, and then—"

"But you already said that," Eric informed him.

"Right, but the new part is that *I'll* join Harry's squad under the new name, see? And..."

"And what?"

"And he'll never know the difference!" Luke announced triumphantly.

"He won't?" said Eric sceptically.

"He won't!" insisted a cheerful and optimistic Luke.

"He won't?" repeated a rather more dour and entirely unconvinced Eric.

"He *will*, I should think," suggested Conor. And, then, to Luke specifically, "Because you're nowhere near as good as Eric's sister," he explained. "In fact you'd be better off getting your *mum* to stand in," he said with a cheeky grin. "Or perhaps even your budgie."

"We don't even have a budgie!" Luke reminded him.

"I know. But even an imaginary budgie would be better at playing than you," Conor told him.

"Ta. Thanks for that, mate. And what a good friend you are to have. I swear, if I had a fish right now—"

"What kind of fish?" Conor interrupted.

"It doesn't matter what kind of fish! A halibut, all right? If I had a halibut, okay?"

"And what would you do with the halibut?" asked Conor, intrigued by this new fish-related line of talk.

"I'd slap you in the face with it! That's what I'd do!" Luke informed his friend.

The two of them had to laugh at this point, and once the giggles had died down, Luke turned his attention again to Eric — who was staring at the two of them like he wondered if they'd lost their marbles, or, in fact, if they'd ever had any to begin with.

"Eric, look, all we need to do is get you through this afternoon and it'll be fine and after Monday it won't matter because Harry will have cleared your name and it won't matter that you're useless after that," Luke said in one breath.

"*Hmm.* I suppose it may be my only option," Eric considered logically.

"Either me or Conor will play on your behalf, Eric, and we'll be able to do enough to at least convince him you're not completely useless at the game..."

Luke trailed off for a moment, his mind evidently elsewhere. He smiled a simple grin to himself.

"What?" the other two asked him in unison.

"I'm just picturing Harry's face on the day of the tournament," Luke explained, waving his hand as if to introduce the image into the collective mind's eye. The three friends huddled closer together, like a group of tramps seeking warmth from a fire. Luke went on...

"Imagine Harry has just taken his seat for the tournament, his teammates now around him, together in the same room for the very first time, playing together..." Luke began.

"Yes?" said the other two.

"... And then Harry looks around with a smug expression, thinking he's compiled the most elite team of Hundred-to-One professionals, when he catches sight of Eric staring down at his controller with literally not one clue of what any of the buttons do."

"Oh. Eric," Conor entered in. "You should totally hold the controller upside down and look confused!" he suggested.

Luke nodded, waving his hand to engage the mind's eye once more. "Harry notices the controller being held upside down in Eric's hands," he said, going with Conor's idea but now tweaking it a little. "But Harry believes this to be some form of arrogance on Eric's part. Perhaps Eric is such a good virtuoso player that he insists on playing with the controller *upside down*, just to show off. He does believe Eric to be, after all, an absolute Hundred-to-One legend, and one that hundreds of Twitch users tune in to watch each week."

"Thousands!" said Conor.

"Thousands," Luke agreed. "You're probably right," he said, going with the flow.

"Oh. Eric," interrupted Conor once again, but Luke was willing to let it go, since this was their collective fantasy they were imagining. "Eric," Conor went on. "Just when Harry's humongous head is about to blow up, from being so swollen with overconfidence, that's just when you mash all of the buttons on the controller, right? And ask him—"

"I'll ask him which character is Sonic the Hedgehog," said Eric, jumping in, and himself getting into the spirit of it all. And, then, after further consideration, "Oh, and then I'll tell him I've forgotten to put batteries in my controller. That should tip him over the edge...?" he offered up.

"It definitely will," replied Conor. "Harry doesn't seem to know that some controllers *do* use batteries in them, so that'll drive him mad!" he said, remembering the previous conversation he'd had with Harry about precisely that subject.

"Oh, I know," Eric told him. "Luke told me about that, so that's why I suggest it."

"Ah. *Noice*," said Conor, suddenly adopting an Irish accent for no reason at all.

"I like it," agreed Luke.

The prospect of tipping Harry over the edge was, it would appear, rather soothing to the soul, judging by the contented expressions spread over their faces.

Now that was all sorted out, "Here we go!" shouted Luke, with his poster readied and his attention firmly returned to the badminton match. "Matchpoint," he whispered now, for fear of distracting his dad. And Tom delivered an expert serve that drew every last ounce of effort from his opponent to return.

A fairly decent-sized crowd remained to support the two finalists, and the match was not disappointing. *"Go on, Dad,"* Luke mouthed. He was proud of his dad, and he 'felt' every shot his dad hit, mirroring it sympathetically with a jerk of his head and twitch of the wrist.

"Come on!" he shouted, out loud again, sensing — as his dad must have been as well — that his father's courageous opponent was tiring, with each return appearing rather more laboured than the last.

Tom dispatched a drop shot with the seemingly effortless practised dexterity of a brain surgeon. It was delivered with such accuracy that the heavy legs of his opponent could do little to react. *Just like Eric did to me in that match before*, thought Luke.

And that was the game.

"*Yes*, Dad!" shouted Luke, running onto the court. "Dad, that was amazing!" he raved, offering a generous embrace — until, that is, he realised how sweaty his dad was.

Luke stepped back, allowing his dad to graciously accept the wider congratulations on offer and wipe himself down. Luke crossed his arms, smacking his lips with a confident nod of the head which said, *Yep, that man there, he's my dad*.

For Luke, his dad could do no wrong. The man in his life that Luke knew would do absolutely anything for him, no question. He was always proud of his dad, but, in that moment, he felt the overwhelming urge to tell him so. His dad was selfless — the first to pick Luke up if he fell, and the first to do something endearingly stupid and immature if Luke needed cheering up.

Luke felt a wave of elation running through him that'd been absent for a considerable time. He reflected for a moment, coming to the realisation that his current emotion — a mixture of adrenalin, pride, and self-confidence — was last experienced when he'd won the badminton trophy with his father the year before. It felt exceptional. It ignited a fire in Luke's belly. And in an instant, he came to the epiphany that this feeling could only be achieved through competitive sport.

He *did* love his game console, of course. But as much as he loved his video games, they had never made him feel, he had to admit, like he did right now.

He was woken from his reverie by his mum dishing out a series of high-fives to anybody that'd return one to her. Seeing mums doing them was a little odd and unnerving. Still, the intention was there, and Luke jumped into action, once it was his turn, to avoid her hand hanging in thin air, unemployed.

"Come on," his mum said. "We're getting burgers on the way home to celebrate," she told him. "Do you want to join us, Conor?" she asked, inviting Conor along.

"You have to ask?" replied Conor, with pupils dilated, and with what appeared to be a trickle of drool already, at the mere suggestion of burgers, running from the corner of his mouth.

"Can Eric come too, Mum?" asked Luke. "Only we have to do one thing for the Hundred-to-One tournament, and he needs to be with us."

"I guess. But you'll need to clear it with his dad," she said. "What are you three up to, anyway?"

"I'm sorry, Mum," replied Luke. "But as far as Hundred-to-One is concerned, you're technically our competition now. So any strategy meetings we may or may not be having are on a strictly need-to-know basis. I hope you understand."

"Oh, it's like that, is it?" she laughed. "Well," she said, pulling out her phone, "I think I'll just have to message the other mums and set up a strategy meeting of our—"

But the boys had gone — already buckling themselves up in the car, most likely — and Sally was left talking to herself. Clearly, the allure of burgers was the boys' current priority.

Luke and Conor had rather underestimated quite how little Eric knew about Hundred-to-One and online gaming in general. The poor chap was in such a state earlier in the day as he'd assumed any gaming activity with his new squad members would have to take place in person and in the same room, though of course that was not the case at all.

"So Eric," explained Luke for the third, possibly fourth time, "You can have four people in their own houses but they can all play in the same game and they never need to see each other, and this helps because Harry won't be able to see how awful you are at the game. No offence."

"None taken," replied Eric. "Now, so let me get this right in my head. You and Conor can join together on a squad, yet each remain in your own bedrooms and with no requirement to leave your house?"

Conor jabbed the air with his forefinger. "Exactly!" he said, but noticed Eric still looked none the wiser. "You still appear confused," suggested Conor, trying his level best to retain his composure and refrain from chucking the game console out the window.

Eric wiped a drip from under his eye with the back of his hand, then scratched his temple. "No, I get it," he said. "Conor, you and Luke live, what, three minutes apart?"

Conor moved to the window. "Correct. You can see my house from here."

Luke joined Conor by the window, looking out, hands clasped behind his back. "Yes, you can. We're only a stone's throw away. In fact, that's how I was able to see Conor wearing his sister's dress that one day," he observed.

Eric knew Luke was joking but still issued a suspicious glance at Conor.

Conor, surprisingly, didn't say anything. He was trying to remember what day that was, and if he really—

"So, you two live a couple of minutes apart," Eric was saying, saving Conor from his own thoughts. "Yet you spend all of your time in your own bedrooms? See, that's what I don't understand. That's the part I'm not getting."

Both Conor and Luke looked like they didn't understand what Eric was getting at. This is because they didn't understand what Eric was getting at.

Eric had to practically paint them a picture. "You're so close. Why don't you go to each other's house to play?" he told them.

Luke and Conor shared a knowing laugh, letting it go on a little too long, until it became fairly clear that they weren't knowing after all. "We can talk to each other," said Luke. "And, besides, I'd need to bring my game console along with me in order for us to be able to both join in and play together at the same time. So that wouldn't work. Not really. I mean, that'd just be weird, you know? So, yeah, we need to each be at home with our consoles. It's better that way."

Eric had an exceptionally expressive sort of face, when he wasn't repressing his emotions. As such, it became abundantly clear when he didn't know what the heck people were talking about, his face contorting into a mask of confusion. This was one of those times.

"You still don't get it, Eric?" asked Conor.

"I totally get it, Conor," Eric informed him. "But why don't you go around to each other's house and do something besides play video games? That's what I don't get. I know it's winter now, so activities might be more limited, but I assume in the summer, you're out playing football, for instance? Or going out on your bikes?"

"Ha!" scoffed Luke, as an automatic response, though he didn't know why. "Eric, you sound like my mum," he joked, but he pondered that thought for moment, rubbing the impression mark thingy beneath his nose and above his top lip, and then absent-mindedly sniffing his fingers. "Ride our bikes," he thought out loud, repeating Eric's words. "*Ehm...* well, no, to be honest. We played Hundred-to-One for most of the summer. And, before that one, we were playing another massively time-consuming online game," he said.

"Don't forget the World Cup soccer game we played for ages," added Conor, drifting off, himself, in fond recollection, and with the toe of one trainer off the floor and wiggling around in an imaginary game of footy.

But now Luke was giving what Eric was saying some serious thought. "Why *don't* we play football or go out on our bikes, Conor?" he considered aloud. "We live next to an old railway line that's twelve miles long. Perfect for bike riding. Like we used to do. But, instead, we're stuck in our rooms," he said. "Right. Look at my head," he instructed.

Eric and Conor exchanged glances. They weren't sure which one of them was supposed to be doing the looking, or what they were meant to be looking for. "Which one of...?" Eric ventured.

"Either of you. Both of you," said Luke, pointing at his head with both hands now, desperately making some point that appeared to be eluding the others. "My head!" he directed again.

"Is it the pimple...?" asked Conor, taking a guess.

"What? I haven't got a pimple," protested Luke.

"Just there," Conor elaborated, pointing to his own face to illustrate where on Luke's face he was seeing it.

"I think that's strawberry jam, actually," speculated Eric.

Both boys peered at Luke's face intently, scouring it for more spots. Or jam, as the case might be.

"Not my face!" Luke shouted. "Okay, look. Look at my hair, is what I'm saying," Luke told them.

"Do I have to?" asked Conor, getting tired of this kind of game already, whatever it was.

"I've still got the imprint from my headset in it," Luke announced, to stop the others having to guess. "I can't seem to get rid of it," he said. "There's bed-head..." he explained further... "And then there's hat-head. And I've got bloody headset-head."

"Oh," said Conor.

"Oh," said Eric.

"I can't even remember what colour my bike is," Luke went on. "Do I actually still own a bike, Conor?"

Conor didn't answer right away, wondering if this was another guessing game he was supposed to be trying at.

Eric ended up speaking first, looking at the two of them and shaking his head. "Maybe, in your case, playing video games is the best thing," he observed. "But it all seems a bit strange to me, to be honest. I mean, I've got no friends, right? And yet I'm the one who's always out on his bike, and who's out playing football — even if it's on my own. If anyone should be stuck inside all of the time, it's me, because, as I say, I've not got any friends. Whereas you pair *do* have friends... and yet you're locked away in this room which smells of sweaty socks. I don't get it."

Conor pointed weakly at the TV screen. He began to protest, but he had nothing. Eventually, he shrugged his shoulders. "He's right, you know," he admitted.

"What, about the smell?" asked Luke, offended.

"No," replied Conor. "Well, yes, that too. But I meant about the whole playing outside thing," he clarified. "Luke. Do you remember when we built the castle near what used to be the old Union Mills' railway station?"

"Ah, yes... from the old building crates," Luke answered him. "Glorious," he said. "Oh. Conor. Do you remember when we brought your metal detector down and dug up all the old coins that the passengers must have dropped from their pockets back when the trains were still running?"

"I sure do," Conor replied, the nostalgia apparent. "We made a fortune that day."

Luke turned to Eric to include him in the recollection. "We made a swing from the old washing line, Eric," he told him. "It was unbelievable! First we doubled it up, then we put a knot in one end, and then we wrapped the other end around a huge tree branch that dangled over the stream near to the old railway line. If you slipped or let go, you'd end up soaked! Which was brilliant on hot days, actually. You should've seen it, that swing was amazing!" he said, a beaming smile all over his face.

"Your mum wasn't best pleased," remarked Conor. "She went out to hang her washing and found two empty poles. It was a cracking swing, though! We should see if it's still there?"

Eric looked quizzically at Luke, and then over to Conor. "You've just told me how excellent your old base was. And yet you've been stuck in here, and for who-knows-how-long. Why?"

Conor, for a moment, looked like he might be playing imaginary footy again. Really, though, he was just shifting uncomfortably from one foot to the other, trying to think of some kind of rational explanation to hand to Eric. He looked over to Luke.

Luke looked right back over to Conor.

"I... *ehm*... we did... no, see it was... well we were going to, except..." he stumbled. "Actually, I've got nothing," he said, finally. "Gosh, why *haven't* we been down to our base, Luke?" he enquired, redirecting, and pushing the blame squarely onto his friend's shoulders.

But before an explanation of any kind could be mustered up by either of them, a ping was heard from Luke's console, indicating a message had just been received.

At that, a grateful Luke jumped into his seat, with Conor stood at one shoulder, and Eric at the other — all staring intently at the screen like launch controllers at NASA.

Luke handed Eric his headset. "Right. Here we go, Eric. That message on the screen is Harry Newbold inviting what he believes to be you to join his squad. Now, to confirm, I'm going to play the game on your behalf, but you'll still need to speak to him on the headset. Got it?"

"What am I supposed to say to him?" asked Eric. "I don't know anything about gaming etiquette. Should I greet him somehow? Make small talk? Say, *Hiya, Harry, all right*? Or, *Lovely day for it*? Or, like, what exactly? Ask him how his day is going or something?"

"You're overthinking this," Luke told him. "Just be cool. Let Harry do most of the talking. That's probably the way he likes it anyway."

Conor moved around the back of Luke's chair and pressed his head closer to Eric's. "Don't worry, Eric. Luke has the hard work to do convincing Harry that you're good at this game. Harry and the rest of the squad will just talk about the game. You know. What they're doing, what guns they've found, tactics — like where to land — that sort of thing."

Luke peered up over his shoulder, adding, "They'll also talk about where in the map to go. Basically, once we leave the hotel foyer—"

"Hold on, what hotel foyer?" interrupted Eric.

"Nevermind, Eric," replied Luke. "All will become clear in a minute or so. Once we land, all four players will do their own thing, looking for guns, ammo, and material. If we see someone from another squad—"

"We?" asked Eric.

"Our squad. Harry's squad, in this case."

"Oh."

"We join together to try and shoot them," Luke went on. "If we get shot at, we'll start building. Someone from your squad will tell you if they've been shot at."

"How will I know if someone's on my—?"

"You'll know who's on your team as their gamer tag, or screenname, will appear above their character on the screen," Conor offered.

"Like Aquaeyepatch was yours," Luke said. "Though now it's Kikureazz1234."

"How do you spell that?" Eric asked.

"Does it matter?" said Luke.

There was a pause. And then, "Kikureazz1234? *Really*?"

"It's all I could think of on short notice!" protested Luke.

"What's this about building, though?" asked Eric. "I don't really—"

"Right, here we go," Luke cut in. "Hold that thought, Eric, okay? And if you need to talk to us, press the mute button," he instructed.

Eric shuffled in place with nervous energy. It wasn't because he cared about the game, because he didn't. Rather, he was anxious because he had to convince Harry of the whole charade and successfully get through this game — and then come Monday morning he'd be in the clear from the whole electrocution episode.

Eric suddenly jumped back, startled by the screech of excitable voices in his earpiece. "I can hear you!" he shouted, wide-eyed, and seemingly impressed and maybe a little overwhelmed by the whole spectacle unfolding onscreen concurrent with the chatter heard through his headset.

"*Shhh*," cautioned Conor, pressing his finger to his lips. "Don't shout," he whispered. "They can hear you perfectly."

Eric nodded to Conor, then cupped his hands around the earpiece. "What?" he asked into the mic, loudly at first, then again at a more normal volume. "What? Who are you calling a Volcano Meltdown?" he protested.

Conor pressed the mute button on Eric's behalf. "That's where you're supposed to land, Eric," Conor explained. "He's not calling you names or anything. You just need to confirm what he's saying," he told Eric, and then pressed the mute button again to turn it off.

Eric, once the mute was cleared, offered a laugh that sounded something akin to a donkey sneezing. "*Ha-ha*, I was only kidding, of course. Magma Meltdown it is, then. Jolly good. Cheers. I'll see you on the ground. Lovely day for it, by the way," he rattled on, overcompensating with the small talk.

Conor rolled his eyes, fearing their deceit would be uncovered before it'd even had chance to properly begin. He moved his ear closer to Eric's and, fortunately, from what he could pick up, it sounded like the rest of the squad were too preoccupied to worry about Eric's faffing.

"I've no idea what they're wittering on about," Eric told Conor, mouthing the words near-silently. "It just doesn't make any sense." Eric moved to get a better view of the screen, hoping the gameplay would mean something to him...

But it didn't. "*Aaaah!*" he screamed, as a bullet whistled past his head. "Help!" he shouted. "Someone's shooting at me!" He reached for the mute button. "Who's shooting me?" he demanded, almost offended at the very thought.

But Luke, in response to the gunfire, was at present busying himself throwing up a hastily constructed wooden fort meant to repel the attack. And Conor's attention was now elsewhere, glued to the action on the screen.

With Luke and Conor's noses positioned virtually inches from the screen, Eric felt somewhat surplus to requirements.

He made an occasional grunting noise into his mouthpiece, as that appeared to be what his fellow squad members did — or at least that's what it sounded like to him.

With the onscreen activity and the noise in his ear offering him very little in the way of interest, Eric took to wandering around Luke's modest bedroom, where eventually he settled in front of a grey wooden corner shelf that was home to an impressive fleet of Lego Star Wars ships. He raised his hand, running his fingers over them. "Oh, my. You've got the Death Star," he said admiringly. "I've always wanted the Death Star."

But his appreciation of Lord Vader's home was naturally lost on his colleagues who were too engrossed in the action, as well as on the squad members in his ear. "Oh," he said, remembering himself, and immediately aware that he'd failed to activate the mute button. "I was just saying, Harry..." he began, trying to explain away his contrary ramblings... "The Death Star, Harry. That's what I call my favourite, *erm*..." he floundered, looking to Luke and Conor for assistance.

"Tell him it's the name of your favourite rifle," Luke offered over his shoulder, whispering so as not to be heard over Eric's headset.

"Ah," replied Eric with a smile. "I was just remarking that the Death Star is my favourite trifle," he said. "Yum," he added for his own benefit, rubbing his belly.

Luke slapped his forehead. "I said *rifle*, Eric. Look, just make some reason up that you want to play the rest of the game on mute, right? That would probably be your best course of action just now," he suggested.

Eric gave a grateful nod, before turning his attention briefly back to his headset. "Harry, this is Eric. I'm going to go on mute for the rest of this game because you lot are seriously boring me, right? Right," he said, not waiting for the answer, and enabling the mute as Luke had advised.

Conor chuckled to himself. "You could have just said you concentrate better without talking but, I have to say, I liked your reason better."

With no further chatter in his ear, Eric continued on with his exploration of Luke's toys, wonderstruck by the depth of Luke's Lego collection. "You don't play with these anymore?" he asked rhetorically, because the layer of dust told him all he needed to know. "Some of these books haven't even been looked at," he said in abject horror, moving over to Luke's bookshelf now. "This one's still got its wrapper on!"

"Harry's been shot," announced Luke suddenly.

"There's a surprise," remarked Eric, without breaking his bibliophilic browsing. "Wow, you've even got all seven books in the series of the whole..."

But Conor was currently clapping his hands in delight. "Harry's not actually that good!" he exclaimed. "Let the other squad finish him off! Let them— Wait, what are you doing?" he asked, in confused reference to Luke running onscreen towards the collapsed figure.

"If I revive him, then Harry might think Eric is a bit of a legend," proposed Luke, and, with that, Harry was soon upright, armed and on his merry way.

Conor slapped his friend's arm. "Don't tell anyone I said this, Luke, but you're actually pretty good at Hundred-to-One!" he said, duly impressed. "What do you reckon, Eric?"

"Yes. Very good," Eric replied automatically, and with little genuine interest, his attention now moved on to an obviously discarded remote-controlled car. "Oh. Are the batteries not working?" he wondered aloud, directed more to himself than to Luke.

In a movement that James Bond might be proud of, Eric produced a miniature tool kit from somewhere on his person, and before he'd sat himself down on the bed, the plastic covering on the car's underbelly had been removed.

"There's no point," said Luke, whipping his head around for a quick look. "My dad had a look and said the motor's broken," he explained, before turning back to the game.

This didn't deter Eric, who now had several car parts resting on his knee. "It's fine," he suggested, prodding the inner workings with a penknife. "I'll have this sorted in no time."

"You're like a walking toolbox," observed a gaping Conor, who'd decided that Eric's pitstop mechanics, at present, were suddenly more interesting than watching Luke.

"Here," said Eric, handing a few components to Conor. "Hold these for a moment, will you?" he instructed. "Don't lose them."

Conor did as he was asked, then watched on as Eric pressed his nose millimetres away from the car chassis, working meticulously. Eric took one mini tool after another from his kit, snipping this, crimping that, taking a jeweller's screwdriver and turning just there. He seemed to know exactly what he was doing, and one by one he asked for the parts in Conor's hands back, taking each and reassembling them into the whole, in turn.

Luke joined the pair of them on the bed once the game was concluded. "You finished a very admirable third place, Eric, well done. There's no chance Harry will think you're rubbish. Just the opposite. And come Monday he'll now tell the headmaster you weren't involved on his assassination attempt."

"Excellent," replied Eric through his teeth, barely breathing, such was the delicate nature of his mission.

Luke and Conor had their heads buried, fascinated by the inner workings of the car, and fascinated as well by Eric's skill. Eric was just finishing things up by this time, making some final adjustments.

"The instructions say never to take that cover off. For safety reasons," Luke offered, timidly.

This was a warning that came far too late, of course, as Eric had in fact just put the plastic covering back into place and was securing the retaining screws.

"Yeah, they nearly always say that," Eric replied, laughing merrily. "And that should be that," he said, serious now, handing the vehicle over.

Luke dropped down onto one knee, looking up hesitantly at Eric and Conor sat on the bed. Then he turned the car over, flicked the power button, and placed it gently down onto its wheels, on the floor. Luke cradled the controller, scarcely able to believe that his beloved childhood toy was about to be resurrected. He took a deep breath and pressed the joystick forward. And then... absolutely nothing.

Luke pressed on the controller again, pushing the joystick back and forth several times in quick succession. But still nothing. "It's still broken," he announced, disappointed, before the car suddenly sprang into action, nearly toppling him over from the surprise. "It works!" he cried. "It works!"

But it didn't work for long, as it soon sputtered out, lifeless again. "Aw, bugger," said Luke.

"I was afraid of that. Not to worry," advised Eric. "Just a lot of dust mucking up the connections. Easily sorted. Next time I'm over, I'll bring with me some rubbing alcohol, cotton buds, and a can of compressed air. Then we'll get it up and running again for good," he said confidently.

"That was brilliant," Luke told him, taking him at his word. He then switched off his video game console — which, without being asked to, might have been considered a minor miracle in itself. "Should we play with this?" he asked, reaching for a box that'd been stuffed into the rear of his wardrobe. "It's an electrical engineering game for kids. My auntie gave it to me for Christmas a couple of years ago. You can wire up an alarm, that sort of thing."

"Is it any good?" asked Conor.

"We'll soon find out," replied Luke. "Are you staying for a bit, Eric? You can help us out?" he suggested hopefully.

Eric joined the two of them on the floor. "Sure. After all, my only other option is playing football on my own. So I'll stay. Just one caveat, though."

"Caveat?" asked Luke, confused.

"It's that thing really posh people sometimes wear around their neck," offered a helpful Conor.

"That's a *cravat*," Eric corrected him. "No, I meant just one thing. One condition. Okay?"

"Sure. What's the condition?" asked Luke.

"You promise to take me to see your castle?" said Eric.

Conor held out his hand. "I don't know about Luke, but I promise," he said, sealing the deal with a firm handshake. "You know what, Eric?" he offered. "You're still pretty weird at times. But you're alright, mate."

"I promise as well," said Luke, nodding in agreement, whilst at the same time unwrapping the cellophane from the box of the electrical engineering game they were about to play with. "And I agree you're alright, too. And, keep in mind, on top of that, you've just come third place in your first ever game of Hundred-to-One. What a legend!" he added with a laugh

Eric smiled. "Thank you," he said, and he meant it. "That may have been my first game, mind you, but I can assure you it'll also be my last game. Well, apart from the one in the tournament."

"*Ahhh*," sighed Conor contentedly. "I cannot *wait* to watch that match."

"When they see Eric playing Hundred-to-One, for real, Harry's face is going to be an absolute picture!" said Luke. "In fact, Conor, speaking of pictures," he said, waving his finger about excitedly, "You need to make sure you have your camera at the ready, in order to capture the exact moment the realisation kicks in!"

LEVEL EIGHT
GRAND THEFT CANINE

The final Saturday before Christmas was rather a jubilant affair, particularly for the younger folk. In general, the schools had broken up for the holidays and it was a few short days until the jolly chap in the red suit came around to eat your mince pies. Children everywhere were filled with wide-eyed wonderment, fuelled by Christmas cheer and generous amounts of sugar.

More specifically, it was also the day of the Union Mills' Christmas Fayre, an annual fundraising event held at the church where the town's local residents had a chance to meet, eat, drink, and be merry, with an occasional carol thrown in for good measure, and where there were also plenty of stalls to pick up last-minute Crimbo bargains. And amongst the enthusiastic retailers plying their wares to the festive bargain hunters, there were Luke and Conor.

Reverend Scott moved effortlessly through the bustling crowd, exchanging pleasantries in the process, with his infectious smile in fine form. It was fairly evident from a cursory glance that a good amount of the products for sale on the tables in the main hall were somewhat less worthwhile, in regard to purchasing, than one might perhaps hope for. The Reverend was, of course, too much of a gentleman to point this out, instead offering a slightly forced yet easy smile as he continued with his rounds, until he reached Luke and Conor's stall. He did a double-take for a moment, running his eyes over the table, then up to the two plucky stallholders who were grinning expectantly.

"Do you like it?" asked Luke, at the same time lifting his chin to introduce the festive dickie bow sat there, ready to impress. He activated a concealed button on the rear of the fabric, sending the device spinning in a whirl of colour. "Conor," Luke said, nudging his friend to action. And with polished perfection, the two boys soon presented a matching set of rotating neckwear that also released, as if the visual display weren't enough in itself, a lovely, abridged audio verse of "The Holly and the Ivy" as well.

The two of them were dressed immaculately in black trousers, school shoes (that'd actually been polished), and white shirts, accompanied by the multi-coloured spinning light show around their necks. The pasting table that was usually sat at home in the cupboard under Luke's stairs was now covered in tinsel, glitter, and fake snow, with a small herd of miniature reindeer completing the presentation. Their old toys were stacked up, with bright yellow stars stuck to them and with the sale price written in thick black marker pen.

"My word," exclaimed Reverend Scott. "This is an absolute sterling effort, boys, I must say. If there were an award for the most festive stall, you'd surely win it."

These words were met with disappointment from Mrs Temple on the neighbouring table. She'd decorated her table with a malnourished Christmas tree and a porcelain robin which appeared to have one broken wing. The Reverend would attend to her next, tending to her ruffled feathers. Mrs Temple's, that is. Not that of the robin's.

"Are you selling some toys to get a bit of money together to buy Christmas gifts?" continued Reverend Scott, to Luke and Conor.

Conor lowered his chin as his neck was sore, having held his head aloft for more time than was comfortable in order to showcase the spinning dickie bow. "We're trying to get as much cash together as we can," he replied, waving his hand over their assembled goods. "We've got a special project which we need to fund," he explained, with a friendly wink.

"Very mysterious, boys. Well, I wish you both good luck," Rev. Scott replied with a jolly laugh. "Oh," he said suddenly, stopping to look again, before he left, and pressing his glasses up the bridge of his nose. He peered just beyond the table, spying something interesting. "Well, I nearly missed this, now didn't I? Quite a festive-looking elf you've got here, I should say," he told them.

Eric looked simply marvellous in his little red hat and shirt accompanied by striped tights.

"It was their idea," Eric informed the Reverend, with an accusatory thumb pointed at grinning friends. Although the truth of it was, though he'd been reluctant at first, he was now rather enjoying getting into character, and had even taken a moment to recently pose for a picture with a young toddler girl who was quite taken with the gold bell on the end of his hat.

The three boys had each brought a quantity of surplus toys to sell, in the hopes that they may find their way to a good home, and more importantly to raise a little cash in the process. Judging by the interest in their stall, the paying public were either impressed by their salesmanship, or, perhaps they'd priced their old toys too cheaply. Whatever the case might be, their table was emptying quicker than the school classroom at home time.

The day had pretty much run its course, after a while, but sensing another, late-day sale, Conor stood at attention to greet an elderly lady who sported a cloud of white hair and glasses so thick they resembled milk bottles. She made her way forward, adjusting her glasses as she did so, glancing in the vague, general direction of Eric, oddly enough.

"Yes, I quite like that. I'll take it," she said, reaching for her purse.

Conor pointed to what remained of their stock. "No problem, madam," he replied, turning on the charm. "What was it you were looking to buy? The Lego house? Or perhaps the Slinky? The Slinky's been well enjoyed, but there's plenty of life left in it," he said, playing up the item like a true salesman. "Though it's not very good if you live in a bungalow," he joked. But his attempt at humour washed right over his potential customer. "That is... no stairs?" he added by way of explanation, pleased with himself for using a new vocabulary word he'd just learned in school, and not wishing a good joke to go to waste. But it wasn't much use.

"What was that?" she replied, pointing to her ears. "My hearing is not the best, I'm afraid. Nor my eyesight for that matter. But I'd definitely like to buy that item."

Conor attempted to work out where her line of sight led to, but with the magnification of her glasses it was all but impossible. The lenses were so substantial in thickness that the old dear's eyes looked like they were floating behind the glass like buoys.

"I'm not sure what you're after, madam," replied Conor with impeccable manners. "Would you mind pointing it out?"

Conor watched her hand steadily rise, and he turned to look where he thought her finger was pointing. The only problem was, it didn't appear she was pointing towards anything on the table. Eager to seal a deal and help the lady,

Conor asked again. "I'm not sure what it is, madam. Is it on here somewhere?"

"The bear," she said, with a shake of her head. "I'll take the bear. For my grandson."

"No problem," replied Conor, assuming it was something one of his two colleagues must have placed out for sale. "Luke," he said out of the corner of his mouth. "Pass me the bear, please, will you?"

"Got it," replied an agreeable Luke, acting as instructed, reaching out for the...

"*Don't* got it, actually. What bear is this, now...?" asked a similarly confused Luke. "Only I'm not seeing any bears, mate?"

Confirming that his eyes were indeed not deceiving him and that there were, in point of fact, no bears to be had at their stall, Conor returned his attention to the elderly lady. "I'm sorry. But we don't have any bears," he told her gently.

What she didn't still have in sight or hearing, the woman nevertheless possessed in persistence. "*There*," she said, throwing a boiled sweet towards where she was looking, which, as it turned out, was only a few paces behind Conor and Luke, where...

"Ow!" Eric then shouted. "What's the idea?" he said, promptly turning around, and assuming the perpetrator to be either Conor or Luke. "That sweet hit me in the head!"

Conor laughed, because Eric getting knocked on the noggin with a boiled sweet was some good, harmless, jolly fun, he was sure everyone would agree. And then he returned his attention to the elderly lady. "Good shot," he commended her.

"Did I hit it?" she asked. "I think I hit it. But I'm not sure I hit it."

"You hit *something*," Conor told her. "But—"

"Did I hit the bear?" she asked, not waiting for him to finish. "I think I hit the bear. That's the bear I want. That one. Yes."

"Sorry, but we don't have..." Conor began. But then the realisation struck him. "Ah. Madam," he said. "That's not a bear. That's an elf."

"A bear dressed up in an elf costume? Does it cost more? You're driving a hard bargain," she scolded him, though she nevertheless took it in stride because, having seen a good many years as she had, she was well accustomed to this sort of haggling. She opened her purse wider. "I'll take it. For my grandson," she told him. "How much?"

"No, madam," replied Conor, shifting awkwardly from one foot to the other, and looking for assistance from Luke — assistance that was not forthcoming, because Luke was too busy laughing silently, his shoulders shaking in mirth like a jiggling blancmange.

Conor was on his own on this one, so he broke the news to the woman as gracefully as he could. "That's not for sale," he said. "That's Eric."

"An Eric? I don't think I've heard of that kind of bear. So it's not for sale after all? Why isn't it for sale?" the pensioner pressed on.

"Well I don't think his mum would be too happy if I sold him to you?" Conor tried to explain. "Wait, how much have you got in there?" he asked abruptly, peering over the table, contemplating for a moment what could very easily be their biggest sale of the day. "No, sorry," Conor corrected himself, shaking the thought off, and regaining his senses. "Eric, will you stand up and dance or something?" he asked, with the intention of demonstrating to the pensioner that Eric was Eric, a small boy, and not an oversized stuffed toy.

Eric did as he was asked, but it wasn't really much of a dance. At least not a very good one, as he wasn't the best of dancers. It was perhaps more of a wobble, really, with arms flailing about for a bit, and finished off, for reasons unknown even to Eric, with a curtsey.

Conor held his hand out in an *and-there-you-have-it* manner. "See, Madam?" he said, certain this will have sorted things out.

"Oh, my," she replied. "It's one of those voice activated ones, isn't it?" she said, tittering delightedly through the hand now placed over her mouth, hardly believing her good fortune. "My grandson will love it. He'll absolutely adore it! Right, then. How much?"

Sensing he was soon to be kidnapped — or elfnapped, or bearnapped, or whatever the case may be — Eric moved forward with caution from around the back of the table, removing his hat and presenting himself for inspection, in order to clear up the confusion.

The pensioner moved her face an inch or so from Eric's, carefully sizing him up. "Here, what are you playing at? That's a real boy!" she told Conor in dismay, her formerly sweet demeanour now turning almost venomous.

"Yes, that's what I've been trying to—" Conor started to say, but to no avail.

"You should be ashamed of yourself, young man!" she said to him, scolding Conor like a disapproving schoolmarm, stared menacingly at him, and then releasing another boiled sweet, this time in his direction. "Fancy trying to sell a boy and pretending it to be a bear!" she continued. "No, a boy and pretending it to be a bear pretending to be an elf," she corrected herself. "Honestly!" she said. And, then, to emphasise the point even further, "Heavens to Betsy!"

Conor stood there taking the full brunt of the attack, taking point as it were — but this was only because his comrades had left him there, as they'd judiciously stepped away by several paces. Seeing he was on his own, he did what he could to appease the distraught woman. "I'm sorry?" he offered eventually, not really sure what he was apologising for or what else to say. But, still, manners were everything.

But the auld one ignored Conor's apology, now glancing around and about her feet instead. "Oh, dear," she was saying. "Now I've gone and lost my Terrance."

Eager to redeem the situation, Conor stepped forward. Or, rather, he stayed where he was, already in the forward position, as he was, by virtue of his compatriots having stepped back. "Where did you last see him?" he asked.

"He was here just a moment ago," she said, completely forgetting to be cross with Conor now that her beloved Terrance had gone missing. "I've just been outside to take him for a poo," she went on, the formidable creases on her forehead growing even deeper than usual, in concern. "I know he was here a moment ago. I felt his nose on my leg."

Conor was seconds away from retreat himself, but he soldiered on. "Your grandson has been outside for a poo?" he asked, with one eye nevertheless cast around, looking for perhaps Reverend Scott to rescue him.

"What? Of course not! Terrance is my dog!" she berated him. "Here, are you having me on? Are you one of those young people who takes pleasure in hectoring a helpless old woman? Some sort of rapscallion?"

"I... I don't even know what those words mean," Conor answered her, raising his hands in submission. He took a deep breath. "I just... I thought..." he said, struggling to come up with anything that might both explain himself and appease her — and failing in it.

But then providence presented itself unexpectedly, but most fortunately. "Nevermind," said Conor. "I think I've just spotted your dog," he replied. "I think I see your Terrance. Is he small, with wiry fur?" he asked, effectively describing likely half the dogs on the Isle of Man.

"That's him!" the pensioner cried. "That's my Terrance!"

"Right, then. I see him," Conor told her. "He's not far. I'll just go and fetch him, madam, shall I?" he said, not waiting for an answer and making a hasty — and grateful — exit to do precisely as he suggested.

Conor made his way across the hall, and sure enough there sat outside the disabled toilets a small, scruffy dog, seemingly abandoned, and waiting patiently for its owner's return. It had to be Terrance, there was no two ways about it. And so Conor took hold of the friendly little doggie's harness leash and escorted him back in the direction of the distressed pensioner.

"There you go, madam," Conor said, once pensioner and pooch were happily reunited, and handing off the dog's harness leash, even going so far as to place it safely in the woman's hand. "All sorted," he said, satisfied, and happy that ordeal was finally over and done with.

With his recovery mission concluded, Conor retreated to where Eric and Luke had, well, retreated. "I think I could have sold you for quite a lot of money," he told Eric. "But in the end, I didn't," he reassured him, proud, apparently, of the restraint he'd shown. "She really liked that dance you did, by the way," he added, emphasising the point, perhaps, that he *could* have sold Eric if he really wanted to. But that he didn't.

"Thanks for that, I guess...? That you didn't sell me...?" offered Eric.

"Wait, is she okay?" asked Luke, in reference to the elderly woman. "Only she's just standing there staring down at her dog. Why is she just standing there staring down at her dog...?"

"Maybe she's overwhelmed to see Terrance?" suggested Conor. "Anyway, it looks like the crowds are leaving. We've got next to no stock left, and we're getting picked up to go to the doubles badminton competition you're playing with your dad in half an hour anyway, Luke. You think we should call it a day? What do you guys reckon? There's not much more happening here at this point, I don't think."

But, just then, as if to prove Conor wrong...

"Help!" called out a trembling male voice, from someone quite obviously suffering great upset. This was followed very quickly thereafter by additional appeals. "Help me! Anybody!"

All eyes turned to the origin of the voice, a gentleman of advanced age, as it happened, stood near to the disabled toilets.

And it was Reverend Scott, still present, who came to the rescue, quickly finding his way to the visibly shaken man, and placing a protective arm around the pensioner's narrow, stooped shoulders. "Whatever is the matter, my fine fellow? Are you all right? How can I help?" he asked. "You're safe here," he assured him. It was the Reverend's job, after all, to provide aid and comfort to his flock. It's what he did, and he did it well.

"I'm nearly blind, I can't see a blessed thing..." explained the old man... "And somebody's only gone and stolen my bloody guide dog while I was in the loo!"

The collective sound of uniformly horrified, disgusted people inhaling through their teeth or gasping in astonishment, in unison, was practically deafening. Conor's shoulders sank, to the point where they almost resembled the osteoarthritic old man's, and if he wasn't already firmly up against a wall he would've taken several steps back.

"Can you shout the dog's name out?" suggested one of the concerned crowd that, along with Reverend Scott, had come to the gentleman's aid. "Disgusting behaviour!" remarked another. "Who would do such a thing!" asked another, as this sort of heinous act was rare in their sleepy little town.

"Yes," agreed Reverend Scott. "Call your dog's name, and if he's in the vicinity, he may hear your voice and return?"

The man ran his hand through erratic, sea-spray wisps of grey hair. "He's never ran away before. Not ever," the old fellow explained. "He's a good, loyal pooch. That's why I think he must've been stolen. But it's worth a try, calling out for him," he said.

Reverend Scott let go of the man, allowing the fellow to fill his lungs as best he could. "Escort," the man said, softly at first, but then louder. "Escort!" he repeated. "There's a good lad! Come here, boy!" he called out hopefully.

Several more voices called out as well, joining in on the endeavour, including Conor, who was inexplicably also shouting for the dog — the dog which he'd stolen in the first place.

And, in fact, after not too terribly long a time at all, Escort did indeed dutifully appear, cutting through the crowd at a respectable clip — several knots, perhaps — the small sea of spectators parting like waves as he passed through them, and a confused and disoriented elderly woman pulled along in the little dog's wake across the church hall.

"Oh, my," she gasped, once the pair had arrived. "Where am I now? I was over there, just there, a moment ago. And now, somehow, I've gotten over here. Where is here...?"

Reverend Scott placed his hands squarely on his hips. "Gladys Wilson," he said sternly. "I can scarcely believe it! You've stolen this poor gentleman's guide dog?" he said, hardly trusting his own eyes.

"What?" asked a muddled Gladys, who then looked down at the leash, still, to her surprise, in her hand. "Oh. I see," she said, the question of her sudden and mysterious intra-church transport now solved, as well as the source of the Reverend's enquiry.

"I've done no such thing!" an indignant Gladys went on. "That young hooligan who tried to sell me the elf-themed giant dancing toy bear handed me this dog, to replace my own missing dearest Terrence," she rightly explained. "As if I wouldn't know the difference!" she cried. And, "Heavens to Betsy!" she added, once again, this time to aid in establishing her obvious innocence.

Reverend Scott looked at his watch. "It's a little early for the gin, Gladys, don't you think?" he said, tut-tutting all the while.

Meanwhile, observing — along with Eric, and, once again, Conor — from a safe distance away, behind the Christmas tree, Luke felt a wet nose through the fabric of his left sock. He looked down. "Ah. So I'm guessing this is Terrance," he said, in reference to the Jack Russell terrier scouring the surface of his socks in search of treats. "You need to deliver him," he suggested to Conor.

"Oh, no thank you very much," replied Conor. "That didn't go so awfully well for me last time I tried it, if you recall," he said. "Eric. Mate. Will you go?" he asked. "There's no way they're going to shout at an elf, yeah?"

"Pixie," corrected Eric. "Or was it an elf? I forget."

Conor picked up what was presumably Terrance, handing the wee doggie off to Eric. "Well whatever you are — elf, pixie, dancing bear — can you please go and hand this dog over to what I very much hope is its rightful owner?" he pleaded. "And can I be arrested at this age?" he asked to nobody in particular, wondering aloud.

Fortunately for Conor, and for everyone involved, the two dogs eventually ended up with each one's rightful owner. And not only that, but the boys' stall was all but emptied of its few remaining contents by a few last-minute bargain hunters.

"How did you get on?" asked Sally, once arrived to pick them up, and beaming with pride at the little gaggle of entrepreneurs.

Luke's face lit up. "Brilliant, Mum. We sold practically everything, and we now have enough money for our project."

Sally offered a round of high-fives to the boys, particularly determined ones. She'd obviously been practising at it. "Well done, boys," she told them. "Now, come on. I need to get Luke to the badminton tournament so he can defend his title with his dad. Luke, your dad's been so nervous all day!"

"We're bringing Eric and Conor?" asked Luke.

"We are. I've already spoken to their mums. Now come on, get packed up. I know how much you've been looking forward to this!"

With their table packed up and now armed with handfuls of cash, it was the end of a relatively good afternoon. "You know..." said Conor thoughtfully. "Aside from the Grand Theft Canine incident, I've had loads of fun today. We should totally do this again, yeah? Maybe at the Easter Fayre?" To which the others couldn't help but agree.

"I know you're on your way out the door. But just a quick word, if I may?" said Reverend Scott, catching Luke's mum before they left. "I wanted to tell you I was watching these young ones in action today, and that they were simply wonderful," he informed her. "You know, Conor and Luke," he said, moving his attention directly to the two boys — and getting their names mixed up yet again. "I've known the both of you for a very long time, and it's such a pleasure to see you growing into polite, friendly young gentlemen."

And, then, to Eric, "And, Eric, although we're of recent acquaintance, I look forward to getting to know you better. But, for now, I'd say you're in exceptionally good company with these two," he told him, in reference to Luke and Conor, and at which point he gave each of them, in turn, a friendly ruffling of the hair. The boys, that is — not Sally.

Once the ruffling of the boys' hair was properly sorted, Reverend Scott stepped to one side, allowing them to pass. In doing so, however, the huge plastic thermometer behind him used for the ongoing roof fundraiser was coincidentally revealed.

"We're almost there," observed Conor, noticing the sand was near to the top line indicating the church's ultimate fundraising goal. "Not long to go now..." he added, trailing off at the end, something on his mind, or a thought occurring to him, perhaps.

Conor shifted his attention to Luke and Eric, and a series of glances and head nods ensued between them, with no words having been exchanged, or needing to be exchanged, and, then, with Conor collecting the notes between them.

At this, Luke then patted each of his friends on the back to acknowledge and seal the deal they'd just silently made. He walked up to the thermometer, reached for the plastic beaker at hand, pressing it into the bucket of sand there at the ready, and then climbed up and carefully emptied the contents into the thermometer until the sand level had risen to indicate an increase of roughly two hundred pounds.

As this was accomplished, Conor reached back into his pocket, paused for a moment, and then kissed the notes he held goodbye, pressing them with purpose into Reverend Scott's palm. "Here," announced Conor. "We'd like to give you this towards the church roof."

Reverend Scott placed his other hand over the money, accepting the gift with, well, reverence, and he bobbed his head in thanks and warm regard.

"Oh, my," said Sally, instantly dabbing her eyes. "Boys, I don't know what to say. That's a wonderful thing to do. Give me a cuddle, you lot!" she said. And, to Luke, after the impromptu cuddling session had concluded, "Right. Now let's get you off to the badminton tournament!"

Luke realised he was still holding the plastic sand beaker, having carried it back with him to witness Conor turning the money over to Reverend Scott. "Just a tick," he told his mum, and then hurried back over to return the beaker to its proper place. As he did so, however, a certain dog with a wiry coat was making a beeline across Luke's path, harness leash trailing behind on the floor. Apparently, Terrance, once tasting freedom, wanted rather more of it.

With Terrance suddenly tangled underfoot, Luke promptly pitched over, heading straight to the floor. He thought he'd be saved by the waiting arms of the Christmas tree just beside him, but he fell right through, his head smacking the hard tiled floor, and the remains of the sand in the plastic beaker he'd been carrying now strewn out across the tiles as well.

"Luke!" shouted his mum, running towards him.

Luke moaned, pressing his hand to his head.

"Don't move," said his mum, kneeling beside him. "Luke, can you hear me?" she asked. "Phone an ambulance!" she shouted out, to anyone nearby. And, then, returning her attention to her son, "It's okay, Luke. I'm here."

"Me too," said Conor, who'd quickly made his way over.

"Me three," said Eric, also appearing by his side.

Unfortunately, as Luke's head began to clear, another area of his body subsequently came into sharp focus. "My ankle!" he yelped in pain.

"Oh dear," whispered Reverend Scott, arriving beside Luke as well. He didn't need to be a doctor to observe from the angle of Luke's foot as compared to his leg that something was truly amiss.

Luke tried to hold back the tears, but the pain was too intense. Conor sat one side of him and Eric the other, with his mum doing her best to remain composed. And yet in spite of his obvious distress, Luke insisted that someone go after Terrance so his owner, Gladys Wilson, wouldn't be too upset.

"Don't you trouble yourself with that," Reverend Scott said as soothingly as possible. "Let's worry about *you* right now, lad." Then he turned to Sally, and said quietly, "I'm sorry to say that'll need to be X-rayed. I'm fairly certain your son's broken a bone in his ankle. He'll need to go to hospital straight away."

"I can't!" sobbed Luke, not helping but to overhear. "I'm supposed to be in a badminton competition!"

Sally took Luke's hand. "Don't worry, Luke," she said softly. "There will be other tournaments. Now, take a deep breath and be brave. I'm going to try and get hold of your father."

"*Noooo*," moaned Luke. "I promised Dad that we'd win our tournament. I need to *goooo...*"

But as Luke attempted to lift his head, a wave of pain ran through his body, alerting him that he wouldn't be going anywhere fast.

Conor lifted Luke's head from the cold floor, placing his folded jacket under it for him to rest on. "Hang in there, mate," he whispered, his eyes welling with tears. "You'll be fine. I promise."

"I can... I can do a dance?" offered Eric hesitantly. "To help cheer you up...?"

Eric wasn't being disrespectful. He was just at a loss as to what to say or do, and wanted to do something, anything, to help.

"*Noooo*," moaned Luke again. And then, "*Ow, ow, ow!* It hurts when I laugh!"

LEVEL NINE
THE TERMUMATORS

Christmas Eve in the Jacobs household was, like with many families, steeped in tradition. Their two cats lay sprawled out in front of a good old-fashioned roaring coal fire in the fireplace, with all of them, cats included, absorbing the gentle melody of traditional Christmas carols, provided graciously, now in this modern age, by Alexa.

"It's eight p.m.!" announced an extremely animated Sally, bouncing into the living room with three presents wrapped immaculately and finished off with tied green bows. "And you know what that means!" she said as a statement rather than a question.

"I can get a whisky?" suggested Tom, poking the fire, but he knew what was coming, of course, as did Luke. It was an annual tradition in the Jacobs household.

"Christmas pyjamas!" announced Sally merrily — just in case they didn't already know — and handing out the presents to the both of them, and one to herself. Tom was sat in his favourite chair, and Luke was laying on the sofa with several pillows under his head and leg propped up with pillows as well. "Don't worry, Luke. I've made a slight adjustment to yours," she said.

"Thanks, Mum," Luke said, ripping open the paper. The pyjama trousers were rolled up like a beach towel, so Luke gripped the waistband and snapped his wrists to unravel them. The left leg dropped to the floor, as one might expect, but half the right leg was missing, and so it fell short. "Aw, thanks, Mum," Luke said again.

"I've taken off the right leg from the knee down and put a little split up the side, so you should be able to get them over your plaster cast," she said, coming over and fluffing up his pillows as mums liked to do. "Do you want some help getting them on?"

"I'm fine, Mum," he said, whipping off the badminton shorts he was lounging around in. Or trying to, at least, because try as he might he couldn't reach down to pull the fabric over his feet in the position he was in, unable, as he was, to bend his right leg.

"Let me," offered Mum. "Is your leg itchy, by the way? I can always get one of my knitting needles down there, if you like? Is there anything else you need me to do for you? Are you very uncomfortable? Is there anything...? I could... Oh, my little baby!" she fussed.

But Luke didn't mind the fussing. And it was a bit of an adjustment, having had his bedroom transported down the stairs, but sleeping in the front room was a better option than traipsing up and down the stairs several times each day, given his present condition. And it was certainly safer, at least until he'd mastered the use of his crutches around the house. And being in the front room, as an extra advantage, at least for now, meant staying up watching TV for longer.

"Why have you got a giraffe drawn on your cast?" Sally asked, spotting something peculiar, and tilting her head sideways like a canine who'd just heard an unusual sound and was trying to work out what it was.

"I... *ehm*..." mumbled Luke, uncertain how to answer her, until Dad returned from the kitchen with his anticipated whisky, and saved him.

"Ah. That would be me. I drew that," announced Tom, throwing Luke a furtive wink in the process.

The truth of it was, however, that Eric and Conor had been around earlier in the day, and, as all children knew, a plaster cast just *has* to be drawn on. While Eric had simply signed his name, Conor, being cheeky Conor, decided it best to draw something one might describe, charitably, as somewhat rude. And so Luke's dad had later expertly used his artistic talent to convert Conor's drawing into a giraffe's neck, with the intent of saving Luke from his mum's embarrassed blushes.

And it worked. And although Tom didn't like dishonesty, he felt that in this instance a little white lie could, he hoped, be forgiven.

The dancing flames from the fire cast a gentle orange glow that shimmered on the tree decorations. "I think I will take that knitting needle after all," suggested Luke after a bit of reflection. "It's a bit itchy down the back of my leg, actually."

The front room was peppered with flickering fairy lights, tinsel, decorations, and every conceivable Christmas plush toy you could possibly imagine. But Luke couldn't keep his eyes from wandering over to the oak shelving unit next to the tree. They say you don't appreciate things until they're gone, and boy was this the case with the annual trophy that previously had sat nestled upon the second shelf. Luke had barely noticed it most days, but the empty space was now all he could see.

It wasn't even a particularly impressive trophy, not much bigger than a Sky TV remote, but it was what it stood for that mattered. It was a visual representation that Luke was good at something — and something he was good at with his dad, most importantly — and it not being there was painful. Not as painful as breaking his ankle, granted. But still painful.

"Don't worry. There's always the next one, champ," said Tom kindly, following the direction of his son's fixed stare. "We've got a full year to get in plenty of training, and there's not a hope there won't be another trophy over there on that shelf."

"Put your singles trophy on there...?" suggested Luke.

"You'll be back on your feet before you know it," Tom assured him, wishing to place the focus more on encouraging his son.

"I know," sighed Luke, digging into the huge tin of sweets sat next to him to soothe his spirits. "Though I'm beginning to think that asking for a trampoline for Christmas a while back was probably not the best idea, in hindsight."

Sally joined him on the settee. "The doctor said you'll be back on your feet in five or six weeks, Luke. You just need to keep any weight off of the ankle for a good while," she cooed, holding his hand as if to comfort him. But Luke wasn't stupid. He suspected she just wanted to keep his hand occupied because she was after the sweets herself.

"Don't forget, we're picking up a wheelchair for you next week, so, that's something to look forward to?" added Tom.

"Trust me, I couldn't forget, Dad," Luke told him. "And Eric and Conor cannot wait. Conor wants to race it. And Eric has some pretty bold plans for it, talking about adding a horn and indicators and such, and even upgrading the wheels! He did mention in passing about wiring it up to an old lawnmower engine, as well. But he was joking about that part. Or at least I think he was."

"I don't think the hospital would like that very much...?" considered Tom. "We'll have to give it back to them once you're done with it, don't forget."

"I've been thinking, Luke. You know. About the whole Hundred-to-One tournament thing," his mum said. She took the tin of sweets between them and placed it on the other side of her, scooting closer to him in the process.

Luke eyed her with suspicion, glanced at the tin of sweets — so conveniently out of reach for him now, he couldn't help but notice — and then back at his mum. "Yes?" he said, his eyes narrowing.

"I was a little bit worried that it wasn't perhaps the best of ideas. Us mums entering a team, I mean. Because the last thing I wanted to do was embarrass you, my little cabbage—"

"If you don't want to embarrass me, maybe you could start by not calling me *my little cabbage*?" Luke cut in, but his mum wasn't quite finished yet...

"So I was wondering if perhaps I should think about withdrawing our entry...?" she said.

"What? No, Mum, there's no need to do that," Luke said, his eyes softening. He lowered the one remaining sweet in his hand, which he'd just been about to pop into his gob. This was remarkable, in itself, as it was the purple one that everyone likes best. So, in other words, a minor miracle that he was holding himself back from dispatching it into his mouth with all due haste. "Embarrass me?" he told his mum. "Not at all. I think it's the coolest thing ever!" he insisted.

"You do?" she asked, obviously relieved.

"Of course I do," Luke assured his mum. "But you should realise one thing," he cautioned her.

"And that is?" she asked.

"That if we're to be in competition together, I'll have to pretend I don't know you at the tournament should we both make it there. Deal?"

"Deal," she readily agreed.

A little *too* readily, thought Luke.

"And I'm so glad you said that," she added, clapping with the tips of her fingers only, in a kind of *I've-got-a-plan,* evil genius sort of way. "I'm glad you said that," she said again, pulling a white plastic bag out from beside the sofa and into view.

As Luke watched on, she pulled out what Luke assumed at first to be more Christmas related attire, but was taken by surprise when it was not. Attire, yes. Christmas related, not exactly.

"What do you think?" she asked, removing the contents of the bag, and handing it over to Luke for his inspection. She threw an excited glance over to her husband as Luke took his time examining it.

Luke held it out in front of him, reviewing it carefully. Then he handed it back to her with a nod. He cleared his throat. "Well it's a t-shirt. And it's got a picture on it of what looks to be Arnold Schwarzenegger. Except, instead of where his head should be, your head is there instead...? Have I got it right?"

"*Yeeesss,*" said Sally, her weird fingertip-clapping once again resuming. "I *knooowww,*" she said. "It's from the film *The Terminator,*" she explained. "Each of the mums has got one printed for the tournament, with their own face rather than mine," she went on, as if there was any need to explain that point. "Our team name is The TerMUMators," she said, her hands ceasing their motion, with fingertips now held firmly pressed together. And then she raised up her chin, as well as her eyebrows, in anticipation of what Luke supposed was the expected response — though what that response might be remained unclear.

"Ah. I see. I like it, Mum. Very clever," said Luke. "And I'm sure... *You'll be back*," he added, certain that would please her. But, instead, she only looked back at him blankly.

"*Em...* You've not actually *watched* the film, at any point. Like, ever. Have you, Mum?" Luke enquired, though already suspecting the answer.

She shook her head, only half listening, still chuckling at the brilliance of the t-shirt design she and her friends had come up with.

Now the seed for the idea had been planted, in general, Luke found himself a little annoyed that he and his mates had not considered t-shirts themselves, actually, and he made a mental note to bring it up at their next squad strategy meeting.

Tom took a sip of his drink. "So now who do I support at the tournament?" he asked. "My son or my wife?"

"I'm sure you can support us *both*," replied Sally.

But the look in her eyes told Tom all he needed to know. Women — particularly wives and mothers — were specialists at saying something without saying anything, and Tom was left with no delusions as to where his allegiances should lie.

"Say, I heard you and the other boys talking about your project earlier, but I didn't catch the details," Tom said to his son, trying to change the subject. "Would you care to fill us in, Luke?"

Luke grabbed the piece of folded paper on the table next to his can of his usual Ribena — this time orange-flavoured. "I think Eric's gone a little bit overboard in the plans," he said, in advance of showing the picture to his dad. "You know the castle — well, fort — we built down by the railway line?"

Tom took the paper, smiling in appreciation at what he saw. Then he looked at Luke, and in answer to his question, said, "Sure I do. That swing was definitely something special."

At this, both men in the Jacobs house looked at Sally, unclear if she knew that's where her washing line ended up.

"We went down there the other day," explained Luke. "And the fort is still there. It was a struggle to get up to it, as the winding path up to it was soaked and slippery from all the rainfall we just had, but the structure itself appears to be intact. We'd built a ladder up the steep ledge from the railway line below to access the fort directly and avoid the other path entirely, but it was barely in one piece. We'll need to make another ladder, I expect." Luke scratched his chin... and then wished he could scratch his leg as well. "*Hmm*," he thought aloud. "Maybe we should just keep the ladder off, now I think on it. "Probably best not to give the fort's location away. You can't see the fort from down on the old railway line. Might be best to keep it that way."

"This," said Tom, looking at the intricate plans drawn on the paper, "This is actually very good. In fact, it's fantastic. You three came up with these plans?"

"Yes, Dad. What did you expect? Something like a pirate treasure map with a big 'X' scrawled in the middle?" Luke asked with a laugh.

Tom pushed out his lower lip in admiration, nodding like a dashboard bobblehead. "I'm telling you, Luke, this is like something an architect would come up with. Seriously, it's pretty darned good," he said, handing the drawing back to his son. "So who's going to do all the building?"

"We are," Luke replied. "We may need a little bit of help, but most of it we can do ourselves, I think. It's not going to be cheap, though, with all the various materials we'll need. So the Hundred-to-One tournament will certainly go a long way towards helping, if we should win."

Sally had a look herself at the plans held in Luke's hands. "You three were raising money to pay for this, and you still decided to give it to the church fundraiser instead?" She took a moment to compose herself, before continuing...

"Luke, seeing as how you gave your money to the church, how about Dad and I help you boys out with the money to complete your fort? And, if you need any muscle power..." she added, casting a cheeky grin at Tom, and waiting a beat before continuing, to Luke... "You can always come and ask your mum."

"Oi! What's this??" said Tom in mock protest. Then, to his son, "Seriously, though, Luke. If you need the money, we're happy to help."

Luke stared down for a moment on the master plans he held, before looking back up. "You know..." he said, chewing the inside of his cheek. "Thanks for that. But I think we want to do this all on our own if at all possible. I think it will mean more that way, you know what I mean?"

"Well, you just need to ask, if you should decide you need help, okay?" said Sally. "Now, you boys will have to excuse me," she said. "I'm going to go chop the veg and such and get organised for tomorrow's dinner."

Once Sally was out of the room and out of earshot, Tom, it turned out, had something else on his mind he wanted to say to Luke. "You know when you get the wheelchair?" he asked. "You're going to let me have a spin in it, right?"

"We'll see, Dad, we'll see," Luke teased. "I'm getting low on sweets over here. Maybe if you went and got me some more, I'll have a think about it...?"

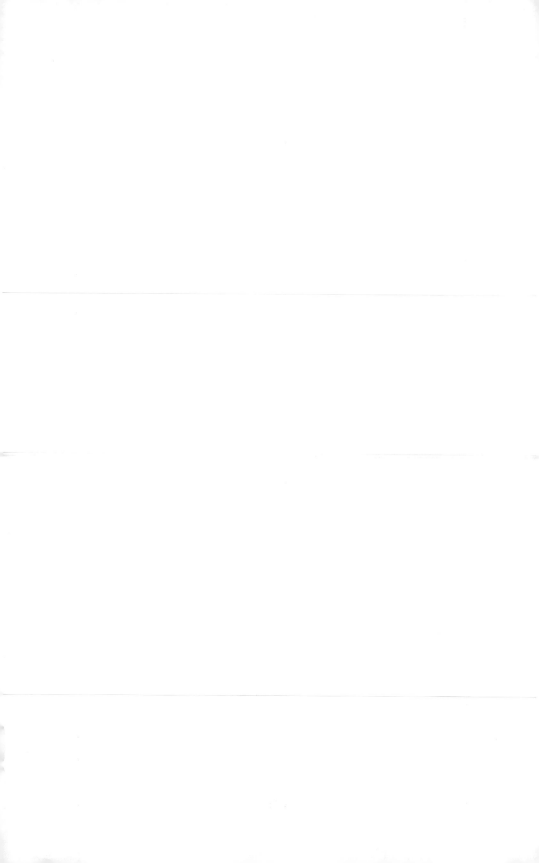

LEVEL TEN
SCYTHED CHARIOT

The festive period for Luke was, well, not very festive. He did his best to keep a stiff upper lip, but the truth was that he was in pain and a little bit miserable. Mum and Dad were brilliant, and he felt guilty — though not too terribly guilty, if he was being honest — for being waited on hand and foot, but the onset of cabin fever was beginning to form. And the irony was not lost on him that he'd been happy as a lark to sit, wasting away, in his room for months at a time when he was perfectly well equipped to go outside and play.

But now he wasn't able to just up and leave, doing just that was all Luke could think about. In fact, they'd opened a skateboard park and BMX track less than two hundred metres from his house, and he'd been near it the grand total of once. That was on opening day, when there was a hot dog stall, and a van that produced those minuscule little scrummy doughnuts that you coat in sugar, he remembered fondly. And as soon as he was back on his feet, he was determined, he was going to pump the tyres on his bike, give it a wash, and take it for a spin around the muddy ramps. Blimey, and thinking about his bike, he couldn't even recall what colour the thing actually was, it'd been so long since he'd been on it. Ages, it seemed like.

At least he could still play video games. If it was a wrist he'd broken instead of an ankle, he'd be absolutely done for. Thank goodness for small favours.

It was the first Tuesday after New Year, and four days until the Hundred-to-One tournament event, and the general excitement over the tournament was palpable. It was all people of his age were talking about on their social media accounts, in fact. And Conor, on one of his regular visits, had confessed to not being able to sleep for thinking about it. Probably the only person not nattering on endlessly on the subject was Eric... who still couldn't care less about it — or, rather, cared only about avoiding it.

While Eric was firmly out of trouble at school after Harry had so graciously cleared his name, Harry, remarkably, remained none the wiser about how utterly useless Eric was at Hundred-to-One. Harry had hosted several training sessions for his squad, which Eric had managed to expertly evade. Or, it could've been more a matter of complete indifference. Either way, Eric hadn't bothered at all to respond to Harry's invitations to the sessions or turn up, so the end result was the same.

Luke and Conor were in a similar situation, in that the rest of their squad displayed absolutely no interest in showing up for training sessions. Though, to be fair, Eric's sister was already a master and so hardly needed to train with them. And if they wanted to see how her practice was coming on, they'd only need to log onto Twitch to watch her in action. The other member of their squad was Eric's older brother, but they'd not met with him again after recruiting him. His involvement in the whole situation was by virtue of his age and not his talent, after all. They would probably see him next on the day of the tournament. And, anyway, it was in the talent department that Luke himself was hoping he was rather fitting into the equation, as opposed to Sam. So not being in touch with Eric's brother was not a huge problem.

But, in spite of all the free time available to him, Luke, while fairly good at the game in general, was still miles away from securing his coveted and long-sought personal goal of a debut Victory Supreme win. If anything, in fact, instead of getting better at playing, it was possible he'd actually gotten slightly worse.

What surprised Luke most about the lack of improvement in his gaming skills was that he wasn't so concerned about it as he thought he might be. A few weeks earlier, he'd spend every waking moment either playing Hundred-to-One, or *thinking* about playing Hundred-to-One, and reviewing his gameplay in his head, analysing any error, and beating himself up for the stupidest of mistakes.

Whereas now it didn't appear to be as important in his life as it used to be. He reflected on the excitement of his dad's badminton tournament, and the disappointment of his own. He also thought about designing the castle with his friends, and about discussions as to how they were going to spend their time down by the old railway line exploring, cycling, building, and making an even better swing as soon as spring came. He still loved Hundred-to-One, mind. He hadn't *completely* lost the plot. It was just that he was seeing scope in his life for something in addition to video games.

"You will be careful, won't you?" asked Sally for the third time. She took a woollen hat she'd crocheted and placed it firmly on Luke's head in a manner that held little regard, it seemed to Luke, for the well-being of his ears.

"It's really cold out there, Luke. Are you sure you don't want to go another day when it's a little warmer?" she asked. "Do you have your gloves? Where are your gloves? Oh, where did I put your gloves?" she said, worrying over him like only a concerned mother can do.

"Mum, calm down," said Luke, releasing his eyes from the woollen prison they'd found themselves in as a result of the overenthusiastic hatting procedure perpetrated upon his person. "I'll be absolutely fine, I promise! I'm only going down to the old railway line with Conor and Eric," he assured her. "And, besides, what possible trouble could I get into while in this thing?" he added, in reference to the new wheelchair in which his bum was now firmly sat.

"Just promise me you'll take care, my little mushy pea," she worried over him, wheeling him to the front door, where, once opened, were revealed Conor and Eric stood waiting like two smirking bookends.

"I'm not sure I like that look," Sally cautioned the pair. "What sort of mischief are you two up to...?"

Conor spoke first. "We're here to show Luke a..." he began.

"... Wheely good time," said Eric, concluding the line, in what was obviously a well-rehearsed bit.

"Nailed it," remarked Conor, with a quick grin to his partner-in-comedy, indicating their delivery had been delivered flawlessly and most satisfactorily.

"Seriously, boys. You will take care of him, won't you?" Sally asked, patting the top of Luke's woollen-covered head. "I'm asking you, especially, as the sensible one," she said to them, looking down, straightening the hat on Luke's head even though it wasn't the least bit crooked.

"I'll look after him, Mrs J, you can count on me!" said Conor, with a smart nod.

Sally looked up. "*Hmm*? Oh, I was referring to Eric, dear, actually," she said. She leaned down, whispering into Luke's ear, "*Nailed it.*"

"Fair play to you, Mum," Luke said with a laugh.

Eric looked chuffed, and Conor looked wounded. But then Conor was laughing too, as was Eric.

"Again. Seriously. You'll be gentle with the wheelchair, boys, won't you?" continued Sally, checking Luke over with some last-minute pokes and prods to make sure he hadn't somehow managed to get his winter clothing undone in the second or two she hadn't been attending to him. "There's a slope down to the park. So you'll be sure to keep a firm grip of the handles?" she advised Conor and Eric.

"Sure," replied Conor, flapping his mittened hands as if fanning himself on a hot day. "We're totally trustworthy and wouldn't do anything stupid that could place Luke in danger. You can be sure of it. Nothing stupid at all, not the slightest bit. He's safe in our hands, don't you worry."

And yet after that most sincerest of pronouncements, Sally observed Conor nudge Eric with his foot.

"Eric," Conor whispered out of the corner of his mouth. "Mate. Hanging out of your coat..."

"What?" Eric whispered back, unsure what Conor was getting at.

"The thingies," Conor told him.

"The thingies?" asked Eric.

"The *thingies*," stressed Conor, worried Luke's mum would overhear. "You know. The *thingies*," he said again, not wishing to say the actual word for reasons between them he felt should be obvious.

"Oh, the *thingies*!" Eric said in recognition, finally. "Why didn't you *say* so?"

"What's all this, then?" asked Sally, stomping forward around Luke's wheelchair and presenting herself to the pair before Eric had chance to conceal what very much needed concealing.

"*Eric*," she said sternly, and on the verge of becoming cross. "Are those *swords*?" she asked, barely able to believe what she was asking. "*Please* tell me those aren't swords."

Eric opened his coat tentatively, like an overly cautious cowboy revealing his gun belt. But instead of guns, two swords fell to the doorstep. They were short, curved swords that looked almost like scimitars.

Conor shifted a pace to his right, tut-tutting as he did so, as if what he was seeing was a complete surprise to him and absolutely *not* something they'd talked about and planned in advance.

But, then, sensing the severity of the situation they were in — and present threat of the police being called — Eric recovered one from off the stoop. "They're not real, Mrs Jacobs," he explained. "They're just made of plastic, see?" he said, holding it out for her inspection. "I only wrapped them in tin foil so they'd look more like real swords," he told her.

"What? Why on earth would you—?" asked Sally.

"We were going to surprise Luke," explained Eric, taking a step over to Luke's wheelchair. "You see, I put this bracket on the base of each sword, and they should... if I've done my calculations correctly..." he went on, dropping to one knee, and deftly — with the sort of expertly efficient pitstop that a Formula One race team would be proud of — outfitted Luke's wheelchair with a blade protruding out from the centre of each wheel.

"I don't understand," said Sally.

That is, she didn't understand until she glanced over at Conor, who was now stood there wearing a plastic Roman centurion's helmet. And where he had hidden it previously, she had no idea.

"We wanted to turn Luke's wheelchair into a gladiator's scythed chariot," explained Conor, producing a homemade spear, as well, from somewhere under the roomy confines of his winter outerwear. "We thought it'd cheer him up."

Sally bit the back of her hand, but it was useless. "What are you two boys like, then?" she said. "Are you determined to make me cry every time you see me? That is a lovely thing to do, the two of you. In general, I mean. Not necessarily the whole sword thing. But, please. I don't want him or either of you to end up with more broken bones, okay?"

Conor confirmed by offering a soldier's salute. The two boys each took a handle on the wheelchair and carefully eased Luke gently from the doorstep, rolling him onto the walkway of the front garden.

But Sally, for her part, had a suspicion that as soon as she was inside the house, the pretence of sensibility on the boys' part would end soon enough. And as if to prove her right...

"One thing, Mrs J," said Conor, pausing on the walkway and looking back over his shoulder in her direction. "We didn't manage to get hold of any horses, so could we possibly borrow the cats?" he enquired.

Sadly, at least as far as the boys' hopes were concerned, this request was answered in the negative.

Luke's house backed onto the once popular and fairly busy Douglas-to-Peel railway line, the only surviving remnant of which was the wide path where the tracks once lay. For those without broken limbs, access from Luke's location would ordinarily be gained via a gap in the wind-battered fence at the foot of the Jacobs' rear garden. But that route was not favourable for those in a wheelchair. As such, while Luke was rather enjoying his trip out, the same could not be said, at least at present, for Conor and Eric, as the path down to the railway line they were now taking included a rather steep uphill climb that had to be managed before the route descended once again to the line.

Conor steadied and braced himself. "We can do this," he said to Eric. "Ready?"

Eric puffed out his narrow chest, like a winter songbird ready to let out an impressive warble. But, then, all he said was a simple, "Yes," his chest once again deflating, and he too set to work at the task at hand.

They ever-so-slowly eased forward, pushing Luke up the incline. But the problem, which soon became apparent, was that Conor was somewhat stronger than Eric. And with the increased force on one handle over the other, the result was that the wheelchair was veering off to one side like it was being piloted by a drink-driver.

"Guys! Hang on!" shouted Luke, fearing he was going to be tipped out into the undergrowth.

"It's not my fault," said Eric, releasing his grip for a moment once they'd gotten Luke to a somewhat level spot in the path. "This helmet keeps dropping over my eyes," he told them, pushing up his centurion's headwear, but then deciding to dispense with it entirely. "Here, let's swop," he said to Luke, pulling off his friend's bobble hat and then replacing it with the helmet. "There," said Eric, patting it down, and then placing Luke's bobble hat on his own head. "Better," he declared, and then saying, "*Ohhh*, this is nice and warm," in reference to the hat hand-crafted by Luke's mum.

But, in spite of his best efforts, it was obvious that Eric wasn't best suited to pushing a wheelchair up a hill. And of course the watery eye and slight limp didn't help matters any. "Here, I've got this," said Conor with a friendly wink, deciding it easier to pick the reins up himself. And before long, the chariot was once again underway and making steady progress.

Luke extended the spear Conor had given him to hold onto, and taking a quick moment to glance from one side of his chariot to the other, appreciating the blades protruding from either wheels, commended, "Top job, boys." And, then, to the current business, "Now press on, and don't spare the horses!" he commanded, prodding the air before them with the tip of the spear. "Onwards and upwards!"

"I'm already onwards and upwardsing!" complained a nevertheless compliant Conor, while Eric, scouting ahead, did his part by clearing away potential obstacles such as twigs, and very small rocks.

Soon, they were at the crest of the hill, where their path split in two — one way leading to the skate park, and the other down to the railway line. The going down was much easier, the boys found, as gravity was their friend.

"I thought we were going to the park? That's what you guys told me?" asked Luke, as they hadn't taken the path he'd expected. "It's a bit bumpy," he commented, which was something of an understatement, since, if he'd had fillings in his teeth, they would surely have been jarred loose.

"Soon," replied Conor, doing his absolute best to keep a grip on the chair. "Eric," he said. "You'll need to grab hold again as well. This path is ridiculously steep. And if I let go, Julius Caesar here will set a new wheelchair chariot land speed record going down it."

Luke relaxed and enjoyed the ride. After all, he was just glad to be out of his house, a house which, looking back over his shoulder, he saw was now out of view. However, he did see something else... "Someone's watching us," said Luke, informing the others.

Once they'd reached the foot of the hill, and could safely rest without fear of Luke taking a major tumble, the three of them squinted their eyes against the harsh winter sun back up in the direction of the top of the path from whence they'd just came.

"Where, exactly?" asked Eric, taking a position of cover behind Conor. "I don't..."

Luke lifted his right hand to shield his eyes. "Over there. Just there," he said, pointing to where he could've sworn he spotted the interloper. "Oh, wait. Hang on," he added. "It's Mum. I think it's..." he said, as the head of the figure rose up from behind some shrubbery, and then once again fell. "Yeah. It's my mum."

"We can see you, Mum!" Luke called out, resulting in the head rising up like a mole peeking out of a hole, but this time remaining in the exposed position.

Sally waved casually, as if she hadn't just been lurking in bushes at all, no, not at all. "I was just, *ehm*..." she floundered. "Oh! You forgot something, Luke!" she said. It was all she could conjure up at a moment's notice. "I had to come, you know..." But she didn't finish her sentence.

"What did I forget?" asked a suspicious Luke.

"Give me a moment, I need to think of something!" Sally called out.

"We're fine, Mum!" Luke answered her with a laugh, reading, of course, between the lines. "Honest, we're just going..." he said, looking up at his chauffeurs. "Well, I'm not sure where we're going exactly just yet. But we'll be fine, I promise!"

Conor moved his head closer to Luke and whispered, "You wouldn't be saying that if you knew how close I came to losing my grip coming down that path."

"Okay, but just... you know!" shouted Sally. "Right, well I'm sure you can get along without this thing you forgot... the thing you forgot that I haven't thought of yet... So, *ehm*, yes, carry on, then! Alright, ta!" she concluded, lowering her head again below the shrubbery, presumably this time for good.

The boys were quiet for a moment as they attempted to process what they'd just witnessed. Finally, Eric remarked, "She wouldn't make a very good spy."

"*Hrmm*, I don't know about that," replied Luke, after considering this for a moment. "She's clearly not very good at surveillance, I have to admit. But let me tell you, her investigative powers are pretty darned amazing. If food goes missing, or anything gets broken in our house, for instance, trust me, she's on it in no time. You haven't got a chance of getting away with anything," he told them. "Wait, hang on," he said, his finger raised up in the air as if he was testing the wind. "Are we going to our castle?"

In answer, Conor set off, away from the railway line and along a route that'd been trampled out of the overgrown grass. "Wait and see," he said, having to use his maximum effort, once more, to navigate this time over the grassy course, and Eric again leading the way, doing his best to clear from their path any further obstacles.

It was probably for the best that Sally was no longer in apparent pursuit, given the uneven terrain. After all, the path they were now using ran parallel to the main railway line, only about ten feet higher and with a sheer drop down to where the tracks once ran. It was the perfect location for a child's den, set back as the fort was upon the ridge and afforded generous cover by the network of trees and assorted greenery, keeping it well hidden. Even in the winter months when the foliage was less dense, if you were walking down along the lower area, unless you knew to look for the fort, you'd likely walk by the location completely unawares.

"The rope's still here!" shouted Luke, pointing to his mum's former washing line, flapping freely in the breeze. He was filled with a wave of nostalgia at the sight of it, recalling how he'd spent most of the previous summer with Conor, dragging old crates and remnants of wood across the railway line to build their den.

Granted, the den wasn't perfect, and never had been. It wasn't completely straight and true, for example, and they had been forever catching their trousers on a rogue nail that hadn't been given perhaps enough attention required at the time of construction. But it was something they'd done all by themselves, and it was something they'd completed and accomplished once they'd started. And it wasn't often that Luke was able to say that.

It'd been a harsh winter, and Luke knew that any plans for the den would likely include a complete rebuild, regardless of what was already intended. The plywood roof was on its last legs the previous time he'd been down, for instance, so he didn't hold out too much hope for it now.

"Have you pair been here and done some gardening?" asked Luke. "Only the area was covered in thorn bushes and stinging nettles last summer. And now... Is this what you've been doing all week, pretending you were too busy to play Hundred-to-One? Well, Eric, not in your case. You're not ever interested in playing it in the first place. But you know what I mean."

"We knew you wouldn't be able to get through — in your present condition, that is — if we didn't clear a path," said Eric. "We turned up with a pair of shears and rusty secateurs but soon realised that the task was a little larger than we'd imagined."

"You can say that again!" Conor entered in. "It was like cutting down an oak tree with a butter knife!"

"I told you they weren't the proper tools for the job!" countered Eric.

"Still. It does look good, in the end, doesn't it?" said Conor, standing back to admire their handiwork. "Fair play to Eric, also. For a little guy, he doesn't half get stuck into it when he needs to."

"Yes, but that's not all," said Eric, unable to contain himself. "There's more than that to show you." Eric glanced at Conor, who smiled and pushed Luke's wheelchair on, a little further towards their ultimate destination.

"What's this meant to be?" asked Luke, in reference to the white bedsheet draped down from a branch above. "Why is this here? You know I *do* know what's behind it already. And if it's supposed to be a ghost, you've forgotten to cut the eyes out...?" he teased them, grinning. "Or was it maybe that your pruning shears were too blunt at that stage?" he offered cheekily.

"This..." announced Conor, holding his hands out like a really poor game show host... "Is the *actual* surprise we've been working on all week." Conor positioned himself on the left side, and Eric the right, both with a fistful of fabric.

"A rubbish ghost?" asked Luke cheekily.

"*Behind* the rubbish ghost, you twit!" said Conor. And Conor nodded over to his young assistant. "Three-two-*one*," he said. And with that, the sheet was promptly yanked down, revealing what it was concealing...

Their once ramshackle castle, falling apart at the seams, had been reborn. Gone were the wonky boards that made up the walls, replaced with uniform sheets of wood, and...

"It's got a *window*," said Luke, after he'd managed to pick his jaw back up. "A *real* one," he went on, feasting his eyes on both it and the rest of the magnificent wooden structure before him. "And it's even got a proper roof, with tiles and everything!" he continued, pointing in the general direction of the roof. "I–I don't know what to say," he stuttered. "This is brilliant. Absolutely brilliant. How on earth did you guys manage this...?"

Eric and Conor stood, arms crossed, like two garden gnomes. "It's good, isn't it?" said Conor, like a proud parent. Well, like a proud garden gnome parent. "It's big enough for six people to stand up in," he offered. "And, twelve, if they're Eric's size!"

Eric, rather than being offended, just gave a shrug of his shoulders along with a crooked grin. "It's a fair cop," he said, and then laughed.

"Do you want to have a look inside?" asked Conor.

"That's a rhetorical question, I'm assuming?" said Luke.

"Oh, good word," offered Eric, impressed.

Luke went to move, until the realisation struck him that in point of fact he couldn't. "Slight problem there, chaps, as far as looking inside" he said, patting the armrests on his wheelchair. "There's three steps heading into the castle, and I don't fancy your chances lugging me up them."

Conor grinned like a Cheshire cat. "Eric, my good man. If you'd be as kind?" he said, waving his hand expansively towards the structure.

Eric, prepared for the request, disappeared inside the structure, reappearing a moment later with a large handle in hand, the kind you use to wind a ratcheting device. He held the tool up for display purposes, followed by several comical extensions of his eyebrows, with all this directed at Luke. Next, Eric gave a quick wink aimed at Conor, for his benefit, and then he disappeared inside the den once again.

"Have you pair been drinking?" asked Luke, but Conor raised a hand for him to hold his thought for a moment.

"Wait," instructed Conor, with his hand still raised aloft. "Wait for it... Wait for it..."

"Here we go!" shouted a muffled voice from inside.

Luke cast a glance up to Conor expectantly, as he couldn't detect anything actually happening and he wasn't sure what he was supposed to be seeing. But the sudden grinding noise from somewhere inside of the fort startled him. It sounded very much like bricks tumbling around inside a washing machine, and then...

"It's coming apart!" screamed Luke. "The wall's coming apart!"

But Conor's calm demeanour told Luke that this was all expected, and Luke relaxed again. He watched on as, little by little, the wall on the near side of the castle opened like a drawbridge. Luke sat mesmerised as the wall slowly eased ever downwards, eventually revealing Eric, inside, winding on the mechanism seemingly with all his might, making a great show of it. "Do you like it?" asked Eric, panting for breath, using his spare hand to wipe imaginary sweat from his brow.

But before Luke had chance to respond, the wood gently kissed the surface of the grass.

"Now, then," said Conor, taking a grip on the wheelchair, "I should be able to push you up into our den."

With access having thus been gained, and Luke in their castle on his wheelchair throne and the drawbridge wall retracted, the new window that'd been installed offered a splendid view of the old railway line. But it wasn't the railway line Luke was admiring...

Twice Luke went to speak, but twice the words evaded him. Presently, Luke couldn't stand up *or* speak. He ran his eyes over the internal carpentry, which included a prominently featured presently-empty shelf, a long bench attached to the wall to sit on, and other assorted examples of fine craftsmanship. The building was quite something. As for Luke's reaction, not for one moment had Luke expected it — boys being trained, as they were, not to show emotion, especially — but, finding himself taken quite by surprise, he couldn't help but notice he had a series of tears running down his cheeks. "My face is leaking," he said.

"I told you we'd get tears!" shouted Conor, punching the air. "Soon we'll be underwater. Which is good, actually. Because watch this," he went on, moving to a large plastic tube fixed vertically in the corner of the room. Conor pulled down into place two handles either side of the tube, grasped them, and with a gentle upwards twisting motion on the tube-shaped device, poked the top of it through a flapped opening cut into the ceiling. "It's only a bloomin' periscope, is what it is!" he said, peering through the viewfinder like a U-boat captain. "We can spy on any would-be intruders!" he explained. "Do you like it, then?" he asked, returning the periscope to its original position, and looking back at Luke. Though the answer to his question was obvious from the gobsmacked expression there on Luke's face.

"I like it!" replied Luke. "Wait, strike that, I *don't* like it," he corrected himself. "I bloody LOVE it!"

Eric pointed up to the empty shelf. "Conor tells me that's where you're going to put your Hundred-to-One trophy."

"How did you...?" Luke asked again, in the absence of any other coherent words, taking the whole place in. "I mean, all of this...?"

Conor took a seat on the bench. "I bet you didn't know that Reverend Scott used to be a carpenter?" he put forth.

"Oh?" replied Luke. "No, he never said. I guess that would be pretty appropriate when you think about it, though, right? I mean, with the other fella..." Luke said, pointing skywards. "With the other fella being a carpenter and all."

"I hadn't thought of that," said Conor, with a chuckle. "Anyway, when we told him you were stuck in a wheelchair for a good while because of your leg, he wanted to know what could be done to cheer you up. I mentioned this place, and Bob's yer uncle. Before you knew it, we had loads of supply materials, not to mention no shortage of volunteers using them to put this thing together!"

Eric pulled out his technical schematics, pointing here and there as he cross-referenced the images on the paper with what he saw before him. "We've still got a lot to do," he announced, tapping the paper for effect. "I'm bidding on a generator on eBay so we can get some lights wired up, and maybe some heating. I need to smooth out and fine-tune that wall-opening mechanism, also, to make it quieter and easier to operate. I'd also like to build some sort of slide down to the lower path that runs below. You know. In case a quick getaway should be necessary at any point in future. Oh, and maybe..."

"A zip line," said Conor, running his finger through the air to illustrate. "For same."

Eric nodded. "That's a good idea, we should totally do that," he confirmed, running his own finger through the air. "We just need to get our hands on some cash to finish the job completely," he said.

"This is entirely amazing, and we've got the best bloody den anywhere, *ever*," Luke observed, to which the others couldn't disagree.

Conor pulled out a piece of paper of his own, chewing on the end of a dog-eared pencil as he looked it over. "Reverend Scott said he'd carve us a door sign. To make our fort all official. And I was thinking about this," he said, holding out his design.

LUKE AND CONOR'S MOMENTOUS MELEE CLUB

"*Hmm*," said Luke, reaching out for the paper, and then motioning for the pencil. "After our Hundred-to-One club? I like it," he said, scribbling for a bit. "But I like this more..."

LUKE AND CONOR'S MOMENTOUS MELEE CLUB
FEATURING ERIC

Conor slapped Luke's shoulder in agreement. "You know, I was going to suggest something like that," he said. "It's just, being our club, I didn't know how you'd feel about it."

Luke looked at each of his friends, in turn. And, then, sitting upon his wheelchair scythed chariot throne, he declared, "Eric is included in everything from now on."

"Here, here," said Conor.

"Huzzah," added Eric.

"We're going to have a lot of fun down here, I should think," observed Luke. "Especially with the zip line," he added, now running his finger through the air himself. "It's going to be totally—"

But as Luke's line of sight passed through the window, he halted mid-sentence.

"It's going to be what?" enquired Eric.

Luke was still looking out the window, his gaze fixed. And then he shouted...

"Mum, you know we can still see you, don't you??"

LEVEL ELEVEN
THE HUNDRED-TO-ONE TOURNAMENT

"Okay, ladies and gentleman, boys and girls, welcome. Can you all hear me?" asked Brad, tapping his finger on the microphone, as people so often feel compelled to do. "Hello, everyone! I'm Brad Masterson from Gaming Tournaments International, and I'd like to welcome all of our friends in the Isle of Man to, I believe, the Isle of Man's first-ever Hundred-to-One tournament!"

This chap was polished, walking from one side to the other across the front of the enormous conference room where row upon row of people sat with their eyes fixed on him. Nerves were clearly not an issue for him as he soon had the audience hanging on his every word. He removed his floppy beanie hat for a moment to run his hand over his shaved scalp. From the looks of him, you wouldn't be surprised to see Brad on the evening news having just sold his latest tech company for several trillion dollars.

"I'd like to welcome you all to the Mount Murray Hotel for what is going to be an absolutely spectacular day!" Brad continued. "Now, before I flew to the Isle of Man, I was told that you're not terribly good at Hundred-to-One over here..."

he said, pausing deliberately in order to give the audience ample opportunity to respond.

As expected, the crowd released a booing noise like the panto villain had just walked on stage.

"Oh!" remarked Brad, feigning surprise and working the crowd. "Is that wrong? You're telling me that the Isle of Man *does* know how to play Hundred-to-One?"

He'd redeemed himself now, of course, with the crowd producing a shrill cheer.

"If that's the case," Brad carried on. "Then you're all certainly in the right place to prove it! We've held twenty-two..." he said, looking over to his colleague at the side of the room. "Sorry, make that twenty-*three*," he corrected himself, "regional Hundred-to-One heats all around the UK and Europe, and now it's the Isle of Man's turn!" He paused to receive further applause, then held out a friendly hand to quieten the room. "If you're sat here," he went on. "Then it's probably because you're in a team who thinks they're good enough to win the heat and progress to the national finals, am I right?"

At this point, he turned his back to the crowd, keeping them in suspense for a moment, before slowly twisting back around — first by turning his head, and then the rest of his body along with it. "Oh!" he said, once he was facing front again. He said it as if he'd forgotten something and had just remembered what it was. "Did I mention that the winning team will receive ONE THOUSAND POUNDS? Yes, you heard that right. *One thousand pounds*, folks. That's a fair bit of dosh, now isn't it?"

And with that, the crowd were on their feet, with some standing up on their chairs — those being Luke and Conor — soaking up every word like a sponge.

Brad pointed to the generous array of bountiful-sized flatscreen TVs set up as monitors on the opposing wall of the room. "For those that aren't actually playing, that's where you'll be watching all of the action unfold. But, first, I'll quickly take you through the order of events for the day."

Once the crowd had settled back down, he continued. "Right. So the format for the tournament is Hundred-to-One Momentous Melee squads, with up to four players in each team. Each team has been allocated into a mini-league, and the team with highest number of points from each league will progress into the knockout stage. We'll then have a quarterfinal, semi-final, and then on to the grand final, with the winning team taking home a cool one thousand quid, as well as an entry into the UK national final."

There was the type of murmuring from the crowd one would of course expect. After this subsided, Brad carried on...

"We've got different age categories for the early phase of the tournament. But after that, once the knockout stages have completed..." he said, shrugging his well-sculpted shoulders... "Age doesn't count. The finalists could be thirteen-year-olds against sixty-year-olds! If you're good enough to be in the final, then you're good enough to go through to the national final!" he explained. "Are you good enough?" he asked, holding his hand to his ear. "Are you *good enough*, I said! What do you reckon...?"

The frenzy was, apparently, not sufficient, as he repeated his question, cupping his ear once more, and getting a second, even *more* frenzied response.

"The final reminder from me before the action begins!" shouted Brad, pointing up to the large placard with the rules printed on it. "With Hundred-to-One, it would be all but impossible to get two different squads from the tournament into the same game. With that in mind, you'll be entering a random game, a match-up generated by Hundred-to-One in the usual fashion. So the squads you'll be up against could be anywhere in the world! As such, it really is about luck of the draw as much as skill! Now, as far as scoring, teams here today will be awarded ten points for a game match victory, with an additional one point awarded for each confirmed kill in the game," he explained. "We'll add all points up at the end of each game, and the team with the highest number of points in each league will top their league and then progress to the next stage of the competition!" he said. *"Phew!"* he added, dramatically clutching his chest as if he felt a turn coming on. "Does that all make sense?"

Some more murmuring from the crowd, and then Brad had a few more things to say...

"Now, if you look on the board, you'll see that your team has been allocated to one of the five different leagues. Each league will be ushered into a room of their own — the smaller study rooms, just there off the main conference room here — where they'll be playing, and where the internet-enabled consoles have all been set up and are ready. So," he instructed with a wave of his hand. "I'll be between the games giving commentary for those logging onto the live streaming of the event, and also to keep those who are watching the action sat in the main room here appraised. Teams, very best of luck!"

Luke's previous comment about pretending he didn't know his mum at the tournament wasn't going to plan. She'd been over to where he was sat at least three times since they'd arrived for registration, once to see if he was hungry, and multiple times, well, just because. But Luke didn't mind so much. In fact, presently, after Brad had concluded his intro speech, Luke had wheeled his chair over to his mum and the rest of the TerMUMators, where he found the four of them, rather than discussing team tactics, as one might expect given the circumstances, admiring the stitching and print quality on their t-shirts.

Luke waited for the appropriate time to interrupt, which, being mums talking about stitching and such, meant he had to sit there for a fair bit. Finally, when the mums had paused to take a breath, and Luke could manage to get in a word edgewise, he said, "Did you understand all the rules, Mum? Only I noticed you weren't listening."

"Oh, yes, of course. Easy-peasy lemon squeezy," she replied to him, tousling his hair, as adults were so keen to do for some reason. It was like there was something in their kids' hair that drew their fingers to it.

"Are you comfortable, should I get you another cushion?" his mum asked, attempting to change the subject. Or, it could have been that making certain Luke was comfortable was simply more important than some silly tournament rules, since mums tended to have a different set of priorities than regular people.

Luke smiled back. "I'm fine, Mum, but thanks," he told her, and then he gave her a look. "You don't really understand the rules, do you?" he asked.

"Not a clue!" she replied happily.

Luke rolled his eyes, but not in an unkind manner. More in an affectionate way. "Just remember, Mum. It's just like playing a normal game at home," he advised her. "You're not directly up against the other teams in your league, you're all in your own random games. You get points for winning your game, and points for each kill you make in the game. Understood?"

But it was fairly evident from the glazed-over eyeballs Luke observed that it wasn't, in fact, entirely understood.

"So we're not playing against the other teams?" she asked, moving her head to look around the room.

"No, Mum. Not directly. Just like at home, when you play a completely random game, that's what you're doing today. Whichever team gets the most points in their game will top the league. Hopefully you'll end up against squads which aren't very good."

Ordinarily, Luke would have glanced over his shoulder to make sure no one was watching before doing what he was about to do. But this time he didn't care. He leaned over to his mum — not the easiest to do, given that he was stuck in a wheelchair — placing a tender little kiss on her cheek. "Good luck, Mum," he told her, then adding, "Or, should I say, *Hasta la vista, baby?*"

Sally smiled, but she didn't really respond. She seemed puzzled as to why Luke was suddenly speaking Spanish.

"Mum, you've still not watched the film, have you?" he asked with a gentle sigh.

"No, Luke, no I've not!" she said merrily.

Luke wheeled his chair back and forth, to simulate pacing, but that was more effort than it was worth, and so finally he settled in one spot, and he switched to slapping his hands impatiently on the wheelchair's armrests instead. The problem was, the competition was due to start in less than five minutes. The other teams were already congregating outside of their respective rooms, eager for the starting bell to chime, and yet...

"Where *are* they?" Luke asked, for the umpteenth time. He pressed his hand on his forehead, gripping his fringe and squeezing it like it was a sponge needed wringing. "Conor, can you go and find Eric and ask him where his brother and sister are? I'm really starting to panic."

Conor gestured with his head only, lifting his chin up in the direction of the main room where they'd come from, still in view. "*That's* Eric's brother. Just *there*," he said, as if this should have been obvious.

There was one person, sitting by himself, amongst the remaining crowd after the competitors had made their way over to their designated gaming rooms.

"Where?" asked Luke.

"Over *there*," said Conor, now pointing directly.

Luke screwed up his face. "*Where*?" he said again, even more frustrated now than before.

"Honestly, Luke. If you keep this up, I'm going to let the air out of your tyres. *Him*," he said. "How can you miss him? He stands out like a..." But then Conor thought for a moment, and said, "Oh, that's right, I forgot. You didn't actually meet him when we were at Eric's house, did you? It was me that spoke with him, wasn't it? But, yeah. That's him. Just there."

"Don't be stupid, Conor," Luke said in response. "Eric's brother is fourteen, that guy is about eight-foot-six and has a beard. I think he must be one of the organisers or something. Or just somebody's dad."

Conor rolled his eyes. "Excuse me. Sam?" he called over, polite as you like.

When Eric's brother did indeed turn around, Conor threw a satisfied grin in Luke's direction. Then he looked back over to Sam. "We're ready to go in when you are," he said to him. "And, once again, we appreciate you joining our team," he added, ever the gentleman.

Sam stood up, which took an awfully long time. He kept rising skyward like Jack's beanstalk, before finally reaching his full prodigious height.

"It's fine," came in return an unusually deep voice. "You two looked out for my little brother. Which is why I said I'd do it," said Sam.

Sam made his way over to them. Which didn't take much time at all, considering his strides were very long and could very likely span the entire width of the Douglas-to-Heysham Manx Sea ferry route.

"You're Eric's brother? But how?" asked a baffled Luke. "You're like... and he's like..." he said, indicating with one of his hands something of great height, and with the other of his hands something of considerably lower altitude.

"Maybe his father's a giant?" suggested Conor cheekily, taking full advantage of his and Sam's obvious familiarity, despite the fact he'd met Sam only just the once.

But Conor was soon realising his error in judgement, via the smouldering look of anger cast down to him from on high, with Conor coming to the conclusion that such jokes might perhaps be life-limiting in nature. Changing tack, a now contrite and somewhat more cautious Conor enquired, "You, eh... that is, you wouldn't happen to possibly know where your sister might be... do you?"

"What's this? You're interested in my sister...?" Sam asked menacingly.

"Well, yes. If that's all right...?" said an increasingly more terrified Conor.

"What??" bellowed Sam, bending over, and over some more, to berate poor Conor at Conor's lower level. "First you take the mickey out of my parentage. And now you're trying to take my sister out?"

Conor gulped, reaching for the collar on his shirt, even though his shirt wasn't the kind that even had a collar. He ran his finger around his neck, as if he had a collar anyway. Or maybe he was marking off, rather helpfully, the line at which Sam might lop off his head.

"I wasn't asking her out. I definitely wouldn't do that," explained Conor, once he'd found his voice again. "Not that I'm saying there's anything wrong with her or anything," he quickly corrected himself. "I mean, she's just fine. Nothing wrong with her at all. Very pretty, some would say, even," he told the older boy. "Not me, though! Definitely not me," he swiftly added. "*Him*, maybe? Maybe him," said a now panicked Conor, pointing at Luke, for no apparent reason other than to perhaps deflect the line of questioning and direct suspicion onto someone else.

At this, Sam slapped his hand across Conor's back. The hand took up almost Conor's entire back, and the force of the blow very nearly sent Conor sprawling to the floor. Conor said his prayers, as he knew, at that moment, that he was done for. He braced himself for the force of the next hand-based assault.

"Dude, I'm kidding! *HA-HA!*" said a laughing Sam, suddenly perfectly jolly now, to Conor's great relief.

"A guy's gotta have some fun, you know," Sam went on. "And when you're my size, and you look like me, what else is there to do but to scare the trousers off of little'uns!" he said. "Although, when you're as tall as I am, everyone's a little'un, aren't they?" He laughed again. "Anyway, calm down, dude! That vein on your forehead looks like it's about to rupture!"

In answer, "I have veins popping out?" a worried Conor asked, nervously pressing and prodding his forehead in search of them. "Luke, do I really have...?" he said, looking to his friend for help.

"I don't see any," Luke assured him. "But you should definitely go and check the contents of your underpants," he suggested.

Then Luke turned his attention to Sam. "Sam," he said. "You wouldn't happen to know where your sister is?" he asked calmly, suddenly now, between he and Conor, the calm, rational one of the pair. "Only she's kind of important to our hopes of having anything remotely resembling a chance in this competition. No offence."

"None taken," replied Sam. "And I've been wondering about Daisy myself," he said, pulling his phone from his pocket. "Yeah. I've been checking periodically. But she's still not answered my texts," he confirmed. He shrugged, which brought to mind a mountain range being formed. "Dunno. Daisy is fickle sometimes. Daisy is... Daisy," he said, as if that should explain everything.

"Come on, then. We'll need to crack on without her, I guess. Otherwise, we'll be eliminated before we begin," Luke said in response. "Oh, and we need the other players to think we're the real deal. So, you know, don't look like you're panicking or anything," he added. Luke looked to Conor, who had only just now stopped searching with his fingertips for bulging veins on his forehead. "Conor, let's play it as cool as we can, yeah?" he advised.

But before they even had an opportunity to put their coolness strategy into practice, a sing-song voice rang out. It was Luke's mum. "Good luck, Luke! And remember I love you!" Sally was calling over, followed by the blowing and sending off of kisses from the palm of her hand.

Despite his earlier open display of affection, Luke could only stop and cradle his face in his hand at this, shaking his head from side to side and letting out a deep sigh in the process.

Conor, stood beside Luke in his wheelchair, patted his friend on the shoulder. "Way to play it cool, Luke. We're off to a good start there, I'd say."

"Ha! Your mum really loves you. That's cool!" said the formerly terrible — and now terribly jolly — giant that was Sam.

With Luke's mum effectively announcing Luke to the entire world, however, Harry Newbold's ears pricked up. He was standing outside his own designated game room. He turned to face them, but, with his head being the size of a planet, it took a moment or two for it to make its complete revolution. "Ah," he said, in his usual smarmy, nasally tone. "I didn't think you muppets would show up today. Is it just the two of you?" he called over.

"That would be the *three* of us, actually," Luke corrected him, aiming his thumb upwards at Sam, indicating that Sam was with them and they with him.

"So who's this yob?" asked Sam, with a sort of casual indifference, since threats from those found at such lower elevations posed a danger to him not at all.

Luke cleared his throat, making a point to speak loudly enough that Harry Newbold couldn't possibly help but overhear. "Sam," he said, looking up, because he was both sitting in a wheelchair and because looking up was the only way to address Sam. "You know the kid in school who was picking on your little brother? Yes, well that would be..."

But before Luke had chance to finish his sentence, Harry had bolted through the door of his room, running away.

"Is that the kid that my brother electrocuted?" asked Sam, looking at the now empty spot where Harry had been. "Did the electricity make his head that big? Or was it always that size?" he wondered aloud.

But before either Luke or Conor could answer, organiser Brad arrived on the scene, rallying the remaining troops not yet in their allocated rooms, and getting them ready for the gaming battle ahead.

Brad raised a clenched fist into the air. "Let's go, team!" he said, allowing his free hand to form a second fist, as well, to keep the first one company. "You've got this, boys!" he told them, staring into Luke and Conor's very souls with his intense blue eyes.

Conor and Luke felt a collective shiver up their spines.

Sam, for his part, remained unmoved. It may not have been his fault, though. Because of the marked difference in their heights, as it happened, Brad had been unable to look both Conor and Luke *and* Sam in the eyes at the same time, and so Sam had to go without the benefit of Brad's piercing, stimulating gaze.

"We've *got* this," said Conor, energised by Brad's infectious passion. "We've *totally* got this," he said further, pumping his fists in front of him like he was a prizefighter.

Brad crossed his arms triumphantly. "Show 'em what you're made of, boys. Make me proud!"

Ordinarily, this style of pep talk would wash over Luke and Conor. But not coming from Brad. Brad had a way about him that fired people up and motivated them, and Team Hundred-to-One-Shot entered their designated room with a spring in their step.

The boys took their seats once inside the room — with Luke already seated in his wheelchair, and so one chair having been removed to accommodate this — with one seat remaining conspicuously empty in Daisy's absence. In the compact room there were four teams altogether, each facing in the direction of one of the four walls so that they all sat with their backs to each other. Loud music was playing from somewhere, filling the room.

Luke had initially avoided eye contact with the other teams as he was wheeling himself into position. But, once situated, he couldn't help but allow his eyes to wander over his shoulder, scanning the opposition. He didn't recognise anyone, but quickly formed the opinion — based on nothing more than appearances alone — that the competition wouldn't, in fact, be much competition to speak of at all.

He leaned over to Conor. "I think we'll be okay without Daisy," he whispered. "This lot look like a bunch of wasters," he observed, but Conor didn't answer him. "Conor," he said, trying to get his friend's attention, but realising now that his teammate had already donned his earphones and, along with the loud music playing, couldn't hear a word he was saying. "Conor," he repeated, only a little louder this time.

Bur Conor was lost in thought. Luke could tell this was the case because Conor had his finger inserted up his nose and was presently searching for anything worth extracting, as this is what Conor did when he was thinking thoughts.

"Conor!" Luke said yet again, and this time prodding his friend in the ribs for good measure.

"What??" shouted Conor, ripping his finger from his nostril. He cast a quick glance to the finger and appeared disappointed that there was nothing there. And then, and only then, did he look over to Luke, giving Luke his full attention. "What??" he said again.

"WE'LL BE OKAY!" shouted Luke, loud enough to be heard over the music and through Conor's earphones.

'Why?' mouthed Conor.

"BECAUSE THIS LOT LOOK LIKE A BUNCH OF WASTERS!" bellowed Luke, unfortunately at the exact same moment the loud piped-in music switched off.

Luke didn't turn around, but he could feel several or more pairs of eyes boring a hole into his neck. "We'll, ah, start, then, shall we...?" he told Conor, along with a nervous cough. "Before I get lynched by this lot," he added.

"HA!" Sam laughed from above. Even seated, the upper portion of him was still well above the others.

Once logged on and waiting patiently in the Hundred-to-One hotel foyer area, Luke and Conor shared a moment of mutual respect. Words were not necessary. These were two warriors going into battle. Two young men whose friendship would stand the test of time, and between them, they were surely an unstoppable force. Well, in the game, anyway. Outside the game, a simple thing such as a regular set of stairs posed an almost insurmountable challenge to Luke, at least at the present time.

As the hotel lift made its laborious ascent, Luke could hear his pulse in his ears, his breathing now forced. He released one hand from the controller, flapping it like a bird's wing to get air circulating on his sweating palms. The buttons on the controller he'd spent months and months hammering with ease were suddenly now completely alien to him for some reason. What was practised fluid motion escaped him now. Rather than being an extension of his hand, the controller felt like a lead weight, trying its best to escape his grip. He felt drunk, even though he'd never been drunk — though he did once eat three packets of wine gums, which Conor convinced him, wrongly, would make him drunk — and the images on his screen blurred into each other.

Sensing a disturbance in the force, as it were, Conor glanced over. He just knew his comrade was struggling, and like Luke Skywalker in an X-wing fighter, Conor swooped in to come to the rescue.

"Deep breath! Relax! Just pretend we're at home playing!" Conor said encouragingly. "Remember what Brad said! Let's make him proud!" By now everyone had jumped from their lifts and were gliding down towards the map below. "Just follow me, buddy, and I'll guide you in!"

Luke wiped a bead of sweat from his forehead with his shirtsleeve, threw his friend a glance, nodded, and did as instructed, following Conor and Sam in the game towards their pre-agreed-upon landing spot at Tropical Turmoil. "Nice and slowly, Luke. Nice and slowly now," Luke said to himself like a mantra.

Safely on the ground, Conor and Sam made their move to collect supplies and weaponry. But it didn't take long, nor take a tactical genius, to quickly realise their team of three was essentially a team of two at present.

"What are you *doing*?" asked Conor out the side of his mouth. He tried to keep one eye on the screen while directing, separately, the other eye over to Luke, the way chameleons do. But he soon discovered that this was not an ability that humans were capable of effectively reproducing, it being anatomically impossible.

Conor dropped his controller onto his lap. "What's going on?" he said, turning to Luke directly. "We've been working for this moment for months, and you're staring at the screen like you've never played this before!" In a moment of insight, he asked, "Wait, is this to confuse this lot here into thinking you're an idiot? Because, if so, then it's a case of mission accomplished, so well done." But then he reconsidered, with one of his fingers travelling upwards towards his nose, but halting at the last second. "No, wait, hang on," he said. "It doesn't matter what this lot think as they're not playing against you," he reasoned. "Come on, Luke. Snap out of it!"

Luke puffed out his cheeks, inflating them fully before then letting them pop. "I'm sorry, General," he said, as that's what Conor liked to be called when they were playing video games of the shooter variety. "It's the flashbacks, General. The lights, the noise, the pressure. Everything," he said distantly, his mind somewhere else.

Conor knew he had a job on his hands. He removed one of the special gaming gloves he was wearing, taking it up and shaking it about for emphasis. "I know, soldier. The pressure gets to us all eventually. But I need you to focus. Look at me, soldier," he demanded. "Look at me!"

In a laboured fashion, as if moving through treacle, Luke turned his head and met Conor's eyes.

"Snap out of it, soldier!" shouted Conor, taking his glove now and slapping his friend across the face with it. That seemed to bring Luke back to reality.

"Ow," said Luke, rubbing his face. "You *hit* me."

"No pain, no gain, soldier!" Conor answered. "Now I want you to imagine Harry Newbold in school, coming up to you, laughing!" he went on. "And I want you to think of Harry Newbold's big fat head grinning in your face because his team has *obliterated* yours, leaving you in tatters! ARE YOU THINKING ABOUT IT??"

In response, Luke ground his teeth together, his left eye twitching for a moment. "Yes, General! *Grrrr!*" he said, baring his teeth now like a rabid dog. "Let's *do* this thing," he said, psyching himself up. "I CAN DO THIS!"

But he couldn't.

Yes, he was motivated. Yes, he was all fired up and ready to wreak havoc...

But, unfortunately, the owner of the bullet that knocked him off his feet, it would seem, was even *more* motivated, having not spent the last couple of minutes, as Luke had, frozen in fear and indecision. And Luke was knocked off his feet with a precision shot less than two minutes into the game. Before Luke's in-game character had time to be revived, his assailant had quickly reloaded, only to deliver a further immaculate shot.

And that was the end of Luke. The pressure had taken its first victim of the game, and now, as a result, the fate of the Hundred-to-One-Shots now rested squarely on the shoulders of Conor and Sam.

The odds were not exactly stacked in their favour.

LEVEL TWELVE
DAISY, WHERE ARE YOU?

n a gradual trickle, one by one the teams made their way from their competition areas and back to the main conference room. There were a small handful of chuffed expressions to be found amongst the participants, but overall most of the players had faces like a wet weekend, with several unhappy, disillusioned teammates quarrelling amongst themselves over each other's performance and necessitating timely intervention by Brad.

"Okay!" shouted Brad to the crowd, in general, once any incidents of potential fisticuffs had been satisfactorily deescalated and sorted out. "If we can keep the noise down, please, as there's still a few games in progress! Thank you!" With the assembly settling down, he advised, "You can make your way over and watch the remaining games unfold on the big screens, if you like. And there's still some room on the front row!" he joked, waving people along.

Then Brad caught sight of something of interest. "Hello, TerMUMators!" he called out, like a carnival barker. "Have a look at their t-shirts when you have an opportunity, folks! They really are top-drawer!" he said. And, then, directed towards the TerMUMators themselves, "I need your clothes, your boots, and your motorcycle!" he laughed. He waited for several seconds, but the ladies in question just sat there, appearing oblivious to the fact he'd just made a joke. "Ah. I take it you've not seen the film?" he asked, before quickly moving on to other banter.

Sally fixed her eyes on one of the humonstrous screens up on the wall, the one featuring her son's team's game. She'd been watching it since her own team had finished their own game and made their way back to the conference room.

"I think they're finished up," Sally said to Conor's mum, once it looked like just that had occurred. And with that they galloped towards the door of the boys' assigned room, coming to a controlled canter as they approached, and then a trot, and then finally the last few steps in a gentle walk as they arrived at their destination.

Conor appeared from the room first, his head bowed as he came through the opened doorway, followed closely by Luke, with his head bowed also, and Sam bringing up the rear. Sam had to bow his head, as well, but this was borne of necessity rather than low spirits, and his head scraped the top of the doorframe as he passed through regardless.

"How did it go?" asked Sally, biting the webbing of her hand between her thumb and forefinger, because, despite her general lack of expertise in matters of gaming, she already had an inkling of the answer based on what she'd seen of their session.

Luke rolled out into the hallway, head still down. "It wasn't pretty, Mum, I'll be honest," he said. "We came in thirteenth, which in the circumstances I don't think was too bad a result, I suppose, considering we were a man — well, a girl, that is — missing."

"That would be my little sister," Sam told the mums, lest there be any confusion. "She hasn't made it here."

"You weren't exactly there, either, Luke, if you know what I mean," suggested Conor. "Even when you *were* there, you weren't really there," he said. "No offence."

Sally adopted a sympathetic *it's-not-all-bad* expression of the sort mums excelled at. But then she managed to pour salt into the wound anyway, when she asked, "I managed to catch a bit of your game after I finished mine, but I didn't see you up on the screen, Luke. Did you get killed very early on in the game?"

"Killed early?" said a not unkind but still somewhat less sympathetic Conor. "The only way he could've been killed quicker is if his parachute didn't open on the way down from the lift."

"Ah," said Sally, stroking Luke's hair. "So long as you had fun, that's all that matters, boys. Do you want to stay, or should we get you home?"

"Home?" asked Luke. "We can't go anywhere, we need to get ready for the quarterfinals. We may have come thirteenth overall, but these two legends..." he said, looking up now and pointing to his two teammates... "Managed to get seven kills between them. And seven points was still better than anyone else in our heats."

"Ah! That's great news, boys!" said Sally.

"What about you, Mum?" asked Luke, tilting his head to one side in preparation to be supportive as needed.

And it was needed, as it turned out.

"We got beat," she admitted, but didn't seem too broken up about it. "Didn't we, Lisa?" she asked Conor's mum. "But we had lots of fun even if we weren't especially good."

"Your mum fell off her chair," Lisa said to Luke, replaying the action, and with mirthful tears instantly in her eyes. "In front of the entire room. And as she fell, she managed to pull down the tracksuit bottoms of some chap making the rounds and checking in on our room! It's been on the video screen every five minutes in the highlights reel, and I'm sure you're going to be very proud when you see it!"

Conor felt compelled to make an observation. "Hey, Luke, I couldn't help noticing. Your mum fell off her chair, and yet she *still* managed to last longer in the game than you."

"HA!" said a voice from above.

Sally leaned over to whisper to Luke. "Who's this again?" she asked, though her 'speaking quietly' voice wasn't very quiet at present.

"It's Eric's brother, Mum," Luke answered. "Weren't you listening? Our teammate — missing teammate, rather — is his little sister, Daisy," he explained.

Sally stared up at Sam in confusion.

"He's big for his age," Conor offered.

Less than discretely, Sally still stared up in wonder.

"And he matured early," Luke added. "Mum, are you feeling okay?" he asked. "Only you're acting kind of funny. You seem pretty cheerful, strangely cheerful, even though you didn't qualify in the knockout stage? And the rest of your team look like they're about to start dancing over there...?" he said, pointing over to where the other members of the TerMUMators were still sat.

"Ah," said Sally, giggling like a schoolgirl. "Well you see these bottles of lemonade we've been drinking?" she said, taking the bottle she had in her hand and raising it up and waving it about. "Well they've not actually got lemonade in them!" she announced quite happily. "Well, they do. But there's more in them than that!"

Before Luke could even try and work out how to respond to this revelation, both his mum and Conor's mum were off to procure more lemon shandys. Not more than a moment or two later, a minor commotion presented itself, attracting everyone's attention. Eric had appeared from one of the other gaming rooms, closely followed by Harry Newbold and the rest of the team. Harry could be heard berating Eric, but the precise words weren't clear since it was suddenly impossible to hear over the raucous laughter, as the replay of his dear mum's falling-and-rudely-accosting-the-event-supervisor incident had come up on one of the large monitors once again.

It looked bad, the situation in front of them. Both of Eric's eyes were watering.

"Oh, look who it is. Luke Jacobs and Conor O'Reilly. Just in time," said Harry Newbold. "Have you come to reclaim this idiot?" he asked. "He's absolutely—"

"Are you okay, Eric?" asked a worried Luke, not allowing Harry to finish.

"I'm absolutely useless, is what I think Harry was going to say," gasped Eric. "But I'm fine," he said, struggling for breath.

Eric was wiping the tears from his cheeks, but as soon as he dried them with the back of his sleeve, they became moistened all over again. He was certainly in a state...

A state of hysterics, that is. He couldn't stop laughing, and he was now bent over, slapping his knees.

"You—you should have seen... you should have seen his face when he... when he realised..." Eric was saying, stuttering and gulping air, struggling to get the words out through sporadic fits of laughter.

"Think it's funny, do you?" shouted Harry, gripping Eric's shirt. "You won't be laughing so much when you've got a limp on both legs instead of just the one!"

Harry's free arm was cocked, and it was ready to start swinging by the looks of it. At this point, Luke and Conor felt they had no choice but to jump in and intervene.

The two of them grappled with Harry's arms, trying to pull them off and away, first making progress, and then not, and then making headway, and then losing it again, the result of which being that Eric bounced back and forth between them, buffeted about like a cork on the ocean. And then Harry's teammates were drawing in, looking very much like they were considering entering the fray.

Sam had seen enough.

"Problem?" boomed his voice from somewhere up near the ceiling, and a hand larger than the blade of a coal shovel appeared through the jumble of limbs, plunging down and taking hold of one of Harry's tiny fingers like a seabird diving into the brine and deftly plucking a small fish from the waves.

Harry screamed in pain as his finger was then bent in such a way as fingers were not meant to bend, and his grip on Eric was thereby effectively released.

Sam retained his grasp, Harry squirming in pain beneath him, alone. He was now alone, in point of fact, because his mates had thought it best, apparently, to form a collective retreat. In other words, they had fled in terror.

"Harry," began Sam. "Or, should I call you melonhead?" he asked, though with Sam already deciding on the answer as soon as he posed the question. "Yes. Melonhead," he said, considering the name aloud and concluding he did indeed like the sound of it. "Melonhead," he said. "I don't usually start a fight with people younger than me," he continued. "But, for you, melonhead, I could easily make an exception. I'm telling you right now, if I ever see your fat pumpkin head again near my brother or his friends, I'll rip this finger I've got hold of right now... *this* one..." he emphasised, giving the finger a further twisting... "Right off of your hand, yeah? and stick it straight up your—"

"Problem, boys?" asked the event supervisor, making his way out of one of the gaming rooms with another group of boys in tow.

"How's that? Oh. No, no problem at all," Sam reassured the fellow quite cheerfully, releasing Newbold's mangled digit and clamping an arm around Harry's shoulders now instead. "We were just sharing some tactics with one of the other teams. All jolly good fun!" declared Sam.

The event supervisor didn't look like he was entirely convinced. Neither, however, did he look brave enough that he wanted to question Sam's sincerity. "Ah. Carry on, then," was all he said. And then he went on his way, the group of boys travelling along in his wake. After they'd gone, Sam released his grip on Harry's shoulders, and Harry made haste, quickly disappearing to wherever it is that unpleasant boys like him disappeared to once they'd been dispatched.

Conor dusted Eric down. "I'm guessing Harry is fully aware at this point that you're not quite the Hundred-to-One expert he thought you were?" he asked him.

"You could say that," Eric said with a chuckle. He was still in high spirits, despite the scuffle. "I thought he was going to literally explode at one point!" he went on. "During the first part of the game I kept asking him, *Which one am I?* He laughed the first time until he realised I was serious. And then he got even angrier when I kept spinning around on my chair. So, yeah," he said. "And it's safe to say he's not overly happy with us three in general."

"So. You didn't qualify, then?" asked Luke, rubbing his hands in glee, certain he knew the answer. But the sudden look of regret on Eric's face told him another story.

"Sadly, they did," Eric told him. "I hate to say this," he explained. "And I'm no expert on the subject, mind you. But even I could tell they're pretty good, and Harry in particular. And oddly enough, I think making him angry may have even improved his game. It seemed to energise him and make him more focused."

"Wazzock," observed Conor.

"Yeah," agreed Eric.

Luke sunk into his chair, his optimism somewhat deflated. He hoped his onset of nerves at hearing this unfavourable news was only temporary, but it wasn't lost on him that his own team had only qualified due to the rest of their league being relatively rubbish. The thought of potentially being in competition with Harry's team in the coming rounds was not an enticing prospect. He looked up at Conor, and it was as if they both knew what the other was thinking.

"Should we just go?" asked Conor.

But before a response was delivered from Luke, Sam's phone rang. Sam pulled the phone out, and, looking at the caller ID displayed on the screen, motioned for the others to hold their thought. Sam put the phone to his ear, and after a moment the others could just make out a voice on the other end. It sounded like a young female voice.

"Is it—?" enquired Eric.

"Daisy," said Sam into his phone calmly, answering Eric's question in the process. "Where are you?" he asked.

Sam went quiet as he listened, his brow furrowing slightly. "You're with mum at the park? Why are you with Mum at the park, Daisy? You promised you'd be here," he said. Sam listened again, and then said, "Daisy. I need to remind you, there are a thousand pounds at stake here, yes? So if you don't get Mum to drop you down here in the next ten minutes..."

"Is she coming...?" asked Luke.

Sam raised his finger for Luke to hold on a moment, and he went quiet again as he listened to Daisy on the other end of the phone. He was still calm, as Sam was largely unflappable, but it did look like he was getting somewhat close to being cross. And then he spoke again...

"Daisy. People are relying on you and anticipating you'd be here. You made a promise. And, again, there's a thousand pounds at stake."

Conor and Luke looked on expectantly.

Sam went on, his hand now cupped over his mouth, "If you're not here by the time our next round begins, then I'm going to tell Eric that you buried Gilbert alive. I'm going to do it, Daisy, I'm not joking. So you best get your bum down here. NOW."

Even though Sam had been covering his mouth, his voice was loud enough that it could be easily heard even when he was trying to speak quietly. And Conor, Luke, and Eric's eyes went wide.

Luke couldn't speak at first.

"Daisy... *killed* somebody?" asked a horrified Conor.

"Daisy killed Gilbert...?" asked a clearly distressed Eric. "Why did she... why would she...?"

"Daisy's a *murderer*?" asked Luke, finding his voice again, and wondering what sort of person they'd unknowingly allied themselves with.

"Daisy buried Gilbert *alive*?" said Eric, still in disbelief.

"Gilbert is — *was*, rather — a hamster," Sam explained to Conor and Luke. This went a small way towards diminishing the look of dismay on their faces, but only a small way. Sam continued, "Okay. So Daisy thought Eric's hamster was dead, right? And so she buried him. Only Gilbert wasn't dead. He was just hibernating, as hamsters sometimes do. I know he was hibernating because I'd just checked on him before I went out. But by the time I got home, they were having a ceremony for him in the back garden, with my Dad having made a little cross to put on his grave and everything."

"*Daisy buried Gilbert alive*??" said Eric again.

"Eric was away on a school trip at the time," Sam explained further. "When he came home, he was gutted."

"I loved Gilbert," said a stunned Eric. His eye wasn't even watering. His eye didn't seem to know what to do. It just darted this way and that.

"Sorry, mate. I didn't mean for you to find out like this," Sam told his brother. "Honestly I didn't."

"It's okay," said Eric, suddenly pulling himself together and a smile on his face once again.

"It is?" asked Conor. "Because she *killed* your hamster," he reminded him.

"Buried him alive!" replied a grinning, unnaturally calm Eric. "But revenge is sweet. Yes. So terribly sweet..." he added thoughtfully.

"Now, Eric," a worried Sam cautioned him. "Don't be doing anything foolish, alright? Like... another electrocution? Don't do that, mate. Just don't, okay?" He stared at Eric hard, trying to read him.

"Of course I wouldn't do anything like that!" chirped Eric. "She's my little sister, after all. I was just joking!" he assured his big brother.

But Luke couldn't help but notice Eric had his fingers crossed, behind his back, as he said it. "Uh... anyway..." Luke said, glancing down at the watch on his wrist — which was somewhat pointless, since he didn't own a watch.

Conor picked up on Luke's meaning. "What time is it?" he asked. "The quarterfinals should be starting in twenty minutes or so, I think?" he said.

As if in answer, another round of laughter filled the hall once more, as Sally's terrible tumble was aired on the big screen yet again.

Luke sighed. "I was going to go tell our mums that we're going to be here a while longer," he said, looking over to the TerMUMators group, now all sat together again in the main area. "But I think they're too interested in their lemon shandys, at present, to even notice or care."

"I guess we'll all be walking home later," said Conor, in reference to the raucous laughter and continued clinking of glass bottles issuing forth from his mum's team. "They've even got Brad drinking with them now," he observed, shaking his head sadly from side to side.

"Mums," remarked Eric sagely, even though his own mum wasn't among the group.

"Mums," the others agreed, and this was accompanied by further sighs and the shaking of heads.

"Well," said Luke, after a few moments of contemplation and the shaking of heads had concluded. He stared at one of the walls, towards the direction of where the hotel car park would be. "We've got one hope of getting through to the final," he declared. "And she's nine years old, has curly locks of brilliant ginger hair, and murders hamsters."

"Buries them alive," Eric reminded them.

"Come on, Daisy, where the heck *are* you?" said Luke. "Please come."

LEVEL THIRTEEN
THE HAMSTER KILLER ARRIVES

Luke and Conor's heads turned this way and that, in quick succession, like they were on the centre court at Wimbledon. At this rate, they were in danger of ending up with a crick neck or even whiplash. "Come on, Daisy," they said, as every door would open — and there were a lot of doors in this place.

The quarterfinal draw had taken place, and to be fair to Brad he was a little generous with the starting time, likely as he was still drinking with the TerMUMators, but also because the boys had informed him of their star player's imminent — they hoped — arrival. *'Two minutes,'* mouthed Brad, looking over to them, and tapping his watch with a shrug of his shoulders. He'd done all he could to accommodate them, but they knew he couldn't keep the proceedings held up forever.

Harry Newbold strutted proudly through the conference room like a peacock, offering a smug grin whenever he and the Hundred-to-One-Shots' eyes should happen to meet. He wasn't entirely stupid or daft, though, and so made a point to keep his distance as he knew Sam would surely string him up by his feet if he ventured too close.

Conor peered up to one of the big TV monitors displaying the teams in the quarterfinal. "Harry's team name is *The Game Controllers*? I have to admit, that's pretty brill–"

Luke's nostrils flared involuntarily. "Rubbish. I know," he said.

"Rubbish. Right. That's what I meant!" Conor answered, abruptly changing tack. "I wasn't going to say brilliant. Not at all. Definitely rubbish. It really is terri–"

"... But only because we didn't think of it first," said Luke, concluding his initial thought.

Conor did not immediately reply. He was waiting to see if Luke was finished.

"But only because we didn't think of it first," reiterated Luke.

"I know, I heard you," Conor told Luke. "It's just... is that your final answer...?"

"What? Yes. Yes, that's my final answer, I guess, if you want to put it like that. What are you about, Conor...?"

"It really is terrible we didn't think of the name first, is all I'm saying," Conor answered him, adjusting course once again, accordingly.

"We're in perfect agreement again, as usual, then," said Luke happily.

"As usual!" said Conor cheerfully.

"Funny how we think so much alike," observed Luke.

"Isn't it!" remarked Conor, now their perfect agreement was a settled matter. "Well. At least they won't have the pleasure of knocking us out in the quarterfinals, at any rate. So there's that," Conor offered. "Right. Anyway," he went on, "So what do we know about the team we've been drawn against? How's our competition, this SyntheticReality, or SimulatedReality, or whatever it is they're called?"

"SyntheticReality, I think it was," Luke offered.

"Correct," Conor agreed.

"If it's them lot over there," Sam entered in, "Then they go to my school. They're into building robotics and stuff. You know, like on that *Robot Wars* program. Fairly decent guys, to be honest. The only thing is..." he said, trailing off.

"The only thing is what?" asked Conor.

"I shouldn't really say," replied Sam. "It wouldn't be very nice."

"The only thing is *what*?" Luke asked, echoing Conor's same question. "C'mon, you *have* to tell us now. You can't just start to say something and then not finish!"

"Okay, okay," Sam relented. "It's just... I'm just trying to think of a delicate way to say it... Right, well they spend so much of their time with robots, see, I think they sometimes don't remember they're human. And sometimes they forget to..." he said, trailing off yet again.

"Forget to *what*??" cried Conor and Luke in unison.

"Look, just don't stand too close to them if you can at all help it, okay? That's all I'm saying," Sam told them.

Before Conor and Luke could question Sam further to explain his cryptic remarks, Brad was glancing over once more, likely to see if Daisy had arrived yet. He held his hands out in submission, tapping his watch once again. He'd done all he could do to wait, and he could wait no more, and so he made his way from where he was sitting with the TerMUMators up to the head of the room.

"Okay, you bunch of legends!" he shouted, grabbing the microphone off the stand and carrying it with him as he walked from one side of the stage area to the other, addressing the crowd. "I hope you're fully refreshed after the brief interval! I know I am! *HA-HA!*" said the by-this-time-well-lubricated presenter. "And so let's hear who's ready for the quarterfinals?" he asked, holding his hand up to his ear.

The response wasn't as clamorous as earlier, but, to be fair, some people had disappeared after the heat stages of the competition.

"If you'd like to make your way into the competition rooms once again, we can get things underway! Best of luck, teams!" said Brad without any more preamble.

Luke and Conor both wore an expression like they were heading to the hangman's noose.

"Right, then. We should go in," said Conor. "You're going to be okay now?" he asked of Luke. "You're not going to have another meltdown and freeze up again or anything?"

"No, General," Luke answered him. "I've sorted myself out by now."

Conor acknowledged this with a smart nod of the head. "You know you don't really need to call me *General* when we're not in game mode. But, well, you can, I suppose, if you really insist," he said.

Conor surveyed the troops. Which, in this case, were just him and Luke and Sam. He felt it was rallying time, and he rose himself up to his full height. This wasn't very high at all, especially in relation to the towering Sam. But still. This was a call to arms. "We can *do* this, chaps," he said. "We've been readying ourselves, training for months—"

"We have?" Sam interrupted.

"Well, okay, not so much you, Sam," Conor conceded. "But if you could just do a little of what you did in the last round, then that'd be great," he offered, a bit of wind taken from his sails at this point. Because try as he might to rouse his troops, Conor knew, deep down, that they were out of their depth in this battle. It wouldn't be so much a full-on assault as it would be a flurry of desperate volleys and a hoping for the best. And the raised middle finger offered in their direction from Harry Newbold, as he sauntered off to his own quarterfinal match, didn't especially help matters either.

Just then, the hushed, nervous tension in the conference room was shattered, much like the hinges on the wooden door which had been suddenly thrown open, scaring those in the immediate vicinity half to death. And there was Daisy, stood framed by the giant doorway, hands on her hips, announcing her arrival in striking fashion, with her curly ribbons of bright ginger hair swaying dramatically in the breeze — made all the more remarkable by the fact there was no breeze in the room to speak of.

Satisfied, once all eyes were upon her, she tilted her head back and produced a chewing gum bubble from her mouth, ever-so-slowly, letting it expand larger and larger until it was nearly the size of Harry Newbold's melon noggin, and then let it pop with a sharp snap, gathering it back up again in her mouth with loud, precocious chewing noises.

Luke grabbed Conor's arm and exclaimed, "It's Daisy!"

At the same time, Conor had reached out to grab Luke's arm. It looked like they were playing a game of tug-of-war without the rope. "She's here!" Conor cried.

Daisy tucked her thumbs into her armpits as she made her way through the room surveying its occupants, and they surveying her. Her elbows bounced up and down with each buoyant step, giving the impression she was flapping her little wings. She chewed furiously as she passed through the crowd. Sam waved her over, but there was hardly a need to do so as he towered several feet above everyone else and so his position in the room already obvious.

Harry Newbold, meanwhile, had just entered his assigned gaming room. But he'd apparently picked up the scent of a younger, smaller child, precisely the right kind for bullying, as he'd suddenly popped back out through the door. He approached the new arrival, now with the others, but kept his distance, circling around like a hyena, throwing insults and taunts. "Is this your great hope?" he laughed. "A girl? A little girl?"

Harry was confident. Perhaps too confident. He acted as if the rest of his team were behind him, backing him up, but they were not. Not this time. But Harry was too focussed on his prey to realise this. Plus it was easy to be that blustering when he had no intention of actually coming any closer. He kept a safe distance away, being wary of Sam as he was, and continued his jeering...

"Is she on your team?" he cackled. "Or, has the ickle girl just wost her widdle dolly and come in search of it?" he sneered. Harry grabbed a pencil from a nearby table, holding it up. "Would you like a pencil to do some colouring in?" he asked, directed straight at Daisy, and wiggling the pencil in the air. "You could draw a pretty picture if you like?" he suggested sarcastically. "Such a shame we don't have any crayons for you to play with."

Sam tensed up, ready to spring into action and defend his sister if need be. But it wasn't necessary...

Daisy, without a second thought, walked right up to Harry, taking the pencil from his hand before he even knew what was happening. She held it by the end, pointing it at him like a wand. "First of all, I *had* a dolly when I was *little*," she said, calm as you please, and despite the fact that she was still very little. "But I tore its head off and chucked it in the bin," she told him, adding, "But not before I'd saved the decapitated head as a souvenir."

Sam whispered down from the side of his mouth to Conor and Luke, "It's true. She's not making that up."

Luke and Conor didn't respond. They were too busy gaping at Daisy.

"And I half think she knew Gilbert was alive when she buried him," Sam added, considering the words aloud for his own benefit as much as he was relaying the thought to Conor and Luke. "But please don't tell Eric I said that."

"... And as for this pencil, I've the perfect use for it," Daisy was saying. And with that, and perhaps taking inspiration from her previous encounter she'd had with Conor, she spat her bubblegum into her fingers and slapped it onto Harry's forehead, where it stuck fast. Then, she jabbed the blunt end of the pencil into the pile of gum, where it then remained, protruding straight outwards.

While this was happening, Harry just stood there like an idiot. While he'd had every intention of keeping his distance, Daisy had been held back by no such proscription. This was something not at all expected on Harry's part, and so he had no idea how to react. And so, again, he just stood there like a rank idiot.

Daisy clapped her hands together in delight. "Right, then. There you go, Harry. It's Harry, isn't it? Yes. Yes, you look like a Dalek now. Now. If you speak to me like that again, or even *think* of speaking to me like that again, I promise you it'll take a surgeon *three hours* to extract that pencil from where I've jammed it next time. Okay? Okay."

"Right," said Daisy, turning to her team. "So show me where this competition is. I'm anxious to get started," she told them. "And *please* tell me I'll have an opportunity to kick this one's butt at some point?" she asked, in reference to Harry the Dalek, who had now skulked back to his room, horn intact.

You could forgive Team SyntheticReality for the apparent confidence they displayed regarding their competition. When Luke & crew entered the game room, after all, it looked as though the team was now being commanded —

her bossy demeanour bringing about this assumption — by a girl not much bigger than a door mouse.

But Luke and Conor were eager to psych their opposition out this time, using Daisy's presence and misleading appearance to their advantage. They threw assured smiles and cordial nods to SyntheticReality, and with Luke greeting them, "Hiya, gents. Lovely day for it, yeah?" This was met, perhaps understandably, with a collective indifference and utter lack of concern. And that was because they did not yet know who they were dealing with.

Conor ambled over, under the pretext of offering them his best wishes. He turned to give a quick wink back to Luke, then pivoted to face the other team once again. "Hi there, guys," he said. "I Just wanted to wish you good luck for the tournament." There were some grunts in reply, but for the most part not much of a response beyond that. Conor made as if he was about to walk away, but then abruptly turned on his heels like he'd forgotten something. "Oh!" he added, snapping his fingers. "I was just wondering. You guys must watch Twitch?"

Any serious Hundred-to-One player worth their salt would have been a regular observer on the website Twitch, if only to steal tactics from the more experienced players online. And so it was a safe assumption that this would be true of SyntheticReality as well. And, indeed, the turning of heads and the sudden attention gained at the word *Twitch* confirmed that this was so.

"Ah," continued Conor. "You'll have heard of Aquaeyepatch, then? The greatest Hundred-to-One player ever to grace the Isle of Man?"

The chap closest to Conor, a fellow with greasy shoulder-length hair and questionable personal hygiene, pondered Conor's question. "Yeah? So what about him, then?" he asked, interested, but not all that interested.

Conor smiled. *"Her,"* he replied. "And that would be her, over there, on our team," Conor added, pointing with his thumb over his shoulder.

The greasy fellow looked confused. This is because he was, in fact, confused. "But that's a *guy*," he said. "He goes to our school."

"No, not Sam," explained Conor. "His little sister. Daisy. *That's* Aquaeyepatch."

There was some mumbling amongst the group, and Larry McSmelly, or whatever his name was, addressed his teammates, confirming what seemed to be their suspicions. "Yeah, so if that's really Aquaeyepatch, then apparently she's one of the best Hundred-to-One players in the Island," he said. "She's pretty good, I guess."

The rest of his crew snorted out dismissive remarks in response, followed by sarcastic expressions of fear.

"Ooooh," said one, like a cheap ghost.

"We're *really* scared," said another.

But it was obvious enough, behind their façade of false bravado, that the members of SyntheticReality were now a bit worried, and a bit less confident than they'd initially been.

Just then, a fellow popped his head through the doorway. It looked like he was maybe hesitant to come any further, and so he just stood there in the entrance. "Take your seats, please," he told them.

He looked familiar, and Luke recognised him, now he was seeing him yet again, as the event supervisor. And then it occurred to Luke as to why this fellow looked, in fact, *particularly* familiar: this was the man his mum had ravaged when she fell off her chair. A small rip on the waistband of his tracksuit confirmed this.

"We're starting in two minutes, guys," continued the violated man. "So if you can all get logged on, that would be just lovely. Cheers," he said. And then he hurried away, back to safety, lest someone else should have a go at his clothing.

Conor returned to his seat. "What do you reckon?" Luke asked him. "Do you think they're spooked now?" he enquired, in reference to the other team.

"Hard to say," replied Luke, logging onto the game. "But I think they were a bit rattled, yeah."

This assertion, however, was not entirely backed up, as the members of SyntheticReality were now bombarding Luke and Conor with volleys of popcorn.

But they didn't care. Their confidence levels were high, for Daisy Robinson was on their team, and she was now in the fold. In fact...

"Are you guys finished faffing about?" she asked them. "Let's get this party started!"

Precisely seventeen minutes and forty-eight seconds later, the event coordinator with the ripped tracksuit bottoms ushered the first of the victorious teams back in from their quarterfinal heat. Those in the main conference room already knew the outcome, having watched the action unfold on the big screen, but the sight of a triumphant Conor, skipping along merrily like a schoolgirl, and Luke, wheeling himself in dizzy circles in his wheelchair, would have made the results obvious anyway.

The SyntheticReality team followed behind, looking far less satisfied. They had no fight left in them. And they'd been completely humiliated by a nine-year-old girl.

"We *told* you we were pretty good," said Conor, looking back over his shoulder.

"You're rubbish," a dejected Larry responded. "It's that *little girl* who's good. She's a bloody team unto herself."

"If only we could build something like that...?" one of the others suggested. And then the robotics group were off, discussing the possibilities as they went regarding how they might construct an artificial being possessing the superior game-playing attributes comparable to those displayed by Daisy Robinson. One imagines much time would be spent on the endeavour, and that personal hygiene would likely be further neglected in the process.

"*That's* how you do it!" announced Daisy, cutting a swath through the assembled crowd.

"*HA-HA*! That is indeed how you do it. Good on ya, sis," said a very pleased Sam.

"Now who's going to get me a Diet Coke?" she asked like a pop diva. And in response her two enthusiastic puppies, Luke and Conor, raced each other to the refreshment stall to accommodate her, Conor on foot and Luke on wheels.

Even Brad, a seasoned veteran on the Hundred-to-One competition circuit, was eager to offer his congratulations. He bounded over, wireless microphone in hand, anxious to applaud the performance he'd just witnessed. "Nine years old!" he told the crowd. "Ladies and gentlemen, how about that for a performance! The Hundred-to-One-Shots are through to the semi-finals, and in some style!"

Then Brad addressed Daisy directly, settling down onto one knee in order to be able to look her in the eye — or Aquaeye, as it were. "Daisy, your team finished up first, and that's largely thanks to you, isn't it?"

"Yes," she replied. "Yes it is." There was no need for false modesty. This was the truth.

"On an individual level," asked Brad. "Can you tell us how many kills you had?"

"Ten," replied Daisy, holding out all ten digits on her hands for emphasis. Then she pulled all her digits in, except her two forefingers which she left extended, turning her hands into pistols. And then she blew on the tip of each gun barrel in turn.

"Spectacular!" said Brad. "I think we may have just seen a real star of this tournament, and one to keep an eye on for the future!" He was now speaking to the audience again, and started to stand up. But, while he may have been done with Daisy, Daisy wasn't finished with him...

"One thing," said Daisy, reaching for the microphone and pulling Brad back down to her level.

Being, as she was, the star of the moment, Brad obliged her.

"I just wanted to say one thing about my teammates," she told both Brad and the audience.

Brad smiled, waiting for the obligatory 'It's not all about me, I couldn't have done it without my teammates' sort of speech. But that isn't really what he got at all.

"Yes. Hello," she said into the mic, tapping to make sure she was being heard. "I'd just like to say to Luke and Conor, *Hurry the heck up with my Diet Coke*. I'm dying with thirst over here!" she declared. "Right, that's all I have to say," she told Brad and the audience with finality, handing the mic back over.

The audience laughed. But Conor and Luke, over at the refreshment stand, knew better than to brush this off as a joke and they were busying themselves doing precisely as she asked.

"That's my sister," said Eric despondently, at a small table by himself nearby. He was sat there with his own fizzy drink, hunched over with elbows on the table and nursing his beverage like an all-day drunk.

"Eric! I didn't see you there, mate," answered Conor. "But why so glum, chum? Did you not hear about our glorious victory?"

"Yeah," replied Eric. "It was great," he said. But he was about as enthusiastic as an ant at an anteater's convention.

"What's up?" asked Luke, wheeling himself over and patting his friend on the back. "Are you annoyed that Harry Newbold has chucked you out of his squad?"

This got a laugh out of Eric, raising his spirits if only for just a moment. Luke just blinked in response, not really understanding what was so funny.

Once Eric had finished laughing, he then said, "Hang on, you're being serious? Well, no. No, I couldn't care less about Harry Newbold. Or about stupid Hundred-to-One." Before Luke had chance to protest such blasphemy, Eric quickly added, "It's those guys you've just wiped the floor with. Or that Daisy wiped the floor with, as the case may be."

"What about them?" asked Luke. "And it wasn't *all* Daisy's doing that led us to victory, you know," Luke reminded him.

"But it was *mostly* her," Eric reminded *him*.

"Okay, fine, it was mostly her, have it your way," Luke conceded unhappily. "Anyway, so what about those guys, then, the SyntheticReality team?"

"They're into robotics."

Luke nodded. "Yes, your brother said."

Eric sighed. "Well, see, what Daisy is to Hundred-to-One? That's what those guys are to robotics. They've got a very exclusive group called the Robonauts. I was hoping to persuade them to let me join their club. But I don't imagine I'd be overly welcome, at this point, after my little sister humiliated them."

"Oi! What's this? Don't forget us!" protested Conor, now joining the conversation. "We were also in the competition, don't forget" he said, his pointing finger darting between Luke and himself.

"Oh, yes. And remind me how many kills you both got?" Eric observed caustically.

But then Eric's tone softened immediately, his shoulders sagging. "Sorry, guys. I don't mean to get cross with you. It's just something I really wanted to do, this whole robotics thing. I think I'd be very good at it."

"You've always got us...?" offered Luke.

"I know, but you two couldn't change a light bulb let alone create artificial intelligence," said Eric. "No offence."

"None taken," replied Conor. "But that light bulb in my utility room was really a difficult one," he mused. "Wasn't it, Luke?" he said, turning to his friend for support.

"Yes, I remember that!" came the reply. "Very difficult," confirmed Luke. "Anyhow," Luke went on, turning back to Eric, "I meant as friends. You've still got us as *friends*. Not as robot builders."

"I know," said Eric. "Anyway. You should get back over, as it looks like my sister is getting increasingly agitated without her fizzy drink. And it also looks like they're going to draw the semi-finals."

Conor and Luke followed Eric's advice and started their journey back, using Daisy's angry gesticulations as a beacon to guide them on their way over.

"I'd love to get drawn up against Harry Newbold in the semi-finals, now Daisy is with us," remarked Luke as he wheeled himself along.

"Even better," replied Conor, keeping pace, "Imagine how sweet it'd be for him to get through all the way to the final. Picture his big fat face full of optimism, dreaming about getting his hands on the trophy and how he's going to spend his prize money, then only for us to whip his dreams away at the last moment!"

"So you're assuming we're going to make it to the final ourselves?" said Luke.

"Anything's possible now that Daisy is with us," Conor answered him.

"*Hmmm,*" Luke pondered.

"*Hmmm,*" Conor agreed. And then they hurried along to deliver Daisy her Diet Coke lest she rupture a gasket.

Meanwhile, Harry Newbold and his crew — now three in number after casting Eric off like jetsam thrown from the deck of a ship — were rather more reserved than earlier. Like those remaining in the competition, they sat with eyes fixed on the stage, anxious to see who they'd be drawn against for the next round. They glanced over to the Hundred-to-One-Shots. But, this time, it wasn't driven by arrogance or a desire to intimidate. On the contrary, they looked apprehensive and noticeably nervous. Daisy wasn't just good, she was *beyond* good. She was a force of nature, as had been made painfully clear to them. And they knew this, as did everyone else.

Up in front, Brad — ever the performer — was holding his hand inside a velvet bag, slowly producing the names of the teams left in an agonisingly drawn-out manner. There were only four teams remaining, but boy did he take his time, eking out every last drop of suspense.

When the last name was revealed, Harry Newbold jumped to his feet in excitement and relief, casting the Hundred-to-One-Shot team a nasty, conceited glance. No doubt Newbold was desperate to dish out a right good thrashing to the Hundred-to-One-Shots. However, the semi-final draw produced a different result. If they were to meet in the competition, the only possibility would now be in the grand final.

In response to Harry, a perfectly-poised Daisy simply extended a finger — the middle one, to be precise — and waved it in his general direction.

LEVEL FOURTEEN
TAI CHI FOR MIND AND BODY

'm so proud of you," declared Sally, leaning Luke forward in his wheelchair and fluffing up the pillow behind his back before settling him into place once again. "Are you okay in this thing? Do you need anything?"

"I'm fine, Mum, thanks," replied Luke. "Hey, Dad," he added, greeting his father, who'd just arrived to offer his support for the two Jacobs-based teams in the competition.

"When's the semi-final?" asked Tom. "Hang on," he said, sniffing the air. Sally blushed as Tom's nose turned in her direction. "Have you been drinking?" he asked with a grin. He moved closer. "You have as well," he confirmed. "And you, Lisa?" he asked Conor's mum, who was still enjoying Sally's company. "My goodness. Honestly," said Tom, tut-tutting in mock disapproval. "What are the pair of you like?"

"You should have seen it when Mum pulled the tracksuit bottoms off the organiser!" Luke offered up enthusiastically. "It's been on a video loop all afternoon, and it should be on again if you keep your eye over there!" he said, pointing to the array of large TV monitors.

Sally prodded Luke's arm. "Thanks for dropping me in it, you little monkey!" she chided him playfully. "Anyway, Tom, it's not what it looks like," she said, regarding the video that was, just as Luke had predicted, now showing the incident yet again. But it was exactly what it looked like, actually, and was all the confirmation that Tom needed.

Tom laughed and held out his car keys. "Guess I'll be driving us all home later?" he asked, jingling them.

"I suppose that might be for the best," Sally admitted. "These shandys we're drinking have an awful lot of shand in them!" she said, leading to a round of merry giggling from both Lisa and herself.

Luke groaned. "Mum, that doesn't even make any sort of—"

"Anyway, I know your mum's out of the competition at this point," Tom told Luke, gracefully changing the subject. "But you're still going strong, I've heard. So who have you got in the semis, Luke? Who are you up against?"

"I'm not sure, exactly," Luke answered, arching his neck to catch a glimpse of the opposition. "It's that group over there," he said, nodding in the direction of a table where sat two boys and two girls. "I mean I don't know who they are. Not personally. But they're called the Hundreds-of-Guns, and I've heard they're pretty good."

"They are!" said Sally, a little too loudly for Luke's liking. "I was watching them on the big screen during their last game! The boy on the left, just there..." she said, pointing rather obviously. "The one with the—"

"Okay, Mum, you don't need to point like that. They're looking over," cautioned an exasperated Luke.

"I was just going to say, Mister Grumpypants, that the boy with the red cap on was especially good!"

"Okay," said Luke. "You just don't need to shout it, all right?"

As Sally turned back around to focus once again on her own table, she couldn't help but notice something peculiar afoot. Conor's foot, to be precise. "*Erm...* does anyone know what exactly Conor is doing?" she asked.

Conor was presently stood on one leg, hopelessly trying to tuck the sole of his other foot into his thigh. He wobbled like a punch-drunk boxer with the grace of an elephant wearing roller skates.

"It's yoga, I think. Or it's meant to be, at least," said Luke, putting one hand over his face like he was trying to shield his eyes from the sun. He sighed a heavy sigh. "Conor read something about yoga relaxing the body and sharpening the mind," Luke went on. "But I didn't think he was going to do it here, right now, *in front* of everybody."

"I think I'm getting it," said Conor to no one in particular. It looked like he was making some small progress in doing whatever the heck it was he was doing.

"Oh, no," Luke muttered, as their next opponents were now looking over, gawping at the spectacle. Luke had hoped to radiate an air of mystique and gaming professionalism, but any chance of that was currently evaporating.

"My foot's stuck, Luke!" squealed Conor, now hopping around like a pogo stick. He'd managed to place his foot where he wanted it, apparently, but could now not get it undone. "Luke, help me!"

Luke glanced around. Maybe there was someone else named Luke who might come to Conor's aid? But no. No, Conor was indeed calling out for him. Reluctantly, Luke wheeled forward. But it was hopeless as there was not an awful lot of assistance he could offer.

Conor ran out of spring in his hop, and he collapsed in an undignified heap. "Oi! You could have helped me?" Conor complained.

"I'm in a wheelchair," Luke had to remind him. "How on earth did you see that happening? What was I meant to do?" he asked. "Anyway, what's with the stupid yoga moves, mate? You promised you'd do them only in private."

Conor picked himself up and dusted himself down. "I did? I don't remember that," he said. "Anyhow, I saw the Hundreds-of-Guns team looking over. So I wanted to, you know, impress them."

"*Impress* them?" asked an incredulous Luke.

"Yeah. Impress them," Conor answered.

"But how—?"

"Right. Remember when we noticed that guy in the park doing that martial art?" Conor explained.

"Tai chi?" said Luke.

"Bless you," replied Conor.

"No, you plonker. That's what it's *called*. Tai chi," Luke told him.

"Ah, that's it!" said Conor. "Well, remember he was doing all those cool super ninja-style moves, and he looked like he could knock out a hippo with one swing of his leg?"

"A hippo?" asked a sceptical Luke. "I've never seen any martial arts people fighting hippos. Why would they—?"

"You know what I mean!" said Conor. "Anyway, so that's what I was trying to do."

"Knock out a hippo?" asked a confused Luke.

"No. Mind games. *Mind games* is what I was trying to do," Conor said in answer, tapping the side of his head at the same time he was nodding sagely. "I was trying to strike fear into the hearts of the opposition."

Luke glanced over to the laughing opposition, and then back to Conor. "Conor," he said, as patiently as he could, "I don't think it's fear you struck into their hearts. I think it's something else entirely, mate."

But before Conor could respond, Eric appeared, along with Sam and Daisy. "Sorry I took so long!" Eric was saying. "I saw you from across the room, and I had to go and fetch Sam. He's a qualified first aider!"

"I am," confirmed Sam, raising one hand like he was swearing an oath.

"*Erhm*... okay?" said Luke.

"For Conor's seizure!" explained Eric, not understanding why Luke wasn't sharing his concern.

"For my what...?" asked a confused Conor.

"Your seizure!" Eric repeated. "Sam knows first aid! He's trained!" he said, still not understanding why he was the only one worried.

"I don't know first aid like Sam does," Daisy interjected, wishing to make this clear, and not wanting them to think she was completely useless. "I'm only good at murdering things, like—"

"Yes, we know!" shouted Eric. "Not now, Daisy!"

"... Like this Diet Coke in my hand," she said, finishing her joke, and wondering why no one was laughing, and why they were all giving her dirty looks. She just shrugged and took another sip of her fizzy drink.

"Eric, mate, I'm fine," said Conor, ignoring Daisy. "Look, I'll prove it," he said, executing a series of star jumps on the spot. "See? Right as rain. That wasn't a seizure you saw. It was..." he said, looking over to Luke for help.

"Tai chi," explained Luke. "Or Conor's strange interpretation of it, at least."

"So no seizure?" asked a somewhat calmer Eric.

"No seizure," Luke confirmed.

"Oh," said Eric, shoulders drooping. He seemed almost disappointed.

Conor pouted. "No, I'm *fine*, thank you," he said, hands on hips. "And that's the very last time I try to inspire you lot with my yoga moves!"

"I thought it was tai chi?" asked a puzzled Sam.

"Whatever!" Conor sulked. "Let's just get ready," he said, rather offended that nobody appreciated the extra effort he'd set forth. "We've got a semi-final to play."

Sam looked around the group. "Is it always like this with them?" he asked.

"*YES*," announced Sally, Tom, and Lisa collectively. They'd all been standing there silently the whole time while this had played out, as they were all well used to this sort of thing by now.

"*Boys*," declared Daisy, rolling her eyes.

To make things more exciting, the organisers had placed all four teams in the semi-final round into the same room. Once again, those remaining would each be entering a random game, and the quality of the squads they'd find themselves playing in that game really was the luck of the draw and left up to chance. A giddy excitement and feverish sense of expectation was worked up like frothy sea foam as Brad directed the crowd. The boys, and Daisy, were in position with controllers in hand and at the ready.

"We can *do* this," Luke said to his teammates, to which Conor and Sam nodded smartly, fully appreciating the gravity of the situation. For Conor and Luke, especially, this tournament was a defining moment in their lives.

Daisy, on the other hand, seemed less concerned about the game and more concerned about other matters. "Let's just get this over with, shall we?" she said, yawning as if this was all a terrible inconvenience for her. "We need to finish this up quickly because I could really murder a—"

"*We know!*" Conor and Luke cut in, in unison.

"... A Diet Coke. I could really murder another Diet Coke right about now," finished Daisy, eyeing Luke and Conor suspiciously. "And why do you guys keep saying that?"

Sam just laughed a big laugh. Then again, everything Sam did was big. He couldn't really help it.

Once the game began, it became apparent the team the Hundred-to-One-Shots discovered themselves battling against were, quite unfortunately, exceptionally good. Or, it may just have been that the magnitude of the whole affair was taking its toll. Either way, attacks that would have been made fluidly in the previous rounds were now executed in a noticeably clunkier fashion. Kills were also virtually impossible to come by, which, judging by the cheering, did not appear to be the case with the other teams playing their own matches in the room, frustratingly enough. Even Daisy was sluggish, uncharacteristically. Shots that would have been certain kills for her previously were now oddly going completely off-target.

Conor was the first to succumb. He battled an onslaught, fighting valiantly — or trying to, anyway — but it wasn't nearly enough. He was eliminated from the game in no time at all, and he cast down his controller in frustration, with some ungentlemanly language thrown in as well for good measure.

For fear of distracting his colleagues any further, Conor pushed his chair back and watched on silently, observing his teammates playing. He darted his eyes between them, and it was evident that they were giving it all they could. It was also evident that, like him, they were getting nowhere fast despite their best efforts.

Conor focused in on Daisy, in particular. Daisy was a cut above Conor, a cut above all of them. And that was putting it mildly. In terms of Hundred-to-One, she was on a different *planet*. But it was soon clear that she was experiencing the same sort of trouble as the others. And this didn't seem to be some sort of weird strategic play on her part, either. No, plain and simple, she was rotten as rubbish.

But how could someone so utterly brilliant a player as Daisy drop to that extraordinarily low standard in such a short space of time? Perhaps she'd burned herself out in the last round, Conor thought. Or perhaps, being so young, maybe the nerves had taken her over as they had with Luke?

Whatever the reason, Daisy was presently as much use to the team as a chocolate teapot. Conor hoped, again, that this was some kind of canny strategic decision on her part, and that she'd turn it all around any minute now... shock and awe, maybe... lull them into a false sense of security, and then *whammo*... any minute now...

But Daisy was falling off her own buildings she'd constructed and parading around in the open for every enemy scope to see. She may as well have been wearing a giant sign above her head saying *SHOOT ME* in flashing pink neon letters. And all hopes of some fantastical alternate master plan on Daisy's part emerging were dashed against the rocks — much like their chances of victory — when Daisy came under a barrage of sustained fire. With an inexplicable inability to build or shoot her way out of trouble, her in-game character reached its inevitable expiry date, succumbed to its unavoidable fate, was put out of its sad pathetic misery, and was just generally killed until very thoroughly dead.

And thus was Daisy eliminated from the game.

Conor sat slack-jawed as Daisy lowered her controller, removed her earphones, and with an indifferent shrug of her shoulders got up to leave. She busily chewed her bubblegum, like she was maybe working her way up to say something important. But all she ended up saying, with another shrug of her shoulders, was a simple, seemingly apathetic, "Sorry." Her true feelings were better revealed, however, when she kicked the back of her seat on her way out the door. "And I don't mean about the chair," she added as she exited. And this final pronouncement was punctuated by a loud *POP!* as she left, the bubblegum bubble she'd just built up having burst.

"Daisy's *out*?" asked Luke, gobsmacked. But the empty chair spinning on its axis beside him told him all he needed to know. "That's impossible!" he cried.

But Luke didn't get to dwell on this unsettling turn of events for more than a short moment because he was under attack and pulled instantly back into the game to try and defend himself, unleashing in response a desperate volley of rapid gunfire.

Sam's demise in the game soon followed. He did the best he could, and he'd managed to make some small amount of progress. But in the end, it was still, well, the end. At least for him it was. "Looks like it's up to you now, Jacobs," he said. "Godspeed, my friend."

"I'm going to bloody need it," said Luke, tucking in. Luke was now the only one of them left in the game, and all the hopes and dreams of the Hundred-to-One-Shot team were now pinned squarely on Luke's shoulders.

The benefit of being both out of the game and seated so closely to the competition was that Conor was able to do a little reconnaissance, to spy on them and see how they were faring. Conor kept his eye on Luke's screen whilst edging his chair over to the right, little by little, inch by sneaky inch. But it was plainly obvious to Sam what Conor was trying to achieve, prompting Sam to ask Conor, "So how many kills have the opposition, the Hundreds-of-Guns team, got? Can you see?"

"Yeah," Conor answered him. "They've got twelve. And we've got the grand total of..." He paused, leaning over Luke's shoulder.

"We've got six," Conor came back. "And I'm not sure how we even managed that. I hate to say it, Sam..." Conor went on. "But I don't think we've got a hope in hell..."

"You do know that I can *hear* you," said Luke, still staring at his screen and not daring to look away.

"... O. *Hell-o,* was what I was going to say," Conor tried, attempting to redeem himself. "As in, *hello,* how's it going there, friend? My best friend. Did I ever tell you you're my best friend?"

"*It's not going well at all,*" Luke answered him. "Now please be quiet, I'm trying to concentrate!"

"Good luck, little man," said Sam encouragingly. It wasn't an insult, either. Everyone was little compared to Sam.

"He's going to need it," Conor mumbled under his breath.

"Yeah, I can still hear you," came Luke's reply. "Even with the headphones on, I can *still* hear you."

But Luke knew Conor was correct. The opposing team onscreen had all four players still in the game, as compared to his not-by-choice solo outing. And so the only chance the Hundred-to-One-Shots would have is if Luke did what he'd never done before and managed a Victory Supreme solo win — picking up the bonus points for doing so in the process. It was their only hope.

In fact hope was virtually all they had left at this point, and little else. Still, miracles had been seen over the course of the day already, in that they'd made it as far in the competition as they'd managed to make it. That was pretty amazing by itself. And Conor closed his eyes and dared to dream, willing the gods of Hundred-to-One to grant his friend Luke and the rest of his team safe passage through to the grand final. He wondered what to say to the unknown pantheon of Hundred-to-One gods, rolling different things over in his head, until finally he came up with the words...

"*I'm out*," sighed Luke, head now down, game over.

"That's... not what I was thinking," said Conor.

"What?" said Luke, looking up.

"Nothing. Sorry," said Conor, motioning for his friend to continue if he should have more to say.

"I couldn't do it," Luke said, his voice weak.

Conor took a moment to collect himself, because the loss was a big blow to him as well. But he mustered together all his strength to hide his own disappointment and to console his best mate.

"Chin up, buddy. Yeah?" Conor told Luke. "Listen, we got to the semi-finals, didn't we? Which is beyond our wildest dreams. We made it all the way through to the last four. Remember that!"

Even Sam, who hadn't been especially keen on the whole tournament thing at the very beginning, offered up his own encouragement and support. "I just want to say. You guys are alright, you know? You are. And I didn't think I would — not at the start, I have to admit — but I really did enjoy this today. And there's always next year, remember, to try again," he said. "And if you're a man short..." he offered, getting up from his chair to take his leave.

"You're never short," observed Conor, looking up from his chair, and up some more. "At least we can say that."

"You can have that one, that's true enough," chuckled Sam. "Well. You know where I am, anyway. For next time around." And, with that, he made his way out the door with a bow. Although, to be fair, he *had* to bow in order to make his way out the door.

Luke and Conor left their station, offering the Hundreds-of-Guns sincere handshakes of congratulations as they left. Sure, the pair were gutted they weren't going through to the final. But they were realistic. While they'd been hopeful and optimistic once Daisy had been in the fold, they knew they would've still had a tough fight to beat Harry Newbold's team in the final. Which, judging by the happy — though idiotic and graceless — dancing across the room, Harry Newbold's team had just succeeded in making it to.

"Come on, mate," said Conor. "Let's get out of here, yeah? I think I've had enough Hundred-to-One for one day, and I don't think I'll even want to *look* at my game console for at least a month."

"Let's just hope the Hundreds-of-Guns destroy Harry's team," Luke said as he wheeled himself back out into the main conference room. "They really deserve it."

"Agreed," said Conor.

"I mean Harry's team deserves to get destroyed," Luke clarified.

"I knew what you meant," laughed Conor.

"Hey," Luke said, a thought occurring to him. "If we're not going to be playing video games for a while, it means we can really get stuck into the castle."

"True enough," agreed Conor.

"Eric said earlier he'd sorted out a generator, and also mentioned something about a solar panel," Luke added, and in an instant all thoughts of defeat were forgotten and plans to spend the next few months making their den the best in the entire Isle of Man were now very much on their minds.

Once back with the others, Sally, Tom, and Lisa were quick to offer their condolences regarding the boys' loss. But, as the boys told them, they genuinely weren't required. They'd had a fantastic day out, they agreed. And their mums had had a grand day out as well, the boys reminded them, drinking loads of 'lemonade,' and with Sally soon to be a viral internet star. All in all, what was there to feel down in the dumps about?

"Do you fancy an ice cream on the way home, boys?" asked Sally.

"I'm driving," Tom reminded them.

Luke looked over to Conor, and then to Eric, who'd joined them once again. "I think we'll walk home, Mum," he said. "If you don't mind? We need to catch up on our plans for the den."

Conor curled up his top lip in mock annoyance. "What do you mean, *walk* home? I think what you mean to say is that me and Eric will go to the great effort of pushing you while you're sat in there like royalty, isn't that right?" he joked, pointing to Luke's wheelchair.

"You don't have to push me on even terrain! I'm perfectly capable of wheeling myself along!" protested Luke.

Tom laughed. "We'll see you when you get home. 'Drive' safely, boys!"

And then Tom and the mums waved as the boys went on their way. Eric and Conor each took a handle of Luke's wheelchair and pushed him along, even though they didn't really have to.

The three boys were almost clear of the hotel when Conor pulled back on the wheelchair, bringing it to an abrupt halt.

"Why'd we stop?" Luke asked. "I was enjoying the ride."

"Why *did* we stop?" asked Eric as well.

"Over by the main entrance doors. Just there," said Conor, pointing to a loitering figure.

"The one facing away?" asked Eric. "Is it Harry Newbold?"

"Newbold," replied Conor. "There's only one person we know with a head that big," he confirmed.

"Just go another way," suggested Luke. "There's got to be another exit, and I really cannot be bothered with that great pumpkin-headed idiot at the moment."

"It's fine, we can make it past," offered Conor. "He's not looking, and I don't know another way out besides."

Eric and Conor pushed the chair as gently as possible, attempting to creep past Harry like burglars in the night. Harry was busy doing something, they couldn't tell exactly what. Their view of him was still partially obscured by the reception desk. But as they eased closer, they could see he was up to something.

"He's talking to somebody," Eric had noticed. "Who's he talking to? I can't see around him."

"I can't tell just yet," replied Conor.

Luke tried to get a look, but from his sitting position his vantage point was worse than that of his friends. "Wheel me a little closer, guys," he told them.

"Are you crazy?" whispered Conor. "We're trying to sneak *past* them without Harry seeing us. Remember?"

But then it didn't matter, because Harry had heard them anyway. He turned around to face them, standing there holding something in his hand, something that looked like pound notes.

Harry's face lit up in an instant. "Ah! This day couldn't possibly get any better if I'd planned it myself!" said Newbold. For someone who was obviously up to some sort of mischief, he didn't seem the slightest bit concerned. "How's it feel to be out of the competition, *losers*?" He said this like it was the most cleverest of insults ever.

"You know what, Harry," replied Conor. "We genuinely couldn't care less, to be honest. In fact, Harry, I'll actually wish you the best of luck in the final as it's pretty clear how much this means to you."

And with that, Conor walked over to shake Newbold's hand. But as Conor got close, he caught a better view of who Harry was speaking to.

"Hang on. Who's that you're with?" Conor asked. "What's going on? Is that...?"

"Daisy?" said a surprised Eric, as Daisy stepped out from behind. "Daisy, what are you—?"

"Oh, yes," Harry cut across, grinning like an idiot. "It's Daisy, alright. You're spot on there, Eric. And I'll leave you to it, as I'm sure you've a lot to catch up with," he said.

The boys just stood there — or in Luke's case, sat there — not sure what to make of all this.

Harry turned his attention back to Daisy momentarily, handing her the notes in his hand to complete whatever transaction was taking place.

"You should count that out, Daisy," Harry instructed her. "I'm sure the fifty pounds is all there, but it never hurts to double check." He made sure to emphasise the words *fifty pounds* to the point that the others would have to hear. "Anyway, I must go," he told her. "I've now got a final to win."

With that taken care of, Harry turned to address Eric again. "Oh, and don't think I've forgotten about you," said Newbold. "Your little fib about being good at Hundred-to-One may have kept you from being expelled from school, but it nearly cost me this tournament. I won't be forgetting that anytime soon, Robinson. I can promise you that."

Once Harry was gone, Daisy didn't say anything right away, instead staring off with a vacant expression.

"Daisy?" enquired Eric, to which he received no reply. "Daisy!" he attempted again, bringing her back into the room. He was clearly looking for an explanation, any explanation, other than that which was currently, glaringly obvious.

"Look," she said, setting out her stall. "This isn't what it seems, okay? It's just..." she began.

But whatever she was going to say, she didn't finish. "So you didn't take money from Harry to lose our game?" asked Conor indignantly.

"Oh. Well I suppose it *is* what it looks like, then?" she answered him. She twirled a ribbon of her brilliant ginger hair in her fingers. It was difficult to tell if it was done nervously or casually. Then she shrugged her shoulders. "It's only a game, after all," she said finally.

Luke surprised himself by laughing. "You know what, Daisy? You're right," he told her. "It's only a game. And I wouldn't have said that only a few days ago, mind. But you're right. Still, you have to admit, though, it's pretty awful what you did to the team. It's bad form," he said.

"*Really* bad form," said a less charitable Conor.

Daisy stared down at her shoes. "Fifty pounds is fifty pounds, though," she said. It wasn't clear if she was looking down because she felt badly or if she was looking down because she'd simply spotted something on her shoe.

Eric was furious. "*Fifty pounds*? Daisy, if you would have only played properly, you probably would've won the entire tournament! That was a thousand pounds split between the four of you! And not to mention a place in the national finals as well!"

"There was no guarantee our team, as it was, would get through to the final," Daisy countered. "I could only carry so much of the load on my end. And that still left the problem of the others," she said, looking back up and casting a glance in Conor and Luke's direction. "Because they're pretty much rubbish."

"Hey!" Conor protested. "That's not fair! We're not *that* bad! And what about Luke? Luke is actually fairly—"

"It doesn't matter now," Luke entered in. "But as Eric said, what about the national finals, Daisy? It's not just this tournament we lost. If we'd won it, we could have gone all the way to the *national* finals, don't forget. So it's quite a lot you've thrown away here."

"Oh. Did I not say?" she giggled. "I'm already *in* the finals."

"What...? How...?" said Luke.

"In view of my status on Twitch," Daisy told them, "I was given a buy-through, an automatic qualification, to the finals. You see, the organisers want the best players in the finals. And that's me," she said, pointing to herself, grinning. "And, sadly for you, not you."

"But that's not fair, how can they...? That's not even—" Conor began to say.

"And I'm in a really fantastic squad, too," Daisy went on, ignoring their confusion. "So... I'll let you know the details so you can cheer me on...?" she said, taking her hair up and twirling it again now.

"Maybe, Daisy. Maybe," Luke said in answer. "Good luck for the finals, I guess," he told her. He wasn't cross, but neither did he say it with terribly much enthusiasm. Then he looked to the others. "Come on, guys, let's go," he told his friends. "We've got a castle to plan for."

Eric didn't move right away. He was still glaring at his sister, his gammy eye watering. "I hope you're happy, Daisy. I hope you're right pleased with yourself," he said to her. "Mum's going to go mad when I tell her about this. You must know that." He stood there a few moments longer, staring at her, staring at a sister he *thought* he knew, before finally breaking away.

Outside, easing Luke down the disabled ramp, Conor asked, "Do you think Harry will win the tournament? I was just thinking about if he won. Because he'll be a nightmare if he does."

Luke pondered this before answering. And then he gave a thoughtful, considered response. "You know what? The guy's a bit of an idiot... Okay, he's a lot of an idiot, actually...

But if that's all he's got in his life, then good luck to him, I say. I hope he does win."

"That's pretty generous of you," replied Conor.

"Thanks," said Luke.

"He's still a pillock, though," said Eric. "We're still agreed about that?"

"Of course!" said Luke with a laugh. "And I know we didn't win, boys," Luke added. "But we had a pretty good day, didn't we?"

"The best," said Eric. "I'm just sorry about my sister, though. That was a filthy thing to do to you."

"Ah, don't worry about it, Eric," said Conor as he started to laugh, his spirits now suddenly raised again.

"What's so funny?" asked Eric.

"Yeah, what's up?" asked Luke.

"I'm just thinking about your mum, Luke, when she fell off her chair and pulled that guy's tracksuit down. Brilliant," he said, snorting through his nose. "I don't know who was more shocked, him or her!" Once he settled down some, Conor added reflectively. "*Ahhh*. What a day, chaps, yeah? What a day..."

LEVEL FIFTEEN
THE END IS NOT THE END

Eric woke early the morning after the tournament and jumped out of bed, delighted to be greeted by glorious sunshine. Unbeknownst to Luke and Conor, he'd spent most of the week preparing for this day, and the only thing that would have gotten in his way was an Isle of Man downpour — or even a bit of snow, which, in January, was a distinct possibility but had fortunately not occurred. The generator he'd gotten off of eBay sat on the floor at the foot of his bed, and although his piggy bank was distinctly lighter than it had previously been, he was satisfied it was worth the sacrifice.

"Mum, can you drop me off?" he shouted, once fully clothed and with teeth brushed.

"You've not had your breakfast!" came the immediate reply. "I will as soon as you've eaten!"

Eric was due to meet his friends at the castle at ten a.m., and he figured the work he needed to do would take about two hours, so he couldn't waste too much time. Still, his mum was his ride, so breakfast it was.

On reflection, as far as his friendship with Luke and Conor was concerned, Eric wasn't one to get overly emotional, but he had to admit it'd changed his life for the better. He knew he wasn't everyone's cup of tea. He was a little strange, perhaps, and with a limp and a watery eye and all. People who didn't know him would often give him a wide berth. But not Luke and Conor. They looked past his imperfections and accepted him right as is, and with that, he'd become a stronger, more confident person. He knew how much the castle meant to them — and to him as well — and with a bit of effort he was going to make their den absolutely perfect. After all, how many boys would be able to say they had a den with electricity?

Eric ate his breakfast the same way a gannet eats a fish — swallowing it whole. Returning to his room to collect the generator, he rounded the corner, stumbling over a metallic object placed on the floor just outside his door.

"What the *heck*?" he cried out, and if his mum hadn't been in it would have been rather stronger a curse he'd just used because his toe was now throbbing. He stooped down to pick up what he now saw was a trophy, just as Daisy appeared there in the hall emerging from her own bedroom door.

"What's this? And what are you looking at?" he said to her. "I'm still cross at you, you know. And I hope you're well pleased with what you did yesterday. Luke and Conor are the first real friends I've ever had, and you could easily have ruined it by being so selfish! It's a good thing they didn't allow your rubbish behaviour to reflect on me, and good on them for that. It just shows what *real* friends are like," he told her, giving her a proper dressing down.

With a nine-year-old such as Daisy, using a guilt trip against her was not usually overly effective. Still, it appeared to be message received, in that Daisy was gentle in her conciliatory response — which wasn't generally like her.

"I'm sorry, Eric," said Daisy. "It was a lousy thing to do," she conceded. "Anyway, I stayed behind and watched the final. Harry Newbold ended up winning," she told him. "His team won."

"So?" Eric asked. "Why should I care?"

Daisy pointed to the trophy in Eric's hand. "That's yours," she said.

"I don't understand," Eric replied, not understanding.

"That's your winner's trophy," she explained. "After all, you *did* win. You were part of Harry's team."

"I suppose I did," replied Eric, a crooked grin spreading across his face. "I must be the only person on earth to win a trophy at Hundred-to-One while being entirely useless at it."

"Don't forget *this*," she said, producing an envelope from behind her back and dangling it millimetres from his nose.

"Is that...?" asked Eric.

"Sure is," replied Daisy. "Two hundred and fifty quid. Your share of the prize money. Harry Newbold wasn't best pleased with the organisers, but they said that as you were part of the team you were entitled to it. I accepted it in your absence, on your behalf, and promised to pass it along."

Eric's eye's widened, feasting on the contents of the envelope like Gollum in a jewellery shop. You could almost hear him say, *My Precious?*

And with that, Daisy was forgiven in an instant and thoughts were now on what improvements this windfall would fund on Eric and his mates' castle. He went into his room, tucking the envelope under his pillow, and cradling his trophy with his other arm like a new-born baby until he'd decided on a place for it. Once that was settled, he put on his backpack, collected his generator, went back downstairs, and then informed his mum that he was ready for the lift she'd so kindly promised him.

"I don't see them. Where are the others?" asked Eric's mum, parking the car to let Eric out. "Should we wait?"

"No, it's okay. They usually meet me at the castle," replied Eric, not being entirely honest with his mum, because of course his plan was to get there well in advance of his friends. "We don't like to all go in at once as we're trying to keep the location secret," he told her.

Eric wasn't ordinarily one to tell a little fib, but today he hoped he might be forgiven for it. It was also a little white lie that worked, considering his mum let him out. And so he thanked her for the ride, said his goodbyes, gathered up his belongings, and limped up the path to the disused railway line, taking periodic breaks because of the rather cumbersome portable generator he was carrying with him. As he made his way along, he wondered to himself if the two hundred and fifty Isle of Man pounds he very recently acquired might possibly be enough to purchase a hot tub! He wasn't sure, but he told himself he'd have to do some googling when he got back home in order to find out.

The part about keeping the location of the fort a secret was true enough, and Eric looked over his shoulder making certain the coast was clear before veering off the beaten track and making his way towards the direction of his intended destination. Once there, the castle presented itself, framed perfectly by the trees and shrubs growing around it. Eric stopped, taking a moment to appreciate the vision of loveliness before him. Yes, he decided. A hot tub would indeed look quite nice nestled inside it.

He set the generator down, reached into his pocket for his key — one of three — and unlocked the castle door. He settled in, taking a seat on the wooden bench and pulling off his backpack. Along with his tools, the backpack also held his gaming trophy, which he now produced. He'd brought it with him because *this* is where he'd decided to put it. The trophy brought a smile to Eric's face, and he already knew exactly where in the den he was going to place it, where it should live.

Eric was unsure what Conor and Luke might think about the trophy staying there. After all, it wasn't something they'd won. And, technically, neither was it something *he'd* won, when you came right down to it. But it was important to Eric that it came to rest in their den. And this was because, for Eric, the trophy didn't represent success or failure in the Hundred-to-One tournament at all. Rather, it was a reminder of what had brought him together with his best friends, Luke and Conor. And for that reason, whenever he looked at it, it wasn't Harry Newbold's tremendously fat head he'd be picturing in his mind. Instead, he'd always see the smiling faces of Conor and Luke.

On tiptoe, Eric used a hammer to tack up some flexible strip lighting he'd brought along in his backpack, running it around the perimeter of the ceiling, and a few other places here and there. With the lights secured, he plugged them into the generator he'd now set up as a power source. He had to resist the urge to switch the lights on because he wanted Luke and Conor to be there for that — which, after a quick glance at his watch, saw would be in about fifteen minutes or so now he'd got some other things done as well. He took his game trophy, used his jacket sleeve to polish out the fingerprints from the chrome finish, and then carefully placed it centred in the middle of the shelf up on the wall. Eric had placed a double layer of lights under the shelf to highlight the trophy, as well as anything else that might be placed there. It should look quite nice, assuming his wiring skills were up to scratch. And he felt most confident that they were.

Eric sat back and admired his handiwork. He couldn't wait to tell his friends about the unexpected prize money. His mind was working overtime, so out came his *Ideas* notebook — which was packed with his ideas, inventions, and drawings. He patted down his trouser pockets, but soon realised he'd forgotten his pencil. He told himself he'd have to write down a reminder to never forget his pencil... that is, as soon as he had a pencil to write with in order to write down the note to, *ehm*, remember to never forget a pencil.

His grand designs would have to wait, however, pencil to write them down or not, as he then picked up the sound of muffled voices coming from somewhere outside the fort. They were getting closer, he could tell, and so he jumped to his feet, pushed his tool kit into the corner, and tried to adopt a casual, relaxed pose like a country squire nursing a glass of brandy next to the coal fire. He may not have been particularly good at it — and there was no brandy, and neither was there a coal fire — but he did his best to look the part.

The voices grew very near, and Eric was beside himself, anxious for the great unveiling. He couldn't wait to show the others what he'd done, and hoped they'd be pleased with his present efforts. "Oh, almost forgot," he muttered to himself in a momentary panic, because time was now short. He may not have had any brandy, but what he did have, he just remembered, was a bottle of sparkling white grape juice he'd brought with him specifically for the occasion. He rummaged through his backpack and produced the bottle, along with three plastic champagne flutes that he had borrowed from his mum's picnic set. A moment like this, after all, was worthy of a formal toast.

The door handle jiggled, and then the door started to slowly creep open. Eric readied himself, adopting, once again, the same nonchalant pose as before. He prepared himself for the appreciative faces that would be greeting him, feasting their eyes upon his magnificent wiring skills. He held the three plastic glasses by the stems in one hand, and the bottle of sparkling grape juice in the other.

"*Tadaaaaa!*" shouted Eric, as the door was pushed all the way open. But his happy, expectant grin evaporated in an instant.

Eric jumped back in surprise and horror, smashing his head on the corner of the shelf in the process. He teetered, but he managed to right himself, as well as managing to keep the objects in his hands and not drop them. "No! Get out!" he shouted. "You're not welcome here!"

It was Harry Newbold. He moved through the doorframe, running his eyes over the interior of the castle. "Very nice, Eric, very nice," he remarked. And as he said this, he was motioning behind him. "Come on in, Wayne, and take a gander at this place," he said, ushering a crony of his into the den as well.

"Well, well, well, very nice indeed," said Wayne, once inside. "Very nice indeed," he said again, because this was about as witty and clever as Harry and the people he associated with, like his friend Wayne, ever got.

"Yeah, so I overheard you wittering on about this place yesterday," Harry continued, directing himself to Eric once again. "I had an idea roughly where it was, but knew you'd be stupid enough to lead us straight through to it."

"We should keep it for ourselves, Harry, yeah?" remarked Wayne. "It's got a swing outside and everything," he said. "Oi! Are these lights?" he asked, reaching up and tugging at a portion of Eric's skilful craftwork.

"Of *course* they're lights, you imbecile," Eric answered him. "What *else* did you think they were?"

Wayne's eyes were drawn to the trophy shelf, and he took a step closer in that direction. "Oh, I like this bit here," he said. "Fancy." And he reached out like he was going to touch it, and possibly the trophy as well.

"Keep your hands off!" Eric demanded.

But of course Wayne took this as nothing more than an invitation, and he reached over and around Eric, snatching the trophy from off the shelf.

"Yes, I imagine with your intellect — or, rather, lack thereof — you're especially attracted to shiny things, aren't you?" suggested Eric sarcastically. He didn't like the fact that Harry's friend was holding his trophy, not one bit, but there wasn't much he could do about it given their difference in size except to cast an insult in Wayne's direction.

"Throw it here!" said an excited Harry, clapping his hands together and then holding them out in anticipation.

But when the trophy was thrown Harry's way, he flailed his hands deliberately, allowing the trophy to glide straight through his grasp. It crashed to the floor, with the trophy breaking into two pieces — the statue portion from its base — as a direct result.

"*Ooops*! I'm *so* sorry, Eric," said an obviously-not-sorry Harry.

Harry came over and lowered his huge planet-sized head so that it rested mere millimetres from Eric's face, eclipsing all else. The image it brought to mind, despite the present circumstances he found himself in, made Eric crack a smile. *Uranus*, he thought to himself.

"What's so funny?" Harry demanded, but didn't give Eric a chance to respond before continuing. "You thought you'd made a bit of a fool of me, Eric, didn't you? What with the whole pretending to help me out on the squad thing and all," he said. "And if you recall, I *did* say I'd get you back, didn't I?" he added, as a statement of fact rather than a question.

Eric didn't answer. He just stared at Harry.

"Oh, and what's this?" he asked, snatching the bottle from Eric's hand. "Look at this, Wayne, Eric's bought us both a drink!" he said, not looking away from Eric. Harry popped open the bottle and held the mouth of it to his nose. "Lovely bouquet!" he taunted Eric. "I suppose you want some?" he asked, proceeding to pour some of the bottle's contents over Eric's head before Eric could respond one way or the other.

Eric wasn't a fighter, but he wasn't a coward either. He moved to grab Harry, but Wayne punched him firmly in the chest, knocking the wind from his lungs.

"Now," continued Harry. "That's a generator?" he asked of Eric, but Eric was too busy gasping for air to make any sort of reply, even if he'd wanted to. "Looks expensive," Harry said to Wayne. "Doesn't it?"

"And thirsty...?" suggested Wayne, with a wicked laugh. "Don't you think that generator looks thirsty?"

"Oh, it does! Indeed it does, I think you're right, Wayne!" said Harry, wiggling the juice bottle in delight. "Good idea, there!" he agreed.

And with that, Harry took a few steps to the generator, tipping the bottle in his hands over, and leisurely releasing sparkling white grape juice right onto the device. When he was finished, he stooped down to inspect the results, making sure the liquid had penetrated the outer casing, as intended, and had made its way inside to the more vulnerable inner workings. "That's better," declared Harry. "Much better."

As Harry had been busy sabotaging the generator, Wayne, meanwhile, had stepped outside to fetch something they'd brought with them. As he returned, Harry took notice.

"I say, what's that you've got there, Wayne?" asked Harry, very obviously knowing full well what Wayne had in hand.

"Paint!" replied Wayne dutifully, tapping at the lid with a fingertip. "Thought we'd spruce the place up a bit!"

"That's very kind of you, Wayne! Offering to help Eric decorate the inside of his little shed! Such community spirit!" said Harry. "But hang on. There's something I wanted to do first," he added. "I wonder...?" he put forth. And then, spotting Eric's backpack on the bench, he rifled through it until he found just what he was hoping he'd find. "Yes! Excellent! A hammer!" he announced. "You came well prepared, Eric!"

Eric, still clutching his chest, eyed Harry coldly. And he looked on helplessly as Harry smashed the now empty trophy shelf on the wall to bits. And then Harry looked around to see what else he could take the hammer to.

"Please stop..." Eric gasped.

But this only encouraged Harry further. He gripped the hammer and carried on swinging at whatever he fancied, even taking a turn at the glass window. And then he looked down to the mechanism Reverend Scott had so very kindly constructed to open the makeshift drawbridge. "I don't know what this is, but it definitely looks like it needs smashing!" Harry gleefully exclaimed, and then had a go at that as well.

There was nothing Eric could do to stop him.

With his hammer-smashing frenzy over, Harry turned to Wayne. "I think it's time for that paint job now, mate!"

"Jolly good!" replied Wayne, reaching in his pocket for a screwdriver to pry off the lid of the paint tin, though, spying the remains of Eric's trophy, deciding to use a pointy bit from that to accomplish the task instead. But then he stood there with the open tin, acting as if there was something that was bothering him.

"What is it, Wayne? What's wrong?" asked Harry, playing along with the ruse.

"Why, I've just realised I've got no paintbrush, Harry!" said Wayne in mock concern.

"Don't need one!" offered Harry happily.

"Jolly good!" Wayne said again, and then set about shaking dollops of paint out, here, there, and everywhere, over every surface he could from where he stood — including Eric, sat miserably on the bench, shielding his eyes.

"You missed a spot!" Harry called out, taking a few steps back towards the door so he himself didn't get covered in spatters of paint from Wayne's enthusiastic undertaking.

"On it!" Wayne replied gaily, carrying on.

After there was no paint in the tin left to distribute, Harry and Wayne stood there admiring their efforts.

"You should be a decorator, Wayne, it looks quite lovely," a jovial Harry remarked.

"Cheers. And you as well," replied Wayne. "The broken bits of glass and wood add so much. An elegant touch."

"That's so very kind of you to say," said Harry. Then, after glancing about, asked, "Now what should we do next...?"

"Haven't you two done enough already?" pleaded Eric, his voice breaking with emotion. "Just get out! Please!" he said, wiping spattered paint from his face.

"We're going soon," Harry answered him. "And there's no need to thank us!" he said. "We're just happy we could help! After all, what are friends for?" And then, receiving no reply from Eric, Harry turned to Wayne for confirmation, asking, "Isn't this what friends are for, Wayne?"

"That's what friends are for, I should think so," declared Wayne most agreeably.

Conor, who'd been pushing Luke along the path on their way to the fort, came to a halt.

"Why'd we stop?" asked Luke.

"I don't get it," Conor said.

Luke raised his head to the heavens, sighed, and looked back down. "Okay, so the barman asked, *Why the long face?*" he said, now using his hands to indicate the elongated shape of a horse's head.

Conor's blank expression remained blank.

"A horse has a long face," Luke explained to him. "But it also means a person looks sad," he said. "See? You get it now?"

"Oh, yes," replied Conor. "I get it." And then he laughed, though not convincingly enough.

"You still don't get it, do you?" asked Luke.

"No. No I don't," admitted Conor.

"Let me explain it again," Luke offered.

But Conor wasn't paying attention to jokes now. "Hang on. What's that?" Conor asked, looking further up the path. "The wall's down. Why is the drawbridge open?"

"Eric set it open for us?" offered Luke, squinting to make out any other details.

"No. It's more than that. Something's not right," Conor told him. "Something's really not right."

Conor took hold of Luke's wheelchair once again, and they resumed their forward progress, quickening their pace up the hill.

They paused cautiously near to the fort, and Conor's observation was confirmed. The drawbridge was open, yes, but the wall panel hung askew, attached to its mechanism in an unnatural position, and just barely, and it was covered in shards of glass and broken-up pieces of wood. It also looked to be thickly spattered with... something. They weren't sure quite what.

"What the...?" whispered Luke, as the magnitude of the damage became apparent.

And then they saw Eric, sat just outside the den with his knees pressed into his chest, sobbing.

"Eric, what's happened?" asked Conor desperately.

"Are you okay?" asked Luke, his voice full of concern.

Eric was covered in what appeared to be white paint, the same substance as that coating the walls and floor of the den. Several or more dashes of red were also apparent, specked here and there about Eric's person. It was blood.

"I'm sorry," Eric said. "I didn't mean to lead them here, honestly. It's all my fault. I've ruined everything!" he told them, with the sobbing increasing in intensity. And then he held his hands out to them. "I tried to clean up. I tried..." he explained. "But the glass..."

Eric showed them his palms, revealing the broken skin there. There was paint across his forehead, creeping its way down and in danger of running into his eyes.

"Here," offered Luke, and he began removing his jacket, and then his shirt.

"*Erm...* I don't think that's really going to cheer him up?" said Conor, somewhat confused.

"Take this," Luke said, handing his t-shirt over, and then pulling his other clothing back on.

"Ah. Sorry. Gotcha," Conor replied. He took hold of Luke's t-shirt and used the fabric to clear the congealing liquid from Eric's face. And then he picked away at Eric's palms, removing the remnants of glass from them, before wiping Eric's hands of blood with a clean section of Luke's shirt.

"I'm sorry, guys," Eric said again. "I'm so sorry," he repeated wretchedly.

"You needn't say that," Conor assured him, dabbing at Eric's palms to stem the flow of returning blood. "Here, now. You've got absolutely nothing to be sorry over, right? Right," he told him as soothingly as he could.

"Eric. Mate. Don't worry, yeah? This here is just a building," Luke added. "It's just a *thing*. We can fix this place up before you know it, we're not worried about that at all. Not one least little bit. What we're worried about is *you*."

"You know, I'm not sure I liked the bare walls anyway," Conor suggested, looking around the den. "A bit of white paint brightens the place right up, I reckon," he said playfully, trying his best to raise Eric's spirits.

But it wasn't working.

"Are you hurt, Eric?" asked Luke. "Besides your hands, are you hurt?"

"No. And it's just scratches," Eric replied. But the emotion washed over him, moving him very near to tears once again, when he caught sight of their sign. It was the club sign that Reverend Scott had so graciously made for them, and it was there on the ground, left in pieces, a deliberate victim of Harry and the hammer.

"Who did this?" asked Conor, taking stock of the damage, not just of the sign, but of everything.

"Newbold," Eric answered, spitting the name out like a curse. "It was Harry Newbold, and some idiot friend of his named Wayne," he said. "And they even broke my trophy— They broke *our* trophy," he stammered, lowering his head. "I've ruined everything," he said again. "And if you don't want anything more to do with me... I'll understand."

"Stuff and nonsense! You need to stop saying that this instant!" Luke told him. And then, to Conor, he said, "Here, pass that over, would you?" in reference to the various pieces of their club sign.

Conor did as asked, and then helped Eric to his feet. "He's right, don't be daft, Eric. And I mean that in the kindest way," Conor assured him. "Listen, mate, you're part of the... of the..." he said, looking over to Luke.

Right on cue, Luke raised up the reassembled sign he was holding together, the sign that read: *Luke and Conor's Momentous Melee Club Featuring Eric.*

"See?" announced Luke. "A little bit of glue and it'll be like new again!"

"Don't forget to put clamps on it while the glue dries," advised Eric with a sniffle. Thinking about proper tool use was at least cheering him up a little.

"We won't forget," said Conor with a laugh.

"You're the expert," Luke added, to Eric, with a grin. But then he turned more serious. "Now, if you read this sign, Eric, this sign here," he said, shaking it for emphasis. "You'll plainly see that you're part of the gang. So I don't want to hear any more of this *it's-all-my-fault* rubbish, yeah? None of this is your fault, and you need to remember that. The only person whose fault it is, is Harry Newbold's, you hear?"

Eric appeared to be coming around.

"Friends stick together, Eric," said Luke, concluding his motivational speech. "And you, Eric, are our friend." And looking over to Conor, he asked, "Am I right, Conor?"

"Right as rain. Spot on," confirmed Conor. And turning to Eric, he said, "He's not right about most things. But about this one thing, he is."

"Hey!" Luke protested, but couldn't help laughing anyway.

"I bought a generator," whispered Eric once Luke and Conor's laughter had subsided. "I think we talked about that already. But it finally came in the post, and I spent the entire morning setting it up, along with some strip lighting and such. I wanted it to be a surprise," he said. "But they've gone and broken it," he told them, pointing back inside the den. "I was going to power up the lighting. I wanted to show you. I put in... they tore some of it down... but I put in lighting," he said, repeating himself now. "All around..."

"*Pffft*," said Luke, playing it down. "We'll get another and get this place looking even better. We'll just need to get a few pence together to pay for it, is all."

"Ah. About that," said Eric, with the outline of a grin now forming. "As it happens, actually, I've received my share of the prize money for the tournament. Harry's group won, and even though they'd chucked me out—"

"So what is that, now? Twenty-five pounds?" Conor cut in. Maths was never his strong suit.

Eric and Luke both looked at Conor like he was barmy. *"Two hundred and fifty,"* Luke corrected his friend.

"Ah. That's what I meant, of course," Conor lied, and not especially well.

"So..." said Luke, after thinking for a moment. "So you're saying... what you're saying is... we've got plenty of money to redo the place — maybe even nicer than before, in fact — and that it's technically Harry Newbold's prize money we'll be doing it with?"

"Yes," confirmed Eric. "I suppose you could go ahead and put it that way if you like."

"Well, then," said Luke. "I think that works out rather nicely, wouldn't you say? Rather nicely indeed."

The three of them sat in silence for a while, surveying what remained of their castle. But it wasn't sombre faces looking out over the splintered wood and broken glass. Not at all. Rather, it was a collection of optimistic faces, happy faces. The faces of true friendship.

"Tell me again, because I still don't really understand?" asked Conor, finally, punctuating the silence. "Why did the horse have a long face?"

The third Saturday in February was an auspicious day in Union Mills. The local community were celebrating the grand reopening of their church.

"It looks good," remarked Conor, chomping down on a hot dog.

"Your hot dog?" said Luke.

"The new roof!" said Conor.

"*Hrmm*, I don't know. It's just a roof, after all," replied Luke. "I mean, can a roof look good? I think it's more about its ability to keep rain out than anything else," he said, teasing Conor rather than any genuine scepticism involved.

"A roof *can* look good," Eric entered in. "If it's done properly, of course, and the right tools are used."

This set both Conor and Luke laughing. "What?" asked Eric, blinking innocently.

The grounds of Union Mills Church were packed. Months of hard work, determination, and community spirit had today paid dividends, culminating in a garden party on the church lawn to officially reopen the building.

"We financed some of them tiles, you know," observed Conor, a proud smile on his face as he motioned up in the direction of the slate roof.

"Which ones?" asked Luke.

"I don't know which ones, exactly!" said Conor. Then, after considering carefully, he said, "*Hrmm*, I'll plump for those ones there," indicating to those just above the entrance hall. "We can see them when we walk past, so I suppose they'll be as good as any."

"It *is* pretty cool that we helped make this happen, by the way," agreed Luke.

Currently, Eric was having difficulty at the food table. He had a hot dog in hand, but otherwise couldn't do what it was he was attempting to do, at least not successfully.

"Allow me," offered Conor, taking the hot dog from Eric's hand. Conor then squeezed the tomato sauce bottle over the tubular delicacy, until Eric's raised eyebrow told him he'd most definitely put on enough. Then he passed the hot dog back, with a, "There. That's sorted, then."

"Cheers," said Eric.

"How's the hands, by the way?" enquired Conor.

"A bit sore," replied Eric. "But mostly it's these darned bandages that are causing me grief. They think they've got most of the glass out, but these bandages make it really difficult to do nearly anything properly."

Conor dwelled on that thought for a moment. Perhaps too long a moment. Because he then asked, "Well, if you can't use your hands, how do you—?"

"Gentlemen!" shouted Reverend Scott, in high spirits, and unknowingly just in the nick of time. "Do you like our new roof?" he asked, beaming like a proud parent.

"I think it's probably the absolute best church roof we've ever seen," replied Luke.

"The best," repeated Conor.

"Ever," added Eric.

The three boys, out of respect, held their appreciative gazes at the roof for as long as Rev. Scott did. In truth, their necks began to ache a fair length of time before Rev. Scott's gaze eventually came back down to ground level.

"I heard all about your den, boys," offered Reverend Scott, after they'd all finished admiring the new roof. "Terrible business. Absolutely dreadful," he said. "Though work has commenced to rebuild it, I understand?"

Conor went to respond, but he'd just crammed his mouth with hot dog, so Luke jumped in. "It's coming on, Reverend Scott, and is starting to take shape," he said. "It should be ready after several weeks' time, I expect."

"We'ff got a fireman's ffpole," spluttered Conor through fragments of meat and bun.

"A fireman's pole? But where...?" asked a confused Rev. Scott, because he had of course seen the layout of the place.

Luke entered in once more, since Conor was again unable to speak, at present, having taken another large bite of mystery meat sausage and bread. "We had our hearts set on a fireman's pole," Luke explained. "So we just had to add a second floor to the castle in order to use it, now didn't we?"

"Ah, I see," replied Rev. Scott with a chuckle.

"And we'll even be getting a hot tub one day soon, I hope!" announced Eric.

"My, it all sounds perfectly wonderful!" observed Reverend Scott happily. "There's just one thing that concerns me," he added after a pause.

"*Mrmph mrmphn*?" asked Conor, not clearing his mouth of obstruction well enough to speak properly yet.

"Yes, how do you mean, Reverend?" echoed Luke.

"Well. A little birdie told me that the sign I carved for you was broken?" came the reply.

"Ah. Yes, I'm sorry, Reverend. We did try gluing it back together..." began Luke.

"With clamps," Eric entered in.

"Yes, held together with clamps and everything," continued Luke. "But it was too badly damaged, and it just—"

"Not to worry, lads," Rev. Scott gently interrupted. "I made you this," he said, handing over a parcel wrapped in white tissue paper he'd been carrying in his hands.

The three boys looked at each other, and then Eric and Conor crowded around Luke — who was given the honour of opening it — as he gingerly unwrapped the package. Their faces lit up when Luke turned the polished wooden sign over to reveal, on its face:

LUKE, CONOR, AND ERIC'S DEN

FRIENDS ALWAYS WELCOME

"Do you like it?" asked Rev. Scott.

"Like it? We love it!" replied Conor.

"Thanks for this, Reverend. Cheers," said a grinning Luke.

"I quite like it," added a very pleased Eric.

Rev. Scott smiled serenely. "Wonderful, boys. I'm sure you'll all be very happy in your den," he proclaimed warmly. "Perhaps we could bring the congregation for an outing for a look one day, once it's finished...?" he suggested.

"You'd be very welcome, Reverend Scott," said Luke. "And thank you again for the sign, it really is brilliant."

With Rev. Scott assuming his rounds, cordially offering his gratitude for the generosity of those parishioners in attendance, shown in regard to the successful fundraising drive towards the new roof, the boys perched themselves on one of the low, very old stone walls that ran along the church grounds, swinging their feet in unison. Well, Conor and Eric did. Luke was still in his wheelchair, though he'd soon be out of it and switched over to crutches, providing greater mobility. But Luke swung his one good foot along in time with the others.

"I brought this," said Eric after a bit of quiet reflection, pulling off his backpack and reaching into it. "It was a little battered, but I managed to put it back together and polish it up again. So none the worse for wear," he told them, pulling out his Hundred-to-One trophy from the tournament. "I wanted to put it back on our shelf?" he said. "I hope you don't mind. But it'll always remind me of how we first met, if you know what I mean?"

Luke and Conor both nodded.

"Is that stupid?" Eric offered, looking down at the trophy and missing their nods of approval.

"No, not at all!" Luke assured Eric.

"You've done a first-class job repairing it," added Conor, in reference to the trophy.

"May I see it?" asked Luke.

"Sure," said Eric, passing it down to him.

"It looks perfect. You'd never know it was broken at all, would you?" observed Luke, admiring the repair job on the trophy. "It'll be the first thing we place in our new den, I should think. What do you reckon, Conor?" he asked, looking up to the two of them sat up on the wall, and handing the trophy back.

"I reckon you're exactly right," agreed Conor.

"I can't wait to get stuck in to the rebuild," Luke went on. "Once I'm out of this chair, I can even help out properly," he told them. "Just make sure Newbold doesn't know about any of this, yeah?"

"Ah. That shouldn't be a problem, actually. I don't think Harry Newbold will be bothering us anytime soon," Eric informed them, a crooked smile across his face.

"Oh?" enquired Conor, leaning in for details.

"Did Sam...?" suggested Luke.

"Beat him up?" answered Eric. "Surprisingly, no. Sam went round to Harry's house, as it turns out, and had a few words with Harry's mum and dad, explaining the situation very calmly, from what he told me. They were not at all pleased with their son, Harry's parents, after learning about his shenanigans."

"Blimey," said Conor.

"Yeah. So it looks as if he won't be leaving the house anytime in the near future, will our Harry," said Eric. "It's straight home from school for him and that's about it."

"But when that ends...?" asked Luke.

"*Weeeell*, there *may* have been some threats of violence privately expressed by my brother in Harry's direction. There could *possibly* have been. But I can neither confirm nor deny that this is true. Given our current location, on church grounds..." Eric said warily, looking around... "It may not be appropriate to discuss such matters."

"Say no more," said Luke, laughing.

"Did you boys see the new roof?" asked Sally, suddenly appearing with three ice creams held expertly in hand.

"Sure did," answered Conor.

"How could we miss it?" replied Luke. "It *is* nicely done, though."

Sally handed out the frozen treats. "So, I've cleared it with all the mums," she told them. "And they've agreed you can come to ours for a sleepover tonight, Eric and Conor. I've got lots of goodies on hand. Then again, after this afternoon, I'm not sure you'll need anything more...?"

"You pair will have to excuse my mum. She talks nonsense sometimes," Luke told the others, smiling.

"Can we watch a film?" asked Eric, optimism painted, as it were, all over his face.

"Of course!" replied Sally. "What do you boys fancy? What about... what's it called, now? ... *Captain Marvellous*, is it?"

"Nearly, Mum," said Luke. "It's Marvel's *Captain America*, but nice try. In fact, Mum, I've got *just* the film that we need to watch."

"Oh?" replied Sally.

"Well," said Luke, extending a scholarly finger in the air. "When I say *we*, I really mean *you*."

Sally turned up her nose. "And which film is this, then?"

"Isn't it obvious by now?" Luke said with a chuckle. "*The Terminator*, Mum. You really need to watch it, honestly," he advised her.

"*I'll be back*," said Sally. It was the only part of the film she knew, and she repeated Arnold's Schwarzenegger's famous catchphrase in the most peculiar of accents that was perhaps part German, part American, and, oddly, possibly even part Irish. What it was definitely *not*, however, was Austrian. "Seriously, though," she added. "You've got about ten more minutes, and then we're on our way, all right?"

With Sally leaving them to their own devices before she'd come and fetch them in ten minutes or so, Luke tucked into his vanilla ice cream. It wasn't the warmest of days, it still being February, but this was hardly a concern. Ice cream was, after all, ice cream, and so welcome anytime at all.

"You know," said Luke thoughtfully, after having made short work of his own cone. "Has anyone missed playing Hundred-to-One lately?" he asked. "Wait, why am I asking you, Eric?" he added, but not in any way unkind. "Conor, what about you, mate?"

"*Mmm*, not so much, to be honest, now I think on it. And I've got so much stuff done without it, too. I even started reading a book yesterday! And not, you know, for school or anything. But just because I wanted to."

"Cheers, mate," said Luke, raising the remnants of his ice cream like an ancient sword. "Here's to Luke, Conor, and Eric's den," he announced.

"To the den!" replied Eric and Conor in unison, with what was left of their own cones held aloft.

"And friendship," added Luke.

"To friendship!" replied Conor and Eric.

After a moment of reverent silence, Eric had a suggestion. "Should we also toast to the hot tub?" he put forth. "Because we're totally getting one."

"About that," said Conor tentatively, not wishing to ruin the moment, but feeling the need to interject. "I don't think we can really afford it under our budget. Also, sorry, but I don't really think the generator could handle that...?"

"No, it's okay," Eric told him. "You're right, of course. Still. One can dream, yeah?" he said wistfully.

"One can always dream," agreed Luke, raising up the last remaining bite of his cone before popping it into his mouth.

They contemplated dreaming for a few moments, and then Conor spoke up again. "Can I ask you something, Eric? A serious question?" he said. "And you don't have to answer if you don't want to."

Eric looked at Conor cautiously, but still said, "Of course. Ask away."

"Well..." began Conor, uncertain how to put what he was going to say delicately. And so finally he just came right out and asked it...

"You know a while ago you mentioned about your limp? And you said it was something that your sister had done? That it was her fault? Well I've been meaning to ask... well, that's not exactly true, I've been *dying* to ask... what actually happened...?"

"Ah. Well," came Eric's reply. "Ah. Yes," he said, jumping down from the wall. He stood there for a moment, tapping his lips with one of his fingers, contemplating the question, preparing to tell the tale. Intended or not, this delay, of course, only served to leave Luke and Conor on tenterhooks, with the both of them sat in their respective positions with jaws swinging loose in anticipation.

"It's a funny story," Eric said finally. "Well, it wasn't terribly funny at the time, of course. And certainly not funny where the welfare of my leg is concerned..."

Luke and Conor looked on expectantly, jaws reattached, but now champing at the bit.

"Right. So we were visiting this old abandoned house, you see, the two of us, Daisy and me, that was ostensibly haunted," Eric continued on. "The kind like you'd see in a horror film, right? Just like that."

Conor and Luke nodded their heads, entranced.

"Or so the stories went, anyway. I don't believe in that sort of nonsense, and neither does Daisy. We're both proper sceptics. But, still, it's interesting to investigate, right? And we thought a thorough debunking was in order. Then again, one never knows, am I right? I mean, ghosts *could* exist, after all. Again, one never knows..."

Luke and Conor both nodded again, encouraging Eric to carry on.

"One never knows," Eric said again. "And, in fact, truth be told, we were just about to open the door that led to the—"

"Come on, boys!" shouted Sally across the church lawn, interrupting the telling of the story abruptly. "That's time for us to go home!"

"Ah. Well, then. Another time, then, chaps," concluded Eric. "Yes? Another time."

THE END

J C Williams
Author

authorjcwilliams@gmail.com
@jcwilliamsbooks
@jcwilliamsauthor

If you've enjoyed this book, you may also wish to check out my other two books aimed at a younger audience, *Cabbage von Dagel*, and *Hamish McScabbard*!

And also my other books...

The *Frank 'n' Stan's Bucket List* series,
featuring The Isle of Man's TT races!

And more...

The Lonely Heart Attack Club series!

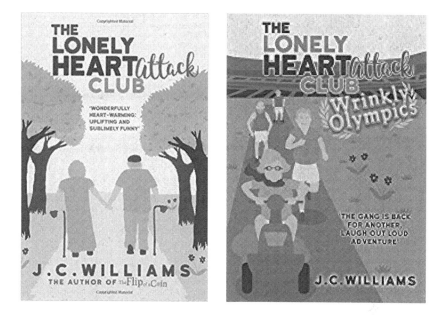

And *The Seaside Detective Agency*, and *The Flip of a Coin*.

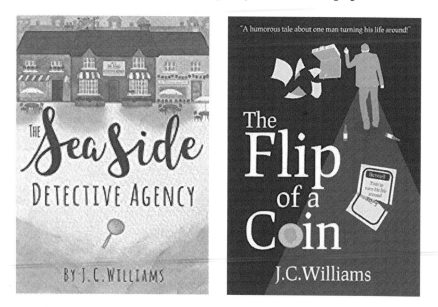

All jolly good fun.

And for the *very* adventurous among you, you may wish to give my hardworking editor's most peculiar book a butcher's. Lavishly illustrated by award-winning artist Tony Millionaire of *Maakies* and *Sock Monkey* fame. Recommended for readers age 14 and up.

Printed in Great Britain
by Amazon